SARAH NEGOVETICH

RITE

of

REVELATION

No part of this publication may be reproduced, stored in a retrieval system, or transmitted in any form without prior written permission of the author.
For information regarding permission, write to : SarahNegovetich@Gmail.com

www.SarahNegovetich.com

ISBN- 13: 978-1519405319
ISBN- 10: 1519405316

The text of this book was set in Garamond 12pt.

Cover design by Deranged Doctor Design

This one's for Ed, for being my first real fan and reminding me to dream big.

Other books by Sarah Negovetich

Rite of Rejection (Acceptance, Book 1)

One

"Ladies and Gentlemen of the Territories, before you stands the future."

My speech from yesterday plays on a continuous loop in my head; a constant reminder of my failure. We hijacked the Acceptance ceremony and told everyone about how the Cardinal locks people away in the Permanent Isolation Territory in a misguided attempt to create a perfect society. I thought it would make a difference. I imagined the people rising up and demanding a change. In a dream I didn't dare speak aloud, Daniel and I would finally have a chance to be together.

I was wrong.

No one came for us except guards with shock sticks and bags to cover our heads.

Daniel's face was the last thing I saw before the world went black. He smiled at me in the way that only Daniel can, and even with the chaos and angry shouts of guards surrounding us, my heart stuttered a moment. The image of his beautiful face was burned into my mind until guards took the hood off my head here in Quarantine.

My brain cuts away the part of the picture where a guard shoves a hard knee into Daniel's back and blurs out where the side of his face digs into the dusty ground. All that's left is his timid smile and dark brown eyes pouring out more love for me than I could possibly deserve.

Long hours of the night spent staring at the bare gray walls, pacing the edge of my tiny, square cell, and wondering what happened to Daniel and all the others who stood with us in front of the camera. I told Elizabeth to run and hide with everyone else, but I have no idea if they managed to get away. I don't know if any of the people I love are still alive, and that's the fear that keeps me sitting in this chair without moving, without resisting. And I really want to resist. Because the alarm bells in my head haven't stopped ringing all morning, screaming at me that this is a huge trap.

The mushy, mostly burned oats the guards brought me for breakfast sit like a sunbaked brick in my stomach. The weight keeps me firmly in the hard metal chair while two stylists try their best to make it look like I haven't been awake for almost forty-eight hours. My face is stiff under the layers of make-up needed to cover the dark circles around my eyes. The men who've been chatting non-stop since they marched in with their cases full of beauty tubes and wands step back and roll their eyes over every square inch of my face. I stay perfectly still through their inspection, my thoughts focused on Daniel. I want to grab their shoulders, shake them, and demand answers. Instead, I turn my head to the left and the right like a trained house pet.

The man in charge nods his head and the other springs into action, packing up all the tools of their trade. He walks to me and snatches away the thin clips holding tiny wisps of hair off my face. He leans down to my ear and whispers, "Show time," before rapping once on the door.

The rusted metal door creaks open and there's Eric. The traitor who lied to us all and made certain I'd never see the outside of this prison again. I can almost hear the spring of the trap falling to catch me.

I jump from the chair as Eric steps into the cell, rubbing his raw knuckles as the stylists hustle out. "Bec— Rebecca, it's time to go."

I like the sound of that about as much as I like the idea of the stylists coming back in here for round two. Eric grabs my arm, but I jerk it back out of reach. His fingers flex as if he's going to grab me again, but instead his closed fist falls to his side.

"I'm not going anywhere until I get some answers. Why all of this?" I fan my hands around my face. "Where is Daniel?"

The last question comes out barely more than a whisper. We hacked into the Acceptance ceremony feed and took over their national broadcast. I went into yesterday's ceremony fully expecting that my act of rebellion would earn me a swift death. I should have known better. The Cardinal has never once shown mercy.

"So the two of you…" Eric lets his question trail off as he stares at every corner of the tiny cell except where I'm standing.

"Seriously? You want to do this now?"

Eric drops his eyes to the ground, but doesn't say a word.

"Fine. You were right. I'm in love with Daniel." I throw my hands up and pace across the small amount of floor space. "I probably always have been. And yet, I was going to run out of here and marry you so we could all have a chance at a little bit of happiness until you ruined it for everyone. There's your answer, now where is Daniel?"

Eric still stands motionless, staring at the floor. I kick my empty chair and it topples over, the metal frame grinding against the concrete floor. "Where is he?"

Another guard, a burly man at least a foot taller than Eric, appears in the door way. "The cameramen said we have about ten minutes until the lighting is, and I quote, 'the perfect shade of sunset Cardinal red.' Whatever that means. We have to get the whole thing shot in under five minutes."

"Better iron out the details here." Eric pulls a small Noteboard from his jacket, hesitating only slightly before he shoves it into my hands. His voice is as stiff and formal as his movements. "Tonight you will film an apology for the Cardinal."

I stare at the screen and force my brain to focus on the words through the hot blood raging through my veins. This isn't an apology; it's a confession letter. They want me to retract everything I said yesterday. "Does the Cardinal think I can be bought with a bit of make-up?" I shove the Noteboard back at Eric.

"The make-up is so you can look halfway human. The Cardinal wants a contrite prisoner, not a victim, and that's what you're going to give him."

"The Cardinal can take his apology letter and—"

Eric grabs my arm, his tug momentarily pulling me off balance. His grip tightens, keeping me standing and pulling me right up against his chest. I struggle against his hold, but his hand clenches tighter on my arm. "Listen very carefully to what I'm about to say." His words are harsh, but the eyes staring into mine are tender. "If you want to make sure the people you love stay safe, you need to do exactly what I say. No questions. No hesitation."

Eric's words are a threat, but all I hear is that Daniel is alive. Daniel, who I love, though it took me way too long to admit it and even longer to let him love me back.

I want to trust Eric. I want to believe he regrets turning us all in. He told the Cardinal about our escape plan last year, ruined our chance to have a real life and got Molly killed. All for his fancy, red, guard jacket. He did tell me about the fence that would separate me and Elizabeth from Daniel. Yesterday, he lied to another guard so I could get away from the courtyard and meet Daniel in time to interrupt the ceremony. And he got my necklace back for me. I rub my thumb over the smooth knot against my chest. But he betrayed all of us, in the worst way imaginable.

I replay his words in my head. "People. Not person?" Not just Daniel is in danger. How many of the others?

Eric nods, but his green eyes never leave mine.

My life is mine to sacrifice and pretty much all I have left to give. Daniel, sweet Daniel, made his choice to stay with my sinking ship. He showed his face on camera and sealed his fate. The others were supposed to run, hide, live the rest of their lives as well as they could in the wasteland of the PIT. Elizabeth, Constance, Thomas, all those people I just met and whose names I can't remember. They all came voluntarily, but if there's something I can do for them, I have to.

I nod and relax the tense arm muscles under his grip. Eric tucks the Noteboard back into his jacket pocket and leads me out the door, the large guard following only a step behind. We're a funeral march, and I'm the overly done-up corpse.

Two

Eric and the other nameless guard weave us through a maze of hallways and out into a grassy nook wedged into the middle of the Quarantine building. The building wraps like a giant U, cutting us off from the decay and desperation of the PIT. My toes itch to kick off these raggedy shoes and run barefoot through the lush green lawn. The inviting grass presents a night and day difference to the yellowish weed grass that sprouts up around the corners of the crumbling bunkhouses on the outer edges of the PIT. Several men fiddle with equipment at a picnic table off to the side, and a little fountain trickles water, creating a natural music in the background.

I can almost imagine we're at a park back in the Territories, except for the giant barbed wire fence that cuts me off from the freedom sprawling to the west.

A third guard watches over a crew of men setting up an array of video equipment. They have several cameras, two large white screens, and a microphone attached to a long pole. This will be a far cry from yesterday's hasty filming.

That was nothing more than Daniel and I with a stolen video camera stacked precariously on some busted crates. We were doomed from the start. Then Elizabeth showed up with Constance, Thomas, and so many others. Dozens of voices blending together to tell the story of a Machine gone wrong and a leader with too much power.

Today is the complete opposite of yesterday.

"Oh good, she's ready." A man from the camera crew takes my arm from Eric, holding barely a pinch of my sleeve. He maneuvers me toward the fence, drops my arm, and backs up, wiping his fingers on his crisply pressed pants. "I want her right here, facing the building. In another minute the sun is going to hit the horizon and this whole area will be awash in perfect red light."

Eric follows us over to the fence, my tense, red-jacketed shadow, never more than a few feet away from me. The cameraman positions me just right, like I'm a department store mannequin, and then walks away to fiddle with a piece of equipment.

Now what? There's no way I can read that message. Even if it wasn't a complete lie, what's to stop the Cardinal from killing me the minute I'm done? I could really use some of Daniel's unwavering support right now. I'd even take a bit of Elizabeth's sarcastic advice, but not if it means putting her in Quarantine.

"Is she ready with the script?" the same man, the director I guess, pipes up again. He looks up from the camera and motions to Eric.

Eric steps between me and the director, cutting off my view of everything but him. He takes the Noteboard back out of his pocket and hands it over, gently this time.

"Resist."

His whispered voice is lost in the noise around us. I must have misheard him. He's so close I have to crane my neck to see his face. I find his eyes and they plead with me. "Resist."

No mistaking it this time. I nod, and Eric steps back into position at my side. The director waves him out of the shot with a sharp flick of his wrist and yells for quiet. As the voices around us fade out, he points at me.

"I won't read this." Our outdoor studio is completely silent, but even I can barely hear my whispered words.

"I can't hear her." The director points at Eric without taking his eyes off the camera. "Tell her she needs to be louder."

It's like I'm not even here. Eric steps closer and leans down to speak directly into my ear. "You can do this. Give them the Rebecca from yesterday."

Eric moves back into position. I barely recognize the girl from yesterday. That feels like a lifetime ago. The director points to me again, and I'm out of time.

"I'm not reading this, and you can't make me." I sound like a petulant child refusing to eat her vegetables. The bustle of the camera crew stops and all eyes fly to me and then the director. I have no idea what to do next, but Eric said to resist. Time to sell it.

I fling the Noteboard back at Eric and he grabs it seconds before it smashes against the plush green grass. For good measure I stomp my foot and cross my arms. Eric covers up a loud, harsh cough that I'm pretty sure was really a laugh. So much for selling it, but I'm committed at this point. What else do I have to lose…except everything.

"I mean it. The Cardinal can beat me, starve me, and kill me if he wants, but he can't make me lie to the people out there." I gesture toward the fence. Saying it out loud makes it more real, and the words come out louder, stronger. "I won't lie. He's done quite enough of that for the both of us."

The tall guard who followed us out of my cell bangs on the door we came through with the heal of his open hand. He marches over until he's right in my face, but doesn't touch me. "Unfortunately for me, with that little stunt you pulled yesterday, the Cardinal needs you in one piece. Trust me when I say there's nothing I'd like more than to slap that smug defiance off your face."

The door swings open and a fourth guard stands in the doorway.

The guard in my face grabs my chin so I can't see what's going on. "Unfortunately for you, the Cardinal doesn't care what that one's face looks like."

He shoves my chin away and marches back to where the director stands waiting.

The fourth guard walks out the door, dragging a man behind him, his dark arms pulled tight in an awkward angle against his back. There's a sack over his head, but I know it's Daniel. No one else could walk with their head held high and their back straight while being led around like a dog on a leash.

The guard jerks him to a stop, and Daniel lets out a moan as he stumbles against the sharp motions. The sack is ripped off his head, and I let out my own moan as I fall to my knees. His face is bloodied and bruised and one of his eyes is swollen shut.

"Get her up and back into position."

Eric lifts me back to my feet, but my eyes don't leave Daniel's beaten face.

"What did you do to him?"

"I'm going to lose my light if we don't get moving here," the director shouts at everyone and no one in particular.

The awful guard shouts from where he stands by the antsy director. He doesn't have to get in my face to scare me now. "That's only the beginning of his pain if you don't get in front of that camera right now."

The guard with Daniel punches him in the stomach and he falls down on all fours. The guard's boot connects with his nose and blood oozes out onto the soft, green grass.

"Stop, please stop." Screams rip from my throat and my fingers tug at the short tufts of hair behind my ears. Lumpy oatmeal from breakfast threatens to come back.

"Keep refusing and we'll beat him more, and then we'll beat him again. And if that doesn't work, we'll round up the rest of your little Reject friends and beat them." The guard spits his words at me, the truth of them written all over his face.

I search the crew for a single sympathetic face, but they're more concerned with adjusting their equipment than the bloodied man bent over in the middle of the grass. Their eyes glaze right over the both of us. The director refuses to speak to me. We are non-entities.

My heart morphs into lead and sinks down into the pit of my stomach. They don't care. Nothing we did yesterday changed anything. I rub at the knotted pendant on my chest. My words, the source of my power against the Cardinal, fell on deaf ears.

"Give her the script."

Eric positions himself between me and the director again and hands me the Noteboard. Cardinal help me, I'm going to do this. They'll probably kill us both, but I can't stand here and watch them torture Daniel.

The words on the screen stare back at me like a taunt, except there is a new line that wasn't there just a moment ago.

Daniel is fine. Read slow.

It takes all my strength not to hurl the Noteboard back at Eric again. Daniel is not fine. Just look at him, barely able to hold his head up. Or not. His head bobs up and down, ever so slightly. Is he nodding? My fingers grip the edge of the board and I follow Daniel's movements like a hawk staring down its prey. Again, his head lifts slightly and then lowers, but it's a controlled movement, not a collapse.

I know better than most that words have power, but I refuse to let these words have power over me. Saying them doesn't make them true. I nod, a strong imitation of Daniel, and turn to face the camera.

The video crew, frozen while they waited to see if I'd throw another fit, scurries into action. They move the white screens into position, flanking the camera in a V to reflect the red light put off by the setting sun. The microphone rests only a foot or two over my head.

"Let's have quiet." The director lifts one hand up and peeks down behind the camera. "And…go." His hand drops and points directly at me.

I have the words on the Noteboard memorized, but the Cardinal's lies don't have a hold on me anymore. I clear my throat and stare right at the camera with all the defiance I can muster. "Ladies and gentlemen of the Territories. My name is Rebecca Collins, and I am a Reject."

Three

Banging erupts to my left. Everyone stops to stare, though all we can see is the wall of the Quarantine building.

"Keep going," the director yells from behind the camera. "I can edit that out later."

"Last night I illegally hacked into the network and, knowing how important the Acceptance ceremony is, I ruined the day for hundreds—"

More banging, and this time from more than just bare hands. It sounds like wooden bats against a wall. Angry shouts join the noise.

"Just keep going."

"Hundreds of society's newest members and their families. I—"

The Noteboard in my hand rings out like an alarm with three sharp buzzes. The Noteboards of the other guards sound as well.

"Now what?" The director steps back from the camera, his hands thrown into the air.

"This recording session is over." The guard next to the director grabs him and his camera and shoves both of them toward the door we all came out of. "Dawson, get this man and his crew back into the guard room."

Eric grabs his Noteboard with one hand and my arm with the other. "I'll get the filth back to their cells."

The guard, whose face I now want very badly to punch, sneers at Eric. "Fine. That should make you feel right at home. Henderson, you're with me."

He doesn't wait for anyone to move before barreling through the door, his hand already reaching for the deadly stick strapped to his belt. With him gone, I lurch toward Daniel, but Eric's grip on my arm is unrelenting. He leans over and whispers in my ear, "Wait till we're alone."

The guard named Henderson dashes through the door, trying like mad to keep up with the guard issuing orders. Dawson herds the protesting camera crew back into the building, leaving the majority of their equipment behind.

The door clicks shut and I'm kneeling at Daniel's side in two seconds flat. I reach to him, but hold back, unsure if my touch will cause him more pain. "Daniel, where does it hurt most?" I choke back a sob. "Are any bones broken?"

"I'm fine, I promise," Daniel croons into the top of my head.

"We have to move." Eric unties Daniel's arms.

He wraps his arms around me, his breath hissing out between clenched teeth. We sit for a minute that doesn't last long enough. Daniel braces his hands against the ground to stand up, but Eric and I have to step in to keep him from falling back down. I rub my hand against his shoulder, afraid anything else will hurt him more.

"Yeah," Daniel says, stretching a bit to the side. "Definitely a cracked rib or two."

The noise from somewhere in the PIT reaches a new level, and shouts from guards mix in with the chaotic screams and sounds of destruction. The loud speaker crackles to life. "All prisoners will report to their bunkhouses immediately."

"Are you okay to walk?" Eric cracks the door open and pokes his head through before pulling it open wide. "They'll have this riot calmed down before we know it. We've got to get moving."

"Is this it?" I grip Daniel's arm like a lifeline. "Are we getting out?"

"Or die trying." There's not a hint of humor to Eric's words. He means it.

Once again, I find myself putting my life into Eric's hands. But what choice do we have? So be it. The Cardinal is probably planning to kill us anyway. I glance up at Daniel, and his dark brown eyes bore into mine.

"I love you," Daniel whispers in my ear.

I nod back at him and swallow down the knot in my throat. "More and more every day."

"We have to move quickly and stay out of sight. Stay right behind me and try not to talk unless you have to." Eric takes off down the hallway. Daniel wraps his arm around my shoulder for balance and we follow behind him.

The three of us move in silence through a labyrinth of hallways. I keep waiting for Eric to stop for Elizabeth and the others, but he barely even slows down.

"Eric, where is everyone else? We're getting them, too." It's not a question. I won't leave them here.

"They aren't in here, not that the whole guard unit hasn't been looking for them. We're heading to them now." Eric pushes open a door and we're outside. The sun fell even lower while we were inside, and its last rays are barely visible off to our left. The dusk-fallen air is filled with a panicked frenzy of shouting, banging, and chaos. We can't see anything from this side of the building, but it's clear there's something awful happening over at the dining hall.

We don't waste time trying to figure it out. Eric runs east, toward the ocean where we tried to escape almost a year ago, weaving between gray, concrete buildings. Every time we run across an intersection, glimpses of the new fence take over the landscape. It's massive. Probably as tall as the exterior fences, but it looks so much bigger up close.

About halfway between the Quarantine building and the eastern fence blocking us from the ocean, Eric takes a sharp left and heads straight for the new dividing fence. The roads are empty, but the loud speaker still blares out the order to report to the bunkhouses. The chaos continues to echo from the courtyard. Daniel huffs next to me, jogging slightly and grimacing against the pain that must be wracking his body. Eric turns again and we come out of a dark alley right next to the fence. A man stands there, quietly staring at the ground and leaning against the fence.

"Nice work, Thomas." Eric pats the man on his back, kneels down, and pulls something metal out of the inside of his jacket.

"Thomas." I drop Daniel's hand and hug Constance's husband, the droopy, pock-marked side of his face rubbing against mine. "You're okay, thank goodness." Thomas and I only spoke once, back when Constance found us stealing her rope. Eons ago. But he came and stood with all of us yesterday. When we hacked into the live feed of the Acceptance ceremony, he joined me in calling the Cardinal out on his lies. He put himself at risk, and that makes him family.

"I could say the same to you." He reaches around me and shakes Daniel's hand. "Now we just need to get the others."

Eric stands up and drops the metal object back into his pocket. Reaching down, he grabs a piece of the brand new, chain-link fence and pulls it back. The metal splits apart and a gap opens up, barely big enough for a person to squeeze through. "Let's catch up over coffee later. Ladies first."

I drop down on my hands and knees and shimmy through the fence, watching so the freshly cut metal doesn't tear a hole in my arm. I'm not even back on my feet before Daniel is squeezing through, followed by Thomas and finally Eric.

Daniel grabs my hand again and we are off, our ragtag foursome winding between the buildings and trying not to run into anything, or anyone, in the dark.

Eric stops in front of a building, but only pauses long enough to push the door open. "In here."

A tiny part of me hesitates to walk inside the dark bunkhouse with Eric. All of the sudden this feels too much like last year. So close to getting out, only for him to take it all away. Daniel pushes a warm hand against the small of my back, and with three steps we're inside and it's too late to reconsider. The door slams shut behind us, and the overwhelming darkness is instantaneous.

A light stick pops on in the middle of the room, and I get my first real look. It's our old bunkhouse, with Daniel's pieced together table and wobbly chairs. And so many people.

"Nice to see you again, princess."

"Elizabeth!" I move to hug her, but Daniel beats me to it.

Constance sobs silently into Thomas's chest. Between fear of being found by the guards and worrying about her husband, the past twenty-four hours must have been torture for her.

Eric grabs a blanket and tears it into strips, wrapping them around Daniel's torso. "It's a far cry from the medical attention you really need, but it should keep you stable for now."

"Patrice? Please, no." Daniel steps away from Eric and wraps his arms around a tall, skinny girl I didn't notice before. She must have been hidden just outside the soft glow of the light stick. Eyes dark as charcoal, the same mouth as Daniel's, pulled into a frown, and the little lines between her brows, just like when he gets mad. Daniel could never deny that Patrice is his sister. "I'm so sorry you're here."

"You should be." There isn't an ounce of teasing or softness to her words. Her arms hang limp at her sides instead of wrapping around to return Daniel's hug.

I can't blame her for being angry. We knew there was a risk she would be Rejected if we hacked into the feed. Of course, we hoped she wouldn't be. Wished it would be too late to adjust her results. We should have known the Cardinal would make sure she paid for our defiance. Her anger is justified, but for Daniel's sake I want her to wrap her arms around his back.

"Who are all these people?" Eric holds a light stick above his head and a dim glow exposes the corners of the room.

At least six women stand huddled at the far end. I recognize them immediately. All of them stood in front of the camera yesterday during the Acceptance ceremony and told everyone in the Territories the ridiculous reasons they were sent to the PIT. I don't remember their names, but each of them holds a special place in my heart.

"I found them yesterday, hiding out in a bunk close to the east edge." Elizabeth walks over and loops her arm around one of the women, a very un-Elizabeth action. "If the guards find them, they'll be in just as much trouble as us. We have to get them out."

"What were you thinking?" Eric grabs Elizabeth's arm and pulls her back over to the door. "I can't get all these people out. It'll be difficult enough to get us out. Plus, I only have supplies ready for the seven of us. They can't come."

"They come."

All eyes in the room flash to me. Daniel squeezes my shoulder and Elizabeth nods her head repeatedly.

"They risked their lives just like the rest of us and we can't leave them here. We all know what happens if they are caught." Eric opens his mouth to protest, but I hold my hand up to stop him. "It's not up for debate. Either we all go or no one goes."

"Fine, but don't blame me when you all end up caught." He runs a shaky hand through his hair. "Try to stay together. If you see a guard, scatter and hide until it's safe to move. If we get separated, go to the fence directly north of here. Okay?"

Daniel grabs my hand and I reach out to grab Patrice standing next to me. All around the room, heads nod in unison. I take another look at their faces, my family. Molly should be here. A sharp knife of pain and loss hits me, and I push it down. No time to deal with that now. There are more of us standing together, and that would make her happy. In the flames of discontent and rebellion, our family grew stronger. And now, we'll get to be the wildflowers we were always meant to be. Eric snaps off the light stick and we plunge into darkness.

I squeeze Daniel's hand and follow the group back into the night. Even this far out, the noise of destruction carries on the salty breeze. I've no idea what's going on, but I don't care so long as it keeps the guards distracted for a little while longer.

My shoes beat out a rhythm on the hard ground just a tad slower than the fast pounding of my heart. We've been here before, so close to freedom I could taste the ocean saltwater on my lips. But that night led to death and disaster. I squeeze Daniel's hand tighter. I can't do that again. Adrenaline speeds through my veins, pumping my legs even faster. I can't decide if it's from excitement or terror.

Eric freezes in front of us and turns, panic radiating from wide eyes. "Run."

Shouting much closer than the courtyard sounds to our left. The guards are here. Daniel pulls me to our right and I chase behind him, my other hand gripping Patrice and hauling her with us. My heart kicks into another level of panic I didn't even know existed. There isn't time to see where everyone else is going.

Daniel runs into a bunkhouse with the door missing. The second I'm inside he pushes me to the floor with Patrice flattening out next to me. Daniel lies on my other side and we wait silently in the dark.

More shouts sound like they could be right outside our hiding spot. "All Rejects must stay inside their bunkhouses. Anyone caught outside will be sent to Quarantine immediately."

I let out a silent breath. These are just guards enforcing the curfew. They aren't looking for us…yet.

Without being able to see, we have no idea if the guards have moved on or not. We wait an eternity with no other sounds from outside. Careful to stay silent, I move to my knees and crawl toward the window. Daniel reaches up to pull me back down, but his battered ribs have him at a disadvantage and I shake off his attempt to stop me. Outside, the night is pitch black with only rough outlines of the buildings visible. Not a soul moves anywhere close to us.

I ease back down to where Daniel and Patrice still lie on the floor and whisper my finding. "It looks clear. We need to keep moving and find the others."

Daniel nods and I help him up from the dirt floor. He lets out a small hiss of pain. I can't imagine how much all this running is hurting him.

The three of us inch back outside, my hands still firmly gripping both Daniel and Patrice. We have to correct course back west a bit, but we manage to make it out to the fence without any more issues. Eric waits there, his head moving from side to side, scanning the PIT non-stop.

"You made it." Eric reaches down and pulls the fence up at another cut. "Everyone else is already through. We need to get going before the guards come back this way."

"Rebecca, let's go." Daniel motions me toward the hole with his free hand. "I'm right behind you."

He always has been. I drop down on all fours again and crawl my way to freedom. In less than a minute, Daniel and Patrice are through and the fence is pushed back down to almost the way it was. I grab Daniel's arm and help him stand. He's got to be ready to drop with all this running.

Somewhere to my right, ocean waves pound against the shore, their soft swooshing matching the swish of the tall grass in the wind. I close my eyes and try to imprint this moment in my memory. No matter what happens next, right now, for this brief moment in time, I'm free.

I open my eyes to find Daniel in front of me, only his concerned eyes visible in the dark. I find his hand and lace my fingers through his. "I love you."

His fingers tighten around mine. "More and more every day."

Four

Eric guides our way with a single light stick. The three of us follow him, our shuffling feet the only sound in the cool spring night air. Whatever noise still coming from the riot in the PIT is lost this far out, eaten up by the sharp wind coming in off the ocean. Without the buildings to slow it down, it pounds into us, nearly pushing me sideways. Daniel trudges beside me, his footsteps occasionally faltering, but never stopping.

Less than fifty yards into freedom, the ground dips into a gully. We ease our way to the bottom, and Eric comes to a sudden stop next to a long vehicle that was hidden in the little valley. It has an arch of fabric across the back like the covered wagons from my old history classes. Thomas, Constance, and Elizabeth stand waiting.

I scan the area, but I don't see anyone else. "Where are the other women? The ones from the bunkhouse?"

"They got separated." Eric moves around to the front of the vehicle and opens a door. "We have to keep moving before the other guards realize you aren't in Quarantine anymore."

Daniel stiffens next to me. "Eric—"

"No, I'm sorry, but we can't wait." Eric kicks at a tire, avoiding looking any of us in the eye. "We have a lot of ground to cover tonight and the longer we stay here the more likely we all end up dead."

I run a hand over the building pain in my chest. Eric's right, but everything about leaving them here feels wrong. I pull Daniel to me until I'm sure he can see the certainty I'm trying to show. "Once everyone else is safe, we come back for them. Promise me."

Daniel stares at a spot over my head. "I promise we'll try."

That has to be good enough for now.

"We can give them another few minutes." Eric reaches into the cab and pulls out a dark red bag, the Cardinal's laurel wreath seal stitched on the front. He turns to face our group, but won't look any of us in the eye. "Before we go, we need to do one more thing."

"Why does that sound like one more thing I'm going to hate?" My shoulders tense, and Daniel tightens his grip around my hand.

Eric takes off his jacket and rolls up his sleeve. "Because it is." He holds the light stick up to his arm just under his shoulder. "When each of us arrived at the PIT, they gave us an inoculation. Said it was to protect us from disease and keep it from spreading. They lied." Eric shifts the light and it highlights a short, silvery line of skin. "They injected each of us with a magnetized capsule filled with a lethal dose of Phenol. Activation magnets are buried in a loop, one hundred yards outside the fence. If you cross it with the capsule still inside, it opens and releases the poison. You'll be unconscious in seconds and dead in under five minutes."

"So last year..." Last year we made big plans to escape on a thrown together raft, on the ocean, the ocean that was much farther than one hundred yards from the fence.

Eric rolls his sleeve back down. "If we had made it past the fence, we would all be dead."

"Did you know?" Daniel asks.

"No, I didn't find out until later when they took my capsule out." Eric opens up the back of the truck and hangs the light stick from a hook in the fabric dome. "And now we need to get rid of yours so we can get out of here."

Thomas and Constance move to the back of the truck without another word. I watch Eric use a small knife to cut a tiny slit in Thomas's arm. Eric grabs a black, round device from the red bag, about the size of a large walnut, and holds it up to the cut. A few seconds later, Thomas flinches and a tiny clink rings out from the device. Eric holds it out so we can all see. In the light from the truck, a bloody, metal splinter sticks to the black ball.

I run my hand over the slight bump on my own arm, there since the night the Machine sent me to the PIT. No wonder no one ever escapes. The Cardinal puts on this big show with the giant fence, disconnected cameras, and guards everywhere, but none of them matter. If anyone gets past all of that, they're as good as dead. One hundred yards of freedom is all they get.

Daniel nudges me with his elbow, his hand holding a small square of gauze on his arm. "You're up."

I step into the light at the end of the truck and hold up my sleeve. Eric moves the knife with a sharp flick, but I barely feel it. My eyes are glued to the darkness.

"How many?"

"What?" Eric holds the black ball to my arm.

"How many people have you found out here who thought they were free?"

Eric is silent while the capsule works its way out of my arm. At the clink, he pulls the device away and hands me some gauze to stop the bleeding. He says nothing while he cleans off the black orb and packs everything away. Everyone else must have gone while I was contemplating just how dark the Cardinal is. Eric zips up the bag, turns off the light, and finally faces me. Wet eyes meet mine for only a second before darting away again.

"At least one every week. Sometimes more. Sometimes a lot more." He throws the bag inside as if it wronged him personally. "It's why we have these trucks. Every morning, just before sunrise, we drive the perimeter and pick up the bodies of anyone desperate enough to escape."

"All those people back there. So many innocent. How many will die tonight?"

"We can't save them all, Rebecca." Eric reaches out a hand, but pulls it back before it reaches my shoulder. "Right now, the best we can do is get ourselves out alive."

I nod in the darkness, but it feels wrong.

"We can't wait any longer. Let's go." Eric climbs into the driver's seat and we all load in, Patrice in the cab with Eric and the rest of us hunched in the back where they pile up the poor souls desperate enough to risk death and uninformed enough to court it.

I help Daniel into the back of the truck. We sink to the floor, our arms wrapped around each other in a silent hug. I can't even begin to process my emotions. Relief, guilt, joy, fear. All of them wrap around my head and spiral around my torso only to somersault in my stomach and swirl up again for another pass. Another set of arms, I don't know whose, wrap around me from behind. More warm bodies crush around us, the overwhelming emotions of freedom pulling us together. The engine fires to life and we ride out, still holding on to each other.

The front of the truck lifts up as we ride out of the gully. A few more minutes of bumpy silence and the wheels hit some kind of paved road.

Eric calls back through the open space behind his seat, "There's an old access road we use to take these in for service. We'll have a smoother ride from here."

The group hug pulls apart, but Daniel's arm stays tight around my shoulder. "Patrice, I'd like for you to meet Rebecca."

From her spot in the seat next to Eric, Patrice gives zero indication that she heard a word of what Daniel said.

"Patrice…" Daniel reaches to the front seat and places a broad hand on her shoulder. She shakes him off without turning around or speaking a word. Daniel tenses for a second before his shoulders sink forward.

I lean in closer and squeeze Daniel's leg. He has so much pain, and there isn't anything I can do to fix it.

"So who wants to explain exactly what happened back there and what the plan is now?" Elizabeth leans forward from her spot on the floor so everyone can hear over the engine. She holds one of the burlap bags that Molly made us close to her chest, the way a small child clings to a teddy bear. "Everything went crazy by the dining hall, so we made a mad dash back to the bunk and waited."

"Thomas," Eric calls back without taking his eyes off the road, "can you fill them in so I can focus up here?"

In the back, we all scoot closer to Thomas. From the front seat, Patrice leans back a little closer, but doesn't turn her head from the front window.

"Everything was chaos on the men's side of the fence. The big bosses were going crazy trying to keep their men under control, but without the women there, they didn't have anything to dangle in front of them. By lunch, the bosses were all dead, killed by the muscle that had been keeping them safe."

Constance nestles up closer to Thomas and he wraps his huge arm around her, kissing the top of her head. "I stayed out of sight as much as possible, and for once I was thankful for the lasting effects of my illness. This face tends to make others uncomfortable, and last night was no exception. No one messed with me during the few times I ventured out for meals. After dinner, Eric found me."

Eric calls back, a touch of humor in his voice, "Hard to miss the guy who stands a head taller than everyone else."

"He told me Constance and the girls were safe for now, but you two," he gestures to me and Daniel, "were in Quarantine and wouldn't last longer than another day."

"If I had read that statement, he was going to kills us both." It's not a question. I already know the truth.

"Son of a…" The truck lurches to the right and bounces off the paved road, sending all of us sprawling around the floor. We pick up speed and it's all I can do to keep from being bounced from one end of the truck to the other.

Just as suddenly as our crazy ride started, it ends, and Eric shuts off the engine. Daniel groans next to me and wraps both his arms around his body.

"Eric, what in the world are you doing?"

"Trucks on the access road." Eric's words come out in between heaving breaths. "They must have called in reinforcements to handle the riot." He shoves Patrice into the back. "Everyone get down on the floor and stay quiet like your life depends on it."

Daniel pulls Patrice down next to him and the six of us lie in the back of the truck. Eric fires the engine back up and the soft hum helps me to not feel so exposed.

"Shit, they saw us. One of the trucks is headed over here. Don't make a sound or we're all as good as dead."

Patrice whimpers softly and Daniel holds her tighter. An engine sounds closer and a door slams shut. I close my eyes as if they can make me quieter.

"Dunstan, what are you doing out here?" A deep, but jovial voice sounds from right outside our vehicle.

"Hey Murphy, they sent me to town to get more supplies. We're almost completely out of restraints and Quarantine is nearing capacity." Eric spits the words out too fast. He needs to calm down before he gives us away.

"Damn animals. Though I guess we were due for something big to happen with the fence going up yesterday. What are you doing driving around in the field with your lights off?"

"I thought I saw someone running around out here, but it must have been my imagination." Eric thumps the steering wheel. "The lights are busted on this one, so it's hard to tell apart the shadows."

I hold my breath. This is where it all goes south if Murphy decides Eric's excuse is full of garbage.

"I doubt it's a Reject. We don't ever find them this far out. Probably a dog."

"I'm sure you're right. Better let you go. They need every guard available in there. It's chaos."

Daniel squeezes my hand in the darkness and I mentally wish Murphy would leave and never look back.

"Great, just how I wanted to spend my evening." Murphy slaps the side of the vehicle and I tense every muscle in my body. "See you back in the PIT."

No one moves. A door slams again and the engine of Murphy's truck fades off into the night. I make it to a count of seventy-four in my head when Eric throws the truck back into gear and sends us bouncing again.

Patrice helps me move Daniel into a sitting position before climbing back into the front with Eric. The rest of us stay on the floor. Every rock under the tire would send us spilling off the benches.

"Is that it? Are we okay?" Elizabeth sticks her head into the front cab and stares out the windshield.

"Who knows? That's why I'm getting us out of here as fast as possible." Eric swivels his head back and forth, scanning the horizon. "The road is too risky if there's a chance they'll send more guards. With the reinforcements, they'll have the riot calmed down faster than I'd planned." Eric tugs his seatbelt on and grips the steering wheel. "We'll just have a bumpy ride for a while."

Elizabeth settles back down on the floor and Eric speeds across the uneven ground.

"So how exactly did this riot get started, anyway?" Elizabeth lounges against a bench as if we didn't just narrowly escape discovery.

"Ah, that would be me." Thomas raises his hand in the darkness. "Eric told me we needed a distraction at just before sunset. Something big enough to pull all the guards away from their assigned tasks. The only thing I could think of was a full scale riot with every man involved. So that's what I did."

"How?" Constance stares at Thomas with a mix of admiration and wonder.

"After lunch, I sneaked into the back of the dining hall and barricaded the door, but only on our side. Dinner time came and none of the men could get in. That should have been enough to get the riot going, but I couldn't take any chances. So, I started a rumor that we got a shipment of fresh bread, but they were only giving it to the women."

Daniel whistles beside me and I agree. There are a few things you don't mess with in the PIT, and food is one of them. If the men thought the women were getting better food and then saw them all able to file into their side of the dining hall while they were locked out...I can't imagine the outrage.

"It was like dropping a lit match onto a pile of firelogs." Thomas smiles in the darkness, as if he enjoyed watching the PIT explode into chaos. "As soon as the violence kicked in, I took off running for the place by the fence where Eric told me to wait. Then you guys came running, and I knew this was it. We were getting out."

"Eric found me, too." Elizabeth's voice cuts into the dark. "My only job was to round up Constance and Patrice and make sure we were in the bunkhouse by nightfall. I was hoping we could get dinner first, but as soon as the shouting started I knew that was out of the question. Any chance you have some food with you?"

Eric turns partially in his seat and it's clear he's smiling. "Not here, but you'll be able to fill up once we get to the city. It should be only a few more minutes."

My head snaps up to meet his eyes. "A city? Is that safe?"

"It's not permanent. We'll stop there to resupply and then head out before the sun comes up."

Patrice comes alive in the front seat. "What do you mean the city's not permanent? You can just drop me off at the nearest Airtrain station. I'm going home."

Home. An image of a cheery, yellow kitchen from my parents' house pops into my brain. It feels like a lifetime ago that I called that home.

"Patrice." Daniel's voice wavers a bit. I wrap his hand in both of mine to lend strength for what he has to tell her. "You can't go home."

"Yes I can. You should have seen Dad after you were Rejected. He would have done anything to get you back, and when I show up, he'll welcome me with open arms. Just you wait and see."

"Let's assume for a minute that you manage to travel all the way back to Cardinal City without a penny to your name or your own OneCard without someone realizing you don't belong and turning you in. Even if you made it home and Dad does let you in. Then what? You spend your entire life hiding inside his house. You couldn't go outside because people would recognize you and know you're supposed to be in the PIT. You could never see your friends, get married, or have any future. You'd live like a caged animal, constantly in fear of being found out." Daniel reaches out a hand, and this time Patrice doesn't shake him off. "I'm so sorry. I know this isn't what you wanted. It's the last thing in the world I wanted for you. But this is reality now, and you can't go home."

Patrice pulls away and leans into the side of the car. "I hate you, Daniel Whedon." Her quiet sobs ring out like tower bells.

Daniel slumps back onto the floor next to me. "Not more than I hate myself."

Five

City lights flood the front of the car. Eric pulls off the main road and down a side street that seems to run around the edge of the city. He drives another few minutes in silence until the road dead ends at the back of a long, low building. Eric cuts the engine, but no one moves. Everything now is one big series of unknowns.

"Welcome to Ricksburg. The lights are from the Airtrain station, but we're hidden behind the utility building. We need to get to my apartment. No one should be out at this hour, but we can't take the chance of someone seeing a PIT truck driving down the road. We'll have to walk, but it isn't too far."

What he doesn't say is that if someone does notice us, that's it. The Cardinal might haul me back to the PIT to film his ridiculous apology video, but everyone else would be dead before the sun comes up. Goosebumps dot my arms and I shiver, though my new dress is plenty warm in the spring night air.

Eric clears his throat and everyone leans a little closer. The lights from the station cast a yellow shadow over his face and he looks even gaunter than he did yesterday. He has just as much to lose as the rest of us. More, even. For us, it's get out or die trying, but Eric didn't have to leave. No matter how hard his new life is, he had a life. That's all forfeited now. The guards from Quarantine will know he helped us the minute they realize Daniel and I aren't in our cells. If we're caught, there won't be any second chances for him either.

His voice is barely more than a whisper, but it feels like he's shouting. "We'll move through the back streets as much as possible. We can talk more when we get to the apartment, but unless there's danger, try to stay silent until we're inside."

We all nod and take off two-by-two, Daniel and I right behind Eric. I've never heard of Ricksburg, but it's got to be part of the AtlanticCoast Territory. This must be where everyone who works in the PIT lives since there isn't any employee housing there. And why would there be? No one would want to live that close to us. All this comfort is probably no more than a quick Airtrain ride to the horrors of the PIT.

Eric leads us through enough small alleys and walking paths that I lose track of how many turns we take. If anyone is following us, they'll have a hard time making sense of our random path. I want to go faster, but I slow my pace to help Daniel. I let Daniel keep an eye on Eric while my head swivels from side to side. Even though the Cardinal lives in the capital, I can't shake the feeling that he's watching us from every corner.

I'm desperate for a break when Eric stops suddenly and holds up his hand for us to wait. He walks casually around the corner where there's a noticeable glow and my heartbeat jumps into overtime. We can't see him and anything could happen out there. Eric never told us the rest of the plan. If he's captured, I have no idea where to go from here.

Eric walks back around the corner and rushes back to where we're waiting, sending my pulse back to its regular frantic pace. "The courtyard in front of my building is empty, but that doesn't mean someone isn't watching from their window. My place is on the second floor, first door on the right. We're going to walk there, quickly, but don't run. Running looks suspicious. No talking. Is everyone ready?"

Daniel grabs my hand and I move into the courtyard, resisting the urge to run. Casual. We're just a group of friends walking to a friend's house for a get together. Nothing to see here.

We head up the stairs, pausing only long enough for Eric to swipe his OneCard against the door reader. He pushes the door open and we all file into the pitch black room. Eric slams the door shut behind Thomas and the lights blink on as he moves through the apartment, revealing a cramped living room filled with a group of dirty and beaten down ex-PIT prisoners.

"Rebecca," Daniel whispers in my ear. He's here, really here right next to me. I reach out and touch his cheek with the palm of my hand, simply because I can. He covers my hand with his and pulls me in with his eyes and wide smile. I could stay like this forever, just keeping him next to me.

"I know this is hard, but we need to keep moving." Eric comes out from another room carrying an armload of clothes. "As soon as the guards get the riot at the dining hall under control, they are going to go back into Quarantine and find you two missing. It won't take long for them to put two and two together and realize I helped you escape. They'll head straight here, which means we have to be long gone before that happens."

I pull Daniel in close to me, my hand on his cheek not enough anymore. I felt safe for half a minute, but Eric brought reality back into focus. We aren't free yet.

"I have clothes for the girls in my room." He lifts up the bundle in his arms. "These are for Daniel and Thomas. None of it is great, but it's the best I could do on such short notice. Anyway, it's better than what you have on now. When you're changed, I have some food in the kitchen and then we need to leave."

Daniel kisses the top of my head and lets go. The separation causes a momentary twinge of pain in my chest. It's silly. He'll be right here in the next room, but yesterday I thought we'd be dead. Every moment now is a bonus I never thought to ask for, and I don't want to let him out of my sight.

Elizabeth loops her arm through mine and we walk together into the bedroom. Laid out are four sets of clothes, but they aren't at all what I was expecting. Long sleeved stretchy shirts without buttons paired with thick pants and men's boots. What in the world was Eric thinking?

"Will you help me?" Elizabeth turns her back to me and points to the buttons on her threadbare dress. I release the last one and she turns back around with a conspiratorial smile and a wink. "Women in pants? The Cardinal would have a fit."

That's all the motivation I need. I turn my back and let Elizabeth return the favor.

The shirt is soft against my skin, even if it is a little big. The material snaps back when I pull on it and despite the light weight, I'm instantly warmer. Encouraged by the shirt, I slide the pants on and struggle to do up the buttons and zipper. It's weird to feel the material move between my legs. Unlike stockings, it doesn't stick to my skin. Instead, the baggy material bunches up at my waist and hips, clearly several sizes too big since they were made for a man. I walk around a bit, testing the feel. Awkward for sure, but these are definitely more practical than a skirt.

Constance turns her torso around to get a better look at her backside in the pants. She turns back, meeting my eyes and shrugs. "Not exactly the most fashionable thing I've ever worn, but my butt looks amazing. Wait until Thomas gets a look at me in these."

There's a beat of silence followed by beautiful gales laughter. It wasn't even that funny, but none of us can stop laughing. Lack of sleep, hours of tension, and a million ways we might all die before tomorrow, and we're in here laughing because Constance thinks Thomas will like her butt in a pair of pants.

A knock on the door silences our laughter. "Is everyone okay in there?"

"Almost done," Elizabeth calls out in response to Eric's question. We all finish lacing up the sturdy boots and head out of the room to find the guys.

In the small square kitchen, Daniel and Thomas stop chewing to stare at the four of us walking in. Daniel swallows down his mouthful of bread and flashes me a smile that warms every inch of my skin.

"Now that's something I haven't seen before." Thomas looks Constance up and down and pulls her onto his lap.

"No," Daniel says, mimicking Thomas's action, "but I think I can get used to it."

"Alright." Patrice nudges past us. "Enough with the kissy face. I was promised food."

Eric passes around a basket filled with bread and hands us each a thick slice of cheese. "Sorry, we don't have time for anything fancier. We can eat this now and I have more packed up to take with us."

The room is silent as we stuff ourselves with bread and cheese. Eric's right that it isn't a feast, but it might as well be a gourmet meal. The bread is still soft without even a hint of mold. The cheese is creamy and a little salty, a perfect match with the bread. It's the best thing I've had to eat in over a year.

Eric passes out backpacks to each of us. Elizabeth slides her burlap bag into hers before sliding it on. I check inside to find a canteen, a bag of food, and a thick blanket. It's enough to last us at least a few days. I'm impressed with how much he was able to pull together so quickly. Eric stands, swinging his own bag onto his shoulders. "Time to go."

Gathered around the door with the lights out, our moment of fun and relaxation disappears. "The truck will stick out like a sore thumb in the city, so we have to move on foot from here on out. We'll take the back roads again, heading west toward the mountains. Just stay close to me and we should be fine. If something does happen, everyone split up and run. They can't chase us all at once."

I grab hold of Daniel's hand and squeeze tighter. No matter what Eric says, I don't plan to separate from Daniel unless someone drags me away kicking and screaming. Eric opens the door and we file out again, two by two, back into the fray.

* * *

Once we leave the courtyard, the streets are dark enough to hide our movements, but not our noise. These boots are much better than my worn out shoes from the PIT, but my feet slide around in all the extra space and they clomp with every step despite my best efforts. I'm not the only one making noise.

The buildings spread out a bit as we head west, but bunch back up again when we hit the edge of the city. The houses and stores are older here, many of them long past the point of a new paint job. None of the buildings back home ever got this bad. I think. I never went to the edge of the city. Everything I needed was no more than a few blocks from my house. Everything feels neglected, as if no one lives here, but there are signs of life everywhere. Wash hanging on a line, a rusted tricycle tilted on its side in a yard that's more weeds than grass. Who lives like this? Are they here by choice or because the Assignment forced them to work at jobs that can't afford them nicer houses?

The street dead-ends at a crossroads, guiding us to the right or left to circle back around the city. We march across the intersection and head into a grassy plain, a copse of trees visible in the distance.

"Stay together," Eric calls softly over his shoulder. Without the road to guide us, it would be all too easy for one of us to wander out of sight in the dark.

The swishing grass absorbs the noise of our footsteps, but the tall reeds slow my progress. Eric increases the pace and my breath puffs out in heavy bursts. I suck air into my lungs, but the cool night air stings my throat and I cough despite my best efforts to stay quiet.

My shoulders ache from running with the added weight of the backpack. Daniel tries to take my bag, but I shake him off. No way am I going to let him carry my extra weight when he's out here with broken ribs and who knows what other injuries. I can be strong, too.

Eric, visible in the moonlight, leads us and we each match his pace. The others are right behind us, I can tell from their labored breathing, but my entire world is the back of Eric's head and Daniel's strong hand in mine.

Leaves crunch off to our right, breaking up the silence. Eric freezes and I drop to my knees out of some survival instinct, pulling Daniel down with me. The top of Eric's head is just visible over the edge of the tall grass. I turn, searching for the others, but they must be buried down, hiding. At least, I hope they're hiding. Eric's head turns from side to side, searching the horizon, and I follow his movements.

I drop back down and focus on making my breaths silent. A cramp builds in my left calf. If we don't get up soon, the rest of my leg will follow suit and I'll be lucky if I can walk the rest of the way.

Eric stands, cocks back his arm and throws something in the direction of the crunching leaves. It's too dark to see, so I close my eyes and strain to hear anything. More leaves crunch and I snap my eyes back open. Several deer jump out of the darkness, bounding into the tree line. Deer, just deer.

I roll my shoulders, then let Daniel help me up. Eric is up and running, but I wait a half a second. Sure that we're all still here, I ignore the building pain in my leg and chase after Eric, moving faster than before.

As my muscles start to give out, we leave the grassy plain and dodge around the first line of trees. It's darker in the forest. A canopy of leaves swallowing up the moonlight that guided us this far. I don't mind. For once, the darkness is welcoming. I lean back against the rough bark of the tree nearest to me and sink down to the ground, my knees tucked up under my chin. Daniel collapses next to me and we sit in silence, catching our breath.

"We have..." Eric puffs out the words from somewhere to my right, "to keep...moving."

He's right, but I hate him for it. The thin line of trees between us and the open plain isn't enough to hide us from searching guards. My legs are lumps of jelly, but more pain is preferable to the alternative.

It takes another minute for everyone to get up. We can't run anymore or risk tripping over roots and fallen branches. Without any light, everyone has to test each step to make sure they stay on their feet.

The silence is unnerving. I want to ask so many questions, but we have to stay quiet. Even if we could talk, I don't have the extra breath to speak. Instead, I run through a hundred different questions in my head. The biggest one being, 'Where are we going?'

Eric said we can't live in the city and, for once, Daniel was in complete agreement. In school we learned a little about the geography of the Territories. There is a ton of unpopulated land in between the cities. So much of it used to hold people, but that was before the violence got out of control and the diminished population flocked to the cities for safety. Before the Machine. But no one lives there now, and it's just forests and wild animals. None of us have the survival skills needed to live on our own in the middle of nowhere.

Daniel squeezes my hand and I focus on the tingling of our contact. The details don't matter so long as Daniel and I are together, right? I can't shake the doubt sitting in the back of my head, but for now I can enjoy every second of this freedom.

Six

It's hard to tell if it's morning yet this deep in the forest, but after walking for what feels like forever, a thin film of light seeps between the trees and casts shadows everywhere. Eric leads us to a huge boulder with a slight overhang, offering a hint of protection.

His feet stop moving and we all fall to the ground in sync. I haven't slept in almost twenty-four hours and the stress of each one of those hours fills up my limbs like sandbags.

"We'll stop here and get some rest. I won't feel safe until we're much farther in, but none of us is going to last much longer unless we stop for a bit." Eric reaches into his backpack and grabs a water bottle and a small bag.

My body fights between sleep and food, but Daniel breaks the tie for me. He grabs the water out of my bag, unscrews the top, and hands it to me, careful not to spill a single drop. I take a mouthful and let the lukewarm liquid coat my tongue before swallowing. One big gulp and I set it back down. Daniel offers me half a bread roll and a small slice of cheese. It's not much, but it will keep my stomach from growling and that's more than I can say about most of the meals we got in the PIT.

Everyone moves in slow motion, eating a few bites of food and spreading out the blankets Eric packed. Daniel spreads his blanket out on the ground and pulls me close so we can both share mine as a cover. Exhaustion pulls at my eyelids, but all the unknowns keep me from giving in to sleep.

"Eric," I prop my head on my elbow with Daniel copying my position behind me. "What are the guards going to do?"

"Once they get the riot quelled and throw a bunch of men in Quarantine, they'll get the film crew out on the last Airtrain. Someone will be sent to check on you and then they'll find you missing. They might search the PIT, but once they realize I'm gone as well, they'll know that we left."

Eric lays out his blanket right beside ours, but doesn't sit down. Elizabeth moves her blanket to the far edge of the overhang. It's not really big enough for her to go far and I'm sure she can still hear every word.

"With no more Airtrains for the night, they'll grab a truck to make the drive and contact the guard in Ricksburg to search my apartment. It won't take long to find it abandoned and realize we're gone."

"Then what?" Patrice asks. She sits on the other side of Daniel. Side by side, there's no denying they're siblings.

Eric shrugs, tossing a small stone between his hands. "As far as I know, there's not a protocol for escaped prisoners. They'll search the city for sure, but I don't know if they'll think to check the forest. We can't risk assuming that they won't."

"But you could go back, right?" Patrice's voice is softer without all the anger painting her every word. "You could tell them that we forced you to help us."

Eric paces back and forth in front of his blanket, his eyes never leaving the stone he's tossing. "Maybe I could have, but not now. We left your clothes at my apartment. They'll understand that means I had to have other clothes there for you already. Most of them barely trust me as is. That will be all they need to know I was a willing participant."

"Then you're an idiot." Elizabeth still has her back to us, but I don't need to see her face to know she's seething with anger. "If the clothes are a giveaway then you should have thrown them away, burned them. Then you could leave us alone and go back to your perfect little world."

Eric stops suddenly and heaves the stone at the boulder. "Maybe I want them to know what I did." Eric's shout echoes against the trees and a flock of birds flies out of a tree, cawing out a reprimand for disturbing them.

"You think I'm a monster, and I can't blame you." Eric rubs his eyes with the tips of his fingers, and the movement ages him another ten years. "The things I've done are horrific and I'd take them back if I could. I hate the Cardinal. I hate what he's done to us. I hate what he does every day, horrible things right under the noses of everyone. I want him to know I helped you escape."

Elizabeth stands up and marches over to Eric. He stands up, arms stretched out, hope lifting his droopy eyes, but when she gets to him, Elizabeth doesn't give him a hug. She pushes him hard enough to knock him back down on the ground and kicks a clump of dirt at him with the toe of her new boots. "Isn't it nice that you finally figured out what a miserable excuse for a human being you are? Looks like you and the Cardinal have a lot in common."

She crouches down in front of him, her face only inches from his. Daniel jerks as if he wants to stop her, but I touch his arm and shake my head. This is between Elizabeth and Eric. It's going to happen eventually, so it might as well be now.

"I don't care if you free the entire PIT and set the Cardinal on fire. I'll never forgive you. I can never forget what you did to me. To her." She swallows hard. "Congratulations on your little act of revolution, but don't expect me to thank you."

She draws back her fist like she's going to punch him, fire writhing in her eyes. She tightens her fingers and smashes her fist into the ground, inches from Eric's head. He opens his mouth, but Elizabeth jumps up and marches away before he can get out the first word.

I smear a dirty finger under my eye to stop the tears before they start. I can't imagine the pain Elizabeth still holds after Molly died. My chest burns even thinking about losing Daniel. I can't imagine doing any of this without him.

Patrice, Constance, and Thomas lie down, and we all settle into an uncomfortable silence as sleep grabs hold. Eric stays sitting up on his blanket, his head scanning back and forth across the forest. Keeping watch so the rest of us can sleep.

His gaze meets mine and I give him a small smile. I hate Eric. I really do. But he's saved my life now, more than once. In almost no time he got a vehicle, the tools needed to remove our poison, new clothes, and packed survival bags. This wasn't a light decision for him, and I can appreciate that. We'd be back in the PIT or dead if it wasn't for him. Maybe that makes me hate him even more.

I drop my head down and ignore the hard ground under my back. It's even less comfortable than the mattresses in the PIT, but my body is too tired to care. I snuggle back against Daniel's chest and let his steady breaths lull me into a calmer state. I have so many questions, but they can wait. We all need sleep, and I don't think I can handle any more honest answers for a while.

I close my eyes and try not to think about the scenarios that Eric didn't offer up. Like what they will do back at the PIT once they realize we're gone. They'll do a search for sure. Will they find all the others who helped me with the hack at the Acceptance ceremony? How many more innocent lives am I responsible for?

* * *

My eyes flutter open and I sit up like a bolt of lightning. Leftover fear from my nightmare tears through my body and my limbs shake uncontrollably. Warm arms wrap around me. Daniel.

What I really want is to stay right here on this sad little blanket and let Daniel hold me forever. But I also don't want to get caught. I force myself to sit up and take in our group. The others are all in varying stages of waking up, including Eric. He must have dozed off at some point, his body's need for sleep winning out over the need to keep watch.

Daniel hands me the water and I take a few swigs. After one day, there is a lot less water than when we started. We need to find a new source today or we won't have to worry about the guards finding us. The other half of my roll from yesterday is hard on the outside, but it will have to do. First, fresh water. Then food.

There isn't much to do to get ready. Just roll up our blankets and put on my shoes. I shove my foot into the boot and immediately regret my action. Blisters on my heel, ankle, and toes rub against the stiff material, sending little stabs of pain into my foot with each movement. What I really need is some antibiotics, a cold compress, and some lambskin wrap to keep those blisters from getting worse. But all I have is a second pair of socks dug out from the bottom of my pack. I put them on and hiss through the pain of putting my shoes on.

I stand and test out the pain. There's no denying it's bad, but I can walk and that's the important part. Daniel finishes adding our blankets to the packs and puts both of them on his back. "Wanna tell me what had you so upset when you woke up?"

"What do you mean?" I know exactly what he means.

"Your face was pale as a bleached sheet and you were shaking like crazy. Something in your dreams had you pretty shaken up." He takes both my hands and rubs his thumb in little circles along the back of my hands.

"It was just a dream."

"Rebecca." His hands give mine a single squeeze and then his thumbs continue their circular pattern. "We're a team, and that means sharing your worries with me, even if you don't think I can help."

"It was a dumb dream. A nightmare." I close my eyes and try to force the image out of my head. "We were back in the grassy area in Quarantine. I told them I wouldn't read the apology letter, but instead of hitting you, they killed you. A guard held a black box up to your arm and you collapsed, your body flooding with poison. I screamed at them that I changed my mind. I would read the letter. But it was too late." I open my eyes and Daniel is even closer, practically flush against me. "I thought I'd lost you."

Daniel lifts my chin up with a strong hand until my eyes meet his. "I'm not going anywhere. You're stuck with me."

He leans down and kisses me gently. And then not so gently. His arms wrap around my waist and pull me closer until there isn't a hair's width between us. I grip his shoulders and lean into him until my arms ache; feeding on the love he passes me with every touch of our lips. I could never get enough of this, and don't care who watches only a few feet away.

"So now what?" Patrice's voice invades my little slice of perfection. We end the kiss and there she is, standing close enough for a group hug, and a smug squint of her eyes confesses her timing wasn't accidental.

Daniel pulls back a little, but doesn't let go of my waist. "We need to talk to Eric."

Daniel leads me over to the boulder and everyone sits down in a little circle.

"So where are we going?" Elizabeth sits on her blanket lacing up her shoes.

"There are rumors...the guards like to tell stories when we pull duty in the middle of the night. Back when everyone migrated to the major cities and the Territories were formed. Not everyone left."

"But that's not new information," Patrice cuts in. "We all learned in history class that there were people who didn't want to let go of the old ways. They all died out decades ago."

"Yeah, the same books that claim we're all a bunch of deranged criminals, too dangerous to live with everyone else?" Elizabeth rolls her eyes and stands up, rubbing shaky hands down her pant legs. "We all know every word from the Cardinal is the truth spoken. Didn't your Rejection teach you anything?"

Patrice stands up, her hands clenched in small, shaking fists. "I guess it taught you how to be a sarcastic bi—"

Daniel, Eric, and I move as a unit to create a living barrier between Elizabeth and Patrice. Thomas wraps his arm around Constance as if to protect her from a fist fight. Daniel turns to me and raises his eyebrows, but I shake my head. I don't have any answers for him. Patrice is livid she was Rejected and she has every right to be. Each of us is at least a little bit responsible that she's out here instead of back at home with her parents. Each of us, except Eric. Which is maybe why he's the only one she's looking at now.

Eric puts an arm around Patrice and walks her to the other end of the boulder, whispering something into her ear. Daniel takes a few steps as if to follow them, and possibly detach Eric's arm from his shoulder, but I put a hand on Daniel's arm and shake my head again. We don't need to break up another fight.

Elizabeth straightens out the pants and shirt that look almost natural on her and sits back down on the blanket. Eric walks back with Patrice and an understood truce washes in silence over us. Thomas nods at Eric to continue.

"The circulated story is that anyone who stayed out of the cities died out within a generation or two. It's easy to believe that survival would be nearly impossible outside of the Territories. But I don't believe it anymore."

I sit up straighter and lift my knees up under my chin.

"After all, we did okay living in the PIT without any of the standards of living we thought were essential before getting there. No indoor plumbing, low-nutrition food, limited clothing and housing. If we survived, who's to say others couldn't do it, too?"

"Wait, are you saying there are people out here living the way we did in the PIT? Who would do that?" I can't tell if Elizabeth's wide eyes are a sign of disbelief or hope. I'm not really sure what I'm feeling either.

"Maybe not," Eric replies, a little overeager to have Elizabeth speaking to him. "They've had a hundred years or more without anyone limiting their actions. They could have communities as advanced as what we'd find in any Territory."

"So that's where we're going. To find these people? Put all our hope on a rumor told around the guard room?" It's the first thing Constance has said all morning.

"Yes." Daniel answers her question, but he's looking at me. "It's the best shot we've got, rumor or not. And if it's true…"

"And if we can't find anyone?" I'm not sure I can hope yet. "What if there's no one out here but us and the Cardinal guards hunting us down."

Daniel runs the back of his fingers down the side of my check. "I'd rather die out here with you, than alone in the PIT."

I scoot over and press the side of my body to his. He's right. "I'm in."

Eric stands and brushes off his pants. "We need to pack up and get moving. We can take advantage of what's left of the daylight and move a little faster. We won't be able to stop again until we're well into the hills." He shakes out his blanket and rolls it into his bag.

Everyone finishes packing up and getting down a bit of food. I can't tell if the mood is hopeful or resigned. I guess it doesn't really matter so long as we keep putting one boot in front of the other.

Seven

I step over a fallen, half-rotted log, but my shoe slips on the damp leaves that cover everything. Daniel grabs my arm and steadies me before I hit the ground yet again. None of us are too steady on our feet with how little we've had to eat over the past four days. Or is it five? I can't keep track. Our irregular sleep pattern blends one day into the next with nothing but more walking through the forest.

Eric's compass tells us we're heading west, but we don't really know where we are. We've been climbing for a while and when the sun goes down, so does the temperature. The night wind stings my face, but our brisk pace keeps me warm enough. For now.

"I'm so cold. Can't we stop and make a small fire to warm up a bit?"

I feel bad for Patrice, really I do. This is her first time away from the comforts of home. But I'm not sure how much longer I can take her constant complaining, Daniel's sister or not.

"Here, take my jacket." Eric slips off the red monstrosity he's been wearing and slips it over Patrice's arms.

Daniel growls next to me, so low I'm probably the only one who heard it. We can't afford for the two of them to get into it. We need to keep moving and putting distance between us and the city.

I slow our pace a bit so there's more distance between us and Eric and fall in line right in front of Constance and Thomas.

"What do you think, Rebecca?" Constance calls out from behind me. "Do these communities exist or are we chasing a fairytale?"

It's a serious question, but Constance's voice is light and cheery, like we aren't marching through the woods at night toward our potential death. I pull out the last of my reserves to match her energy.

"Yep, great big old cities filled with hot showers, feather beds, and buffet restaurants as far as the eye can see."

Daniel laughs beside me. "What, no shopping malls or spa treatments?"

"I've got my priorities, but a clean set of clothes for after that hot shower would be just about perfect." I look over my shoulder. "What about you, Thomas? What does your perfect city look like?"

"Okay, let's see. I'm going to join you at that buffet, and I don't even care what's on it. I'd eat a squirrel right now if we could catch one."

Genuine laughter fills our little space in the trees and it feels good. There hasn't been much to laugh about in too long.

"After that buffet I'm going to hunt down a little house," Thomas says, a laugh still floating on his words. "Nothing fancy, mind you. I'm not greedy. Just a little cottage would do, big enough for me and Constance. Our own space, like the bunk in the PIT, minus the leaky roof and bad neighborhood."

I can picture it in my head. A clapboard house with a stone walk up to the front door. Cozy rooms painted cheerful colors like yellow or the green of spring grass. A place just for me and Daniel. I never allowed myself to imagine the two of us actually spending a life together, but I can imagine it now. A perfect little house for two rises to the top of my priority list.

Daniel squeezes my hand. Is he picturing the same thing? "You're awfully quiet, Constance. What does the perfect city hold for you?"

"Kids." Her voice is as soft as the wind. "Lots and lots of kids."

My chest constricts. For Constance, the fairytale city can never give her what she really wants. A child of her own. It's the reason she was sent to the PIT, and while it's a horrible reason to throw away a person, escaping the Cardinal's rule won't change the fact that she's barren.

"Don't stop dreaming on my account," Constance says, her bubbly voice back to normal. "We all have our dreams, some more attainable than others. But we can't predict what life is going to hand us. This little group knows better than most that you can't predict the future and your reality can change in a heartbeat."

She's right. Two weeks ago, our current situation would have sounded completely implausible.

"After all the surgeries, when the doctors said I would never have children, my mother told me that life for me wouldn't be about dreams and making plans. I don't think she was talking about the PIT, though her words fit. She said much of life is deciding what you can live with and making peace with everything else."

We walk in silence, the wet leaves dampening our heavy footfalls as the first hints of daybreak peek in through the dense trees. After the PIT, I know exactly what I can live with. But Cardinal help me, I'm really bad at the making peace with everything else part.

* * *

The sun is fully up, and I'm fully exhausted. Up ahead Patrice trips and hits the ground on her hands and knees. Eric and Daniel both jump to help her, but Eric backs off with a death glare from Daniel. Despite orchestrating our escape, there's still an uneasy alliance between those two. Eric's attention to Patrice is only fueling the animosity.

Daniel helps Patrice to stand, but her legs are wobbly. She's spent.

"Let's take a break."

Everyone sinks to the ground where they stand at Eric's words, creating a circle of bodies among several large boulders. After walking all night, we're all running on empty.

Thomas crawls over to a tree and strips some of the moss off the bark. Like he's done at every rest stop, he grabs two rocks, makes a small pile of debris and strikes the rocks together repeatedly until a flicker of a spark shoots off and grabs on to the dried moss. Without taking his eyes off the smolder, he grabs a handful of twigs and sticks them into the flame, making a cone shape for the fire to climb.

Eric and Daniel walk over with an armload each of various sticks and branches, and within minutes we're all sitting around a steady blaze, our hands stuck in front of us to soak up the warmth.

"Where did you learn to build a fire like that?" My father would sometimes build a fire in our fireplace, but he only stuck the fabricated logs in and lit it. Thomas's fire required knowledge and skill that would have been useless in the Territories.

"My father taught me when I was a kid." Thomas's voice is low against the crackle of burning wood. "I didn't exactly grow up like the rest of you."

"What do you mean?"

"Remember when we left Ricksburg and there were all those rundown buildings at the edge of city?"

I nod, but Thomas isn't looking at me.

"That's how I grew up. My father worked in a little repair shop that fixed items for people who couldn't afford to buy new when something broke. I would sit with him in his workshop and watch him tinker with everything from ancient Noteboards to coffee pots. When I got older, he taught me how to search out what was broken and figure out how to fix it. And when there wasn't enough money to keep the heat on, he taught me how to make a fire so we didn't freeze in the winter."

I reach out a hand to his arm. "I'm so sorry."

"Don't be." Thomas prods the fire with a long stick and sparks shoot up into the air around us. "The Assignment made sure my family would struggle to get by, but we had a good life. My father is the smartest man I know. He could fix anything, and he taught me more than I ever learned in school. Even without tons of money, there was so much love. No one in my house ever treated me like I was less because of the scars left over from my illness. We didn't have much to eat or new clothes, but we had plenty of laughter. Growing up in my family made me who I am today. I'm not sorry for that and you shouldn't be either."

It's like Thomas and I grew up on different planets. My father's job provided everything we needed, even if it was never enough for what my mother wanted. But we never had laughter.

We all stare into the fire, but without anything more to eat there's really nothing else to do but try to get some rest. Daniel takes out our blankets and the others settle down as well.

Thomas stands, brushing the dirt away from his pants. "I'll go get a bit more wood for the fire and take first watch."

"You should stay right where you are."

My head jerks up at the unfamiliar voice. A man stands a few yards away, a bow and arrow pointed directly at Thomas's head.

Eight

Daniel jumps to his feet and pulls me up without asking, shoving me behind his tall frame. "Patrice. Here, now."

The sharp cold whip of his words isn't Daniel. Gone is any softness. His voice demands compliance and Patrice doesn't question it. His arm moves her next to me and I wrap my arm around her shoulder. Now isn't the time for petty arguments.

Eric, Elizabeth, and Constance run to our little group, but Thomas is still frozen in place as a second man steps from behind a tree and points his arrow at us. I grab Daniel's hand from behind and stare through a gap between his arm and Elizabeth's. We found them, or rather, they found us.

"Hi there, my name is Thomas—"

"Shut up." The taller of the two men pulls his bow tighter and lifts it so the taught string is pressed against his bearded face. "Get over there by the others."

Thomas backs up and joins our group without another word.

All this time we've been looking for these people. The rumored cities living outside of Cardinal control. They were supposed to be our saviors. I never stopped to think they might not want us.

The shorter of the two men steps forward, his weapon sweeping around our campsite. His clean, smooth face pegs him at about our age. "All of you, down on your knees. Hands on your head."

Daniel steps forward, out of reach of my hands. Constance grabs my arm and the pressure of her hand is the only thing keeping me still. "We aren't here to hurt anyone. Mind telling us who you are?"

"We told you to shut up." The younger man lifts his bow, his stance matching that of the older man.

"Okay, you win." Daniel backs up, his hands in the air. He gets down on both knees and motions with his hands for the rest of us to follow suit.

The older, bearded man walks around behind us, his guarded eyes taking in everything from our ill-fitting clothes to the cluster of blankets, still laid out from where we all were about to sleep just minutes ago. He swings back around to the front, but pauses in front of Patrice, his expression frozen in indifference. "You." His booted foot nudges Daniel and Eric aside to stand right in front of her. "Up, now. Move over there."

Both men have their weapons trained on Patrice like she might attack them any minute. She whimpers once, but gets up and stumbles out in front of us. Every muscle in Daniel's back, neck, and arms tenses like a cat waiting to pounce on an unaware mouse.

"Where did you get that jacket?"

Eric moans so low the men can't hear him.

"I…" Patrice turns to us, her eyes pleading for help, several tears spilling over to run down her cheeks.

The younger of the two men drops his bow and moves to stand inches from Patrice's face. "It's a simple question. You aren't a Cardinal guard. Where did you get one of their jackets?"

"It's mine." Eric stands up, his arms lifted above his head.

Before any of us can move, the men shove Patrice aside and point both their weapons at Eric, motioning with the sharp point of their arrows for him to step away from the rest of us.

"Over there, by the rocks. On your knees. Face the rocks."

"No, what are you doing?" Elizabeth jumps up and runs to her brother, but a quick elbow to her cheek sends her falling to the ground with a thump. Daniel turns and wraps both arms around me. I'm frozen in place, my mind screaming to get up and save them. Both of them.

"We don't recognize the Cardinal's authority. His evil minions aren't welcome here."

The older man kicks Eric in the back, forcing him to his knees. Patrice sobs from where she fell across from us. Elizabeth crawls a few inches, but her blinking eyes have trouble staying open. Both men lift their bows, and level them down at Eric.

Despite Daniel's strong arms, I shove up and run toward them. "Stop it. You can't."

They ignore me and lift the weapons up to aim right at the back of Eric's head.

"You're worse than the Cardinal."

Both men spin, their arrows now pointed right at my head. I skid to a stop, my arms flying up over my head. I'm faintly aware of Daniel and the others shouting from their position a few feet away, but I can barely hear them over the pounding of blood in my head.

"What did you say?"

My throat is swollen shut, stopping any air from getting in or words getting out. I open my mouth, but close it again like a fish pulled from a cold creek.

"She said you're a bunch of numb-skulled bullies that make the Cardinal look like a benevolent ruler on high."

I spin on my heels to stare at the girl, probably our age, walking out of the forest into the clearing. Her hair is a wild, curly mound surrounding her head. Green eyes narrow at the two men, their weapons still pointing at my head.

"Put those down, you idiots."

"He's a Cardinal guard." They lower their weapons, but keep them pulled tight, ready to fire.

"Is he now? You searched him and found a shock stick?" Her empty hands rest on her hips. Her own bow sticks up over her shoulder, held on by a series of straps. "He's got a Noteboard order to transport a bunch of PIT prisoners to the middle of nowhere?"

"No." The older man drops his arrow into a cylinder hanging off his hip then points to Patrice. "But that one over there is wearing his jacket. What do you call that?"

"It's a mistake." Without the weapons pointing at me, I've got my voice back. "A painful, costly mistake. It's already responsible for one life lost. Please don't make it pay again."

The woman stares at me, her steely green eyes running over me from my cropped hair, over my baggy men's clothes, down to the obviously too large boots. She takes all of us in, her lips moving silently like she's arguing with herself. Nodding once, she motions at both men and they stow their weapons.

"We'll take them back to the village. Alan can sort this out there."

The men nod back, neither of them questioning her decision. The younger of the two pulls Eric up by the back of his shirt. Eric runs to where Patrice is still sobbing and helps her to stand.

Strong arms wrap around my waist and I know it's Daniel without looking. I turn and let my raised arms fall onto his shoulders. He wraps me up, his cheek resting on the top of my head until I'm surrounded by his warmth.

"Get their stuff and let's go home."

Home. She says it like it's a real thing.

Fabric rips behind me and I turn out of Daniel's arms to see the woman tearing one of our thin blankets into strips of material.

"What are you doing?"

She stands up, one of the strips stretched between her hands. "We aren't going to shoot you out here, but I'm not about to trust you."

Before I can flinch away, she reaches out and wraps the scratchy fabric around my eyes. "My home, my rules." She ties off the blindfold in a rough knot behind my head. "The rest of you get over here and line up behind her."

Footsteps shuffle behind me, but I can't see anything. Daniel's hands grab my shoulders and give a soft squeeze. "You're amazing." Lips kiss the crown of my head and I lean back into him before calloused hands grab my wrist.

I'm tugged forward and the others follow close behind me. Led blindly through the forest to Cardinal knows what, I don't feel amazing.

Nine

We haven't marched far, but my energy is sapped, an entire night of walking through the forest hitting me with every step. My feet throb where blisters have split open and new blisters have formed.

"Hail, Mary." A baritone voice calls from above us. I lift my head up even though I can't see anything.

"Hail, John," the woman with the green eyes calls back. Her voice is friendly, but holds the hint of command she had talking to the men who captured us. "Run to tell Alan we come with guests."

Funny. I don't feel like a guest.

The ground evens out beneath us. If I didn't know better, I'd swear we were walking on a man-made surface. Whatever it is, at least I'm not tripping over tree roots or sliding on fallen leaves.

"Hail, Mary. What do you bring us?" a new man's voice rings out, carrying easily in the warming air. It holds the same sense of command that Mary's does.

Her hand comes down on my shoulder, halting our bone-tired passage. "We found them down by Jacob's rocks. From the look of things, they've been traveling a while."

Strong hands grab my upper right arm, pushing back the stretchy fabric. A finger runs over the small incision where Eric removed our poison capsules, the gauze long gone. I hiss in a sharp breath against the stinging pain. "Rejects." The hands let go and grab the blindfold off my head.

I blink from the sudden onslaught of light and try to take in everything. Daniel gasps behind me. He's seeing the same thing I am. We're still in the middle of the forest, the mile high trees acting like a fence around the large cleared area in front of us. We're standing on an old road and small buildings line both sides. It's a village.

Another man, his temples already graying, stands in front of us. This must be Alan. He stares at me like he's trying to see beneath the grime I've accumulated over the past week in the woods. "Get them over to Marcus to get these cuts cleaned up and something to eat. Then send this one to me." He jerks his thumb at me and Daniel's hand tenses on my shoulder.

"Let's go." Mary walks off, clearly expecting us to follow her.

Daniel grabs my hand, our eyes meeting briefly before we head deeper into the city.

Mary leads us down a paved street. I wasn't wrong about the surface evening out. There are cracks running through the hard dark surface, but only a few spots have weeds popping through them. Someone has taken a lot of effort to maintain the road.

Buildings of various sizes and conditions line the street. Most of them could be houses from back home, with some smaller buildings mixed in, rough wooden signs hung on the doors. Everything could use some repairs and a coat of paint, but besides the slightly shabby state, we could be in any city in the Territories. The only differences are the trees…and the people.

Men, women, and children walk everywhere, traveling alone and in small groups, their voices calling greetings out to each other, laughing and shouting. The people here are genuinely happy.

Several older men sit in rocking chairs in front of what could be a small store. They lean in toward each other, whispering comments before calling out to the people walking by them.

"Hail, Linda. Anything good for lunch today? A stew would be mighty fine."

A woman wearing sturdy pants and carrying a basket of potatoes pauses in front of the trio of men. "You know as well as anyone else we have baked spuds on Tuesdays. Stew is on Friday and not a day before." Her voice is stern, but she winks at the men before walking on, a laugh on her lips.

The sound is infectious, and I smile along with her. This is like the Territories, but with people really living instead of playing out some elaborate Cardinal choreographed dance. When women stopped to chat back home, it was never filled with this much joy. Every contact presented an opportunity for cataloging eyes and critical analysis. Not here. The people talking in the streets look like they're actually enjoying each other's company. My heart surges and I can't hold back a small giggle. We made it and it's so much more than I had thought to hope for.

Mary stops in front of a squat building without any windows in the front. She pushes open the door and a tinkling sound rings through the room. Not an electric chime like the shops back in the capitol, but an actual bell that vibrates above our heads.

"Hail, Marcus," Mary calls out while ushering us all into the mostly empty room. "I've got some actual work for you today."

An older man with wrinkles lining his face and glasses perched on his thin nose comes out of a back room. "Hail, Mary." He wraps her in a brief hug and pushes his glasses up. They have the same green eyes. "Getting a little sassy there, little lady. Don't think you're too old for me to turn you over a knee." He swats at her backside, but she scoots away, laughing.

"You'd have to catch me first, Grandfather."

Matching green eyes.

"Stars guide the man who catches you." He winks at her stuck out tongue. "Now, what do you have for me?"

"Watch found them this morning. Escaped from the PIT. Alan sent them over to have their cuts cleaned up."

Marcus eyes us like a group of abandoned puppies. "Starving by the looks of 'em. Too early for lunch, but run over to Cook and see what you can rustle up. I'll get started here."

Mary heads back outside, her exit announced by the ringing bell.

Marcus lifts my sleeve and shines a tiny light at the cut. "Mhm. Sure enough, there's some early signs of infection. These cuts need cleaned up and closed up. Come on back."

"Wait. How do all of you know about the poison?" Eric pushes up to the front of the group. "I didn't find out until they made me a guard."

Marcus blinks at us, his eyes wide. "Do you think you're the first PIT runaways to find their way here?"

I shuffle back a few steps and bump into Daniel. No one has ever escaped from the PIT. That's what kept everyone in the Territories safe. But we know the Cardinal lies. Is it possible?

* * *

Mary is waiting for us with a basket of bread and cheese when we file out of Marcus's exam room. My arm stings from the antiseptic and stitches, but the sight of food shoves the pain to the back of my head.

"Lunch is still an hour off, but I was able to talk the cooking crew into some bread and cheese. It's not much." Mary sets the basket down on the counter with a jug of water and cups.

We don't wait for an invitation. Constance grabs the basket and hands out bread to each of us while Patrice heads straight to the water. None of us even bother finding chairs, as we cram food into our mouths as fast as we can swallow. Mary and Marcus must think we're a bunch of savages, sitting on the floor in our filthy clothes and dirt smeared everywhere, but that doesn't stop me from licking the bread crumbs out of my hand.

With all the food gone, Mary taps me on the shoulder. "If you're done, Alan wants a word."

Daniel wipes his mouth with the back of his hand and nods. He stands up and reaches down to help me to my feet. Mary raises her eyebrows at us, but doesn't say a word.

"Marcus, Alan thought they'd all like to get some rest. Would you mind taking the others over to the rider's house."

"I imagine they could probably all use a nap. I'll walk them over just as soon as I finish cleaning up in here."

"Perfect." Mary offers him a smile before heading outside, Daniel and I following close behind.

Ten

Mary walks down the street, her shoes tapping against the cracked roadway, and stops a few minutes later in front of a modest house with a sturdy roof. There are curtains in the windows and a line of wet wash hangs out in a rare spot of sunshine. Short of the white picket fence and garish garden decor, this could be my parents' house.

A quick knock on the door is answered almost immediately by a woman in a floral print dress, her hair tied back from a worn, yet beautiful face.

"Morning, Margaret." Mary leans in and gives her a small peck on the cheek. "Alan asked to see one of the newcomers."

"Of course," Margaret says, wiping her hands on a worn rag. "He's in the study. I'll take them from here." She steps back to let us in.

Mary follows us through the door and leans in to whisper to Margaret. Margaret nods and Mary takes a seat on a couch that looks old, but well cared for. She pulls a bit of wood and a small knife out of her pocket and pretends we aren't in the room.

Margaret closes the door and turns her bright eyes and warm smile to us. "This way, dears."

Their home is missing the collections of vases, photographs, and dust catchers that line the shelves and walls back home. Yet, even without all the 'necessities' my mother insisted on having, the rooms feel homey, lived in.

In my mind, I pictured a very different situation when Eric first mentioned people living outside the Cardinal's control. The people here don't live in squalor and none of them are skinny enough to be starving.

Margaret knocks once on a solid wood door before pushing it open. Alan sits at a heavy desk scrolling through something on a Noteboard. There's something else I didn't expect to see out here. He lifts his head as we walk in and shares a warm smile followed by drawn brows. "I only asked to speak to the young lady."

"I'm Daniel, Rebecca's husband." Daniel wraps an arm around my shoulder and my chest warms at his words. This might be the first time he's called himself that. It sounds weird to my ears, but I like it. "We come as a package deal."

"Well, that's a new one. Fine, fine, come in." Alan pulls another chair out of the corner so we all have a seat. "Margaret, please don't let us miss lunch, dear."

"And listen to you complain until dinner? I wouldn't dream of it." She winks at him and smiles again before closing the door behind her.

"That woman could tease a mule, but I'd starve without her." Alan waves at the chairs and spins his own around to face us. "Now that we're settled, why don't you tell me your story, Rebecca Collins and Daniel Whedon?"

Daniel's arms tense where they rest on the chair. "How do you know our names?"

"That's easy." Alan points to Daniel. "You're the spitting image of your father. There was quite the kerfuffle in Cardinal City when you failed Acceptance. And then with your sister this year." He gives us a gentle smile then gestures to me. "Of course, with your little video it was only to be expected. It's hard to forget a transgression like that."

"You saw the video?" My voice is softer than I intended. How in the world would they know all of this all the way out here in the middle of nowhere?

"Of course. We make it a point to stay up to date with the activities of the Cardinal. Brilliant idea, by the way, even if it was doomed. We toasted in your honor that night."

Alan pauses as if waiting for us to ask another question, but my mind is blank. They know us. They saw what we did. They knew we would fail.

"We broke out about a week ago. Eric helped us get out right before the Cardinal planned to kill me and Rebecca."

"I'm surprised he let you live past an hour. Of course, I gave up trying to understand his actions years ago." Alan leans forward, his elbows resting on his knees and his hands steepled just below his chin. "Tell me more about Eric."

I'm at a loss for words and I'm guessing by Daniel's silence, he is as well. How do you explain Eric? He was our friend, a part of our family, and almost my husband. But he threw all that away to save himself. Based on that alone, he's a lying snake. But he's also the person who told us about the fence and got us out of the PIT. He was a Reject, but he left the PIT as a member of the Cardinal's guard. He's risked our lives and saved them.

The silence stretches on until Alan finally puts us out of our misery. "Different question. Do you trust him?"

"He got us out." It's the best I can offer.

"That's not what I asked," Alan says, giving his full attention to Daniel.

"I don't like him, but that's not the same thing. I have my reasons for hating him if I'm going to be completely honest." I grab Daniel's hand, but he keeps his eyes on Alan. "But the escape plan was his idea. Without him we'd still be in there or dead. So, yes, I trust him."

Alan stands to stretch. "That's good enough. I didn't want to have to kill him, but I have a community here to protect. You can stay here tonight to rest, get cleaned up, and sleep in a real bed. But you'll need to be gone tomorrow."

Wait, leave? We just got here. "No...I mean...I just thought we'd stay here. Join your city or whatever you call it." I stand up and Daniel stands with me. "We can't survive out there. A week nearly killed us. I know we don't look like much, but I promise that we can be a helpful addition to your city. You won't find anyone who works harder."

"I'm sorry." Alan shakes his head, but he doesn't really look sorry. "We would let you stay, but we're at capacity as it is. I'm afraid Arbor Glen just can't support anyone else. But there are other villages that would be more than happy to take you in."

"Other villages? You mean there are more people out there living in cities like this?"

"Sure." Alan leans over his desk, his eyes staring at a blank spot on the wall. "The Cardinal and his cabinet have worked very hard over the years to make sure everyone believes he's essential. It's drilled into you from the day you're born until the day you die. But it's a lie. The Cardinal's rule is precarious at best. There's a whole world out there, and it's about time you knew it."

Margaret knocks twice on the door and sticks her head in the room. "Lunch time."

Alan walks over and opens the door all the way. "Perfect timing as usual, my dear. I imagine our guests could use a good hot meal about now."

Clearly the conversation is over, and I'm suddenly not all that hungry.

Mary is still sitting on the couch, carving the little piece of wood, when we make it back to the front door. Her head pops up at our entrance and she jumps to her feet, tucking the carving away. "You two follow me and I'll lead you over to where the others are."

She heads out the door and Daniel and I rush to follow her. Mary doesn't say a word as she turns down a side street and leads us deeper into the village. We pass several other people heading in the opposite direction, and an uneasiness builds in my stomach. Mary pushes open the door of a building shaped like a barn. The others are inside, lounging on sparsely made-up cots.

"Come on, guys," I call out. "Time for lunch."

Mary freezes, her eyes boring a hole into the floor. "Actually, you are all going to stay here and I'll bring lunch to you."

Daniel growls next to me, but so low I'm probably the only one who hears it. His words come out between clenched teeth. "You don't have to serve us. We aren't so tired we can't walk to lunch."

The others stand to form a semi-circle around Mary, and a silence settles around the open room. Nothing good can happen next.

"You'll need to stay here and I'll bring you a meal." She shakes her head slowly as she walks back out the door. She closes it behind her and there's no missing the audible click of a lock sliding into place.

"What's going on?" Elizabeth springs into action, grabbing at the door handle and confirming our captivity. "What exactly happened in that meeting with Alan?"

I open my mouth, but words fail me.

"They aren't letting us stay." Daniel takes care of it for me.

Everyone starts talking at once and I can't make sense of any of it. I hold my hands up and wait for everyone to quiet down. "We told Alan we want to stay here, but he said they don't have enough housing for us."

"Horse shit." I've never heard Daniel outright curse, but I've also never seen his face scrunched up like that either. "They don't want us here. Plain and simple. We're nothing but Rejects to them and that's not going to change. We're better off getting out of here."

"And going where exactly?" Eric chimes in.

"Alan said there are more villages out there like this one." I push a smile onto my face, but I don't feel like smiling. "We'll find one of them. We can sleep here tonight and get some rest and a bit more food in our bellies. Tomorrow morning, we leave first thing."

"So that's it. They're just kicking us out." Constance grips Thomas's hand so tightly his fingers turn white around the edges.

"Yes. They're kicking us out, but we're going to be fine. The good news is Eric was right. There are people living out here, and if we found one village, we can find another." My jaw hurts from holding onto this smile. I don't want to put on a brave face. I want to stand on one of the beds and scream until my throat turns raw, then curl into a ball and cry. But we rarely get what we want. You'd think I'd be used to it by now.

Eleven

I pull the straps of my backpack a little tighter. It's heavy again with the supplies Mary brought us this morning, before the sun was more than an orange tint on the horizon. A clean change of clothes, smoked meat and cheese, and a canteen full of water. I just hope it's enough to get us to another village.

Several other members of the village, including Marcus and Margaret, stand off to the left, beside a large boulder that seems to indicate the entrance to town. None of them have said a word to us. They aren't here to say goodbye. They're here to make sure we leave.

Mary is missing. I really thought she'd be here to see us off, but she dropped off the supplies this morning and then rushed out, claiming she had to get to work without even a parting wave goodbye.

"You should get going so you can take advantage of the sunlight while you have it. There's another village called Allmore almost directly west of here. If you keep a steady pace, you should reach it in a day and a half." Alan holds his hand out and Daniel shakes it, though from the pinched look on his face, he doesn't even want to do that much.

Alan nods, turns, and walks off, most of the other villagers trailing behind him. Only a handful stay to watch us walk out past the boulder. Within minutes we are all swept back up into the forest and alone again.

Daniel and I take the lead, more by default than any real sense of leadership. Constance and Thomas fall in line behind us, with Elizabeth beside them, still clutching the burlap bag she brought out of the PIT. Eric and Patrice pull up the rear. Right back at square zero, almost.

A shrill whistle rings out, bouncing between the trees. I pull up short as Mary steps from behind a thick trunk that had kept her hidden.

"You didn't think I'd let you leave without saying goodbye, did you?" Mary wears a warm smile that puts me instantly at ease. "I know you need to get moving, but I have something for you. I couldn't give it to you back in the village. Actually, my father specifically forbade me from giving it to you." She winks at me as she digs a hand into her pocket. "I'm not the most obedient daughter."

She pulls her hand out and holds it to me. Pinched in her fingers is a braided leather circle. It's roughly made and I have no idea what I'm supposed to do with it.

"You guys are a quiet bunch when you're getting kicked out of civilization."

My eyes flare up at hers. I'm not in the mood to be taunted this morning.

"Easy, it was a joke. Apparently a bad one." She slides the circle around my wrist. "This is a bracelet, obviously. It's used as a bit of a recognition symbol among the Freemen."

"Is that what you call yourselves?" I finger the twisted leather circle.

Mary nods. "We wear these bracelets when we travel outside our own village as a way to let others know who we are." She tightens the bracelet on my wrist and gives it a tug to test the fit. "When you get to Allmore, show this to them and they'll know that you came through us first and we trusted you."

"I think 'we' is a bit of an exaggeration," Daniel says, twisting the bracelet around my wrist to examine it.

"Fine." Mary throws her arms out to her sides. "I trust you."

"Why?"

"Let's just say I haven't forgotten why we live out here and not in the Territories. My father and the others know the Cardinal is dangerous, but they seem to forget that he's also a self-interested liar and master manipulator."

I hold my arm up in front of me. "So this bracelet is our free ticket to Allmore?"

"The bracelet makes sure you don't get shot before you have a chance to plead your case." Mary looks off to the west, almost longingly. "But they are much more open there. I know their leader and he isn't going to send you packing just because you were Cardinal Rejects. Now, you should get going while you still have good light."

I grab Mary's wrist before she can walk back to the village and wait until she meets my eyes. "Thank you."

"We really owe you one," Eric says.

"Out here we have a saying; there are no debts to pay, just favors to be forwarded." She nods at me and the others, then runs back east toward Arbor Glen.

"You know, I would have thought I'd be used to rejection by now."

I wait for Constance to say more, but she only grabs Thomas's elbow and stares straight ahead. The sun lifts off the horizon, casting long shadows in front of us, guiding us deeper into the forest. Daniel squeezes my hand and I squeeze back. We can do this, together.

We walk all morning, heading due west per Alan's instructions. It's all we can do. When the sun stretches up high above our heads, peaking down through the leaves like a yellow spotlight, we stop for lunch. No one has the energy for conversation, and we eat our cheese and dried fish in the quiet peace of the forest around us.

The walk gets harder as the afternoon stretches into evening. The thickness of trees everywhere makes the landscape blend into itself, but it's still clear we're climbing. With the higher elevation and the constant threat of tree roots and fallen branches sending us to the ground with a sprained ankle, there isn't much conversation. Everyone is focused on staying upright.

The deep red sun is barely visible through the trees when the rush of water signals the end of our first leg. The bank of the river is less dense with trees, so we can see up and down for a ways. It doesn't look deep. We'll have to cross it eventually, but it can wait until tomorrow.

We all dump our bags in a little circle, but Patrice is the only one to sit down.

Daniel and I grab the canteens and head down to the river to get everyone a refill. Constance and Elizabeth follow us to gather up sticks for a fire while Thomas gets the kindling going. By the time the canteens are full, a blazing fire lights the way back for us. Daniel passes out the water and I grab blankets out of our bags. Other than the occasional 'thank you,' the whole group is silent. The sounds of the forest are soothing, but the silence of our camp is less than comforting. Everyone is exhausted, but the shooting looks at Patrice, who has yet to offer an ounce of help, is what keeps conversation at bay.

I don't have the energy for a fight tonight, but if I don't say anything now, this is only going to get worse. Tomorrow we have to convince Allmore to let us stay, and we'll have a much better chance of that if we don't hate each other.

I sit down and rummage through my bag for the food we have left. "Patrice, if you want any of this cheese, you'll need to come get it."

Movement in the camp freezes and all eyes turn to Patrice.

"I'm exhausted. Can't you just bring it here?"

Like a tennis match, all eyes shift back to me.

"No. We're all exhausted. Especially since we had to get camp ready without your help. If you want the cheese, you'll need to come get it."

All eyes shift again, and Daniel scoots a little closer to me, as if he's preparing for a nasty volley from Patrice.

"Then keep the cheese." Patrice lies down and turns her back to me, but everyone can hear her add 'bitch' to the end of her response.

Daniel jumps up beside me and is in Patrice's face before I can move. "You ungrateful little brat. Do you have any idea how much everyone in this group has done for you?"

"How much they've done for me?" Patrice stands up, and at almost Daniel's height her narrowed eyes are just about level with his. "You mean the way they helped me get Rejected and sent to the PIT in the first place? The way you all dragged me out into the middle of nowhere, made me a run away, and then got us stuck out here where no one will let us live with them? That kind of help? 'Cause I'm perfectly aware of what a tremendous help you've all been."

"I had hoped you'd grown up since I last saw you, but maybe that was too much to ask."

"And maybe I thought being Rejected would have knocked out that superiority complex Dad instilled in you, but I guess that was too much to hope for."

"If we weren't here right now, then all of us would probably be dead." Daniel motions to the group sitting in a little semi-circle around the fire. "You think you'd be better off in the PIT? Someday you should ask Rebecca what happened to her and the other girls stuck alone in the PIT. You think because the men were on the other side of the fence you would have been safe? Ask Eric how the guards treated pretty, young Rejects."

"I'll just ask you since you seem to know everything, Mr. Council-member's son."

Well, that went much worse than I expected. "Enough." I insert myself between Daniel and Patrice until they're forced to break their staring contest. "Patrice, you can complain all you want, but it isn't going to change anything."

I hold up my hand when she opens her mouth to protest. "But I'm sorry. I'm sorry you're stuck out here. And you're right. You wouldn't be out here if it wasn't for me. I'm the one that insisted on hacking the Acceptance ceremony. I thought it would help. I was wrong. I'm sorry."

Patrice flops down onto her blanket at the same time Eric stands up beside me. "This is just as much my fault. We wouldn't be out here without a place to live if I hadn't broken you all out."

"But you wouldn't have had to do that if I hadn't played a very dangerous game of chicken with the Cardinal."

Daniel grabs my hand. "You couldn't have hacked the feed if I hadn't stolen a video camera and re-routed the signal. I'll take some of that blame, too."

"Wouldn't have been much of a video if Thomas and I hadn't shown up with some of our friends." Constance pulls Thomas up beside her and nods at me.

Elizabeth lets out a hearty laugh. "You wouldn't have even been there if I hadn't hunted down every innocent person I could find inside the PIT and pretty much begged you to come."

Thomas takes one step closer to the fire so the flames highlight the contours of the ruined side of his face. "You wouldn't have had any innocent people to find if the Cardinal hadn't sent so many of us there."

We all make eye contact across the glow of the fire. Each of us had a part to play in getting to where we are, but we'll never forget that the Cardinal is the one who really holds the blame. Everyone goes back to their blankets, and Patrice pulls hers over her head.

I kneel down and set a piece of cheese by her hand. My words are soft, meant only for her. "You're still mad, and that's fine. You'll probably still be mad tomorrow, and the day after that, and the day after that. But one of these days you're going to get it. That we aren't the ones you're really mad at. And when that day comes, you'll realize how lucky you are to be stuck in the middle of nowhere with such an amazing group of people. And we'll be here, waiting and ready to be your family."

I stand up and take Daniel's hand as we walk back to our blankets. I nod at each person as we pass, and thank the stars that each of them is willing to be my family.

Twelve

My stomach growls, but there's nothing for it. Lunch was hours ago and we finished off what was left of our meager supplies. Beside me, Daniel's stomach echoes mine, but neither of us says a word. All we can do is keep walking west and hope there's a village with food willing to take us in.

No one has said a word all day about last night's confrontation with Patrice, but she has been less surly. She even said 'thank you' to Constance earlier when she was passing out refilled canteens. I can't bank on a full change of heart just yet, but I can thank the stars that we're keeping it civil. My nerves are on edge enough with the constant worry of what happens if and when we finally find this village.

Daniel steps over a log and reaches back to help me over. I only have one leg over, straddling the half-rotten log, but Daniel puts a hand on my shoulder and pushes me down until I'm sitting on the soft wood.

His eyes dart all over the forest, and everyone else stops, freezing in their tracks. Thomas pulls Constance behind him, and Eric steps in front of Patrice.

"Hail, strangers," a loud, but cheerful voice calls out from somewhere up ahead. "I can see you, so there's no point in hiding now."

I stand up, but Daniel gently pushes me back down. His voice is steady, but his hand trembles against my shoulder. "Hail, stranger. You can see us, but we can't see you."

A young man, armed with a bow, but with it strapped to his back instead of pointing at us, steps out from behind a crop of trees. His dark-green and brown clothing allow him to blend into the natural habitat. He lifts a hand and smiles in greeting as he walks effortlessly and silently over the uneven forest floor. So different from the last time we were discovered.

"I'm Ethander, but you can call me Ethan." He holds his hand out to Daniel. "Everyone else does, at least to my face. No telling what they call me behind my back." Ethan grins as if we're all best friends, his sable eyes crinkling at the corners.

Daniel swallows hard, but shakes Ethan's hand, Ethan's skin tone only a few shades lighter than his own. "My name is Daniel and these are my friends…and family."

"You all look like you've had a hard time of it. Have you been traveling long?"

I push my way past Daniel's arm. "Two days." I hold out my arm so he can see the leather bracelet Mary gave us. "Alan sent us."

Ethan runs his thumb over the bracelet, frowning at the worn strips. "That explains a lot." He looks right at me as if the others aren't there. "When did you escape?"

We can't hide who we are, and I don't want to anymore.

"It's been about a week."

"A whole week?" Ethan whistles and his smile is back. "If the Cardinal hasn't found you by now, you're as good as safe."

I nod and soak in the warmth filling me from the inside out. Safe. I can't remember the last time that even felt like a possibility.

"Better head into the village then. You're probably tired of sleeping on the ground, and I bet dinner is almost ready."

Ethan turns and walks back in the direction he came from.

Daniel grabs my arm before I can take my first step and the others group around us. "Did that feel a little too easy to anyone else? Are you sure about this, Rebecca?"

No, I'm not. But I've stopped thinking any of us can ever be sure of anything. Ethan is far enough ahead that I can whisper without being heard. "If they treat us like Arbor Glen, we'll be gone before the sun comes up. Until then, this is our best option."

"Are you coming?" Ethan calls out from up ahead.

Daniel grabs my hand and wraps his fingers through mine. At least I can be sure of him.

Thirteen

The smell hits me first. Something spicy and rich floats in the evening air as the trees thin out, revealing the broken up roadway leading into town. If I squint, I can almost imagine we're back at Arbor Glen. Same neglected road lined with buildings of various sizes. Same hustle of people walking about, finishing up whatever they're doing before the meal.

Except this isn't Arbor Glen. More weeds poke up between the cracked asphalt and the buildings are more worn. Splintered wood and empty doorways are a common sight. There isn't a fresh coat of paint in sight. Midway down the street, one building stands out. Warm yellow light flows out of the empty windows and joyful voices mingle with the rich aroma.

"Just in time for dinner." Ethan stops by a lean-to shack and drops off his bow, not even checking to see if any of us go for it. So trusting. What kind of place is this?

Daniel meets my gaze and it's clear he's thinking the same thing I am. Ethan knows we came from the PIT. Alan and the others treated us like we were ticking time bombs that would destroy them any minute. Ethan acts like we're the invited guests of honor.

He pushes open the door where all the noise is coming from. Inside is a whole new world.

Long wooden tables and benches line the deep hall. Warm light floods out of sconces placed along the walls and one huge chandelier hangs from the ceiling. Platters and kettles of food move around the room, everyone taking just enough to fill a plate before passing the food on down the row. Happy voices and laughter mix in the air with the rich aromas of cooked meat, vegetables, and fresh bread.

Several men and women at the front of the room turn, welcoming Ethan with a warm smile or wave. They nod to us and scoot down to make room at the table. A few people lift up off the bench to get a look at us and offer smiles, but no one looks worried by our presence. A woman scurries out of a back room and sets out plates, forks, and cups at the newly empty spots.

"Have a seat," Ethan says, gesturing to the table. "The food should be down this way in a minute. I'll be right back."

Ethan moves deeper into the hall, pausing as he goes to share a word, smile, or pat on the back with the others sitting down for their meals. Several of those he passes look down our way, but all of them have smiles to share with us. In minutes, he disappears into the throng of people.

Eric, Patrice, and Elizabeth don't waste any time claiming a spot at the table. Daniel squeezes my hand, and I squeeze back. There are so many questions, but they can wait until after we eat. My stomach growls and I let out a giggle as I lift my clunky boots over the bench and sit next to a woman who must be only a few years older than us.

Daniel, Constance, and Thomas follow suit, and it isn't long before platters of food arrive. The woman next to me hands over a steaming bowl of fresh meat, potatoes, and carrots.

"Please, take as much as you want," she says, smiling as if she really means it. "I'm sure you're all starving and there's plenty here for everyone. Welcome to Allmore."

Sliding a juicy piece of meat on to my plate, I pass the bowl over to Daniel. Eric is already tearing into his meal, and Elizabeth looks like she might cry, her eyes closed while she savors a bite of something.

Patrice tops off her plate, and Ethan slides onto the bench just in time to take the bowl from her. "You guys picked a great night to show up. Beef isn't super common here yet. We're still working on building up our herd."

"Herd?" Daniel asks around a mouthful of carrot.

"Our cows. We have a small pasture just outside of town." Ethan fills his plate and digs in. "It will be another year before we're ready to slaughter our own, so for now we have to get our beef in trade."

Trade? Just how organized are these villages? In Arbor Glen we only saw a tiny portion of the village. After lunch, Alan kept us contained to the rider's rooms, so we never really saw how everything worked. When I pictured what these cities would look like, I dreamed of a place like where I grew up, but expected to be completely disappointed. So far, this place feels pretty close to perfect.

We all fill up on the best food we've had in who knows how long. They were kind enough to feed us in Arbor Glen, but none of the food was even close to this good. Of course, the joyful atmosphere could be making the food taste better. As many questions as I have, it's hard not to get caught up in the festive feeling of the room.

Next to me, the kind woman who welcomed us is talking to another woman about the same age about a new chicken coop. "Samuel figured out a great new way to insulate the walls so we don't lose as many hens this winter. Last year was a challenge. And Thad is going to show us how to set up traps around the coop at night. We might get lucky and add a few foxes to our menu."

The other woman nods with approval. "I'm sure Stewart and Karen can come up with some good recipes for anything you catch. They'll welcome any fresh meat we can find."

Their conversation is cut off by a dinging of forks on plates. Around the room, more people join in the clatter until a man standing at the end of the room quiets the din by raising his hands in front of him.

"Hail, friends!" The man's smile is infectious.

"Hail, Liam!" the room shouts back at him.

"Let's thank Stewart and Karen for tonight's delicious meal. I'm sure I speak for everyone when I say it was a special treat."

The room breaks into applause as a young man and woman at another table stand up and lift their hands in recognition of the thanks.

"I want to get a few quick progress reports in before we get to the most exciting part of dinner." Liam nods to the woman sitting next to him. "Ana, how is the PE office doing?"

Ana bounces up from her seat, her young face smiling out at the group. Looking around the room, I realize for the first time just how young everyone is. A few could be our age, while most are a bit older, maybe mid-thirties. Only a few might pass for any older than that. There are even fewer children.

Ana sits back down. I've missed all of her report, but I doubt any of it would have made much sense anyway. Several others stand and talk for a few minutes about various areas of the village; farming, animals, infrastructure, medicine. It all comes out as a blur of noise as I scan the crowd for any face that doesn't fall between twenty and forty years old. As the last man finishes his talk about clothing manufacturing, I'm certain I've looked at every face in the room. Only a handful of older people and fewer than thirty children.

Liam stands back up and thanks the speakers. "Now on to what most of you are looking forward to. Would our visitors please join me up here?" The entire room turns to catch a glance at the seven of us as we inch off the wooden benches. Everyone is smiling, but it doesn't stop the suspicion that we are somehow under inspection.

"Our new friends were able to escape from the Cardinal in a brave rebellion of his evil rule."

The entire room bursts into applause. The way Liam puts it, we went out in a blaze of glory instead of sneaking through a fence in the dark of night.

"Arbor Glen found them, but it will come as no surprise that Alan wouldn't let them stay."

The applause stops to be replaced with solemn nods and pinched faces of concern.

Liam turns to face us as we shuffle in a herd to stand next to him. "Before we decide if you have a place here with us, we'd ask that you tell us about yourselves."

My stomach turns over the food I just put in there. "What do you want to know?"

Liam smiles, but his words don't match. "We'd like you to tell us why you were sent to the PIT."

Fourteen

No way. I'm done with this. I turn away from him and motion for the others to head to the door.

"Wait." Liam grabs my arm and speaks softly so only we can hear. "Where are you going?"

"We aren't a carnival side show. You'll have to get your fun torturing someone else tonight." I pull my arm out of his grasp and hold on to Daniel. I'll need all of his support to walk out of the place that was supposed to become our home.

"The Cardinal Rejected me because I didn't want to marry a girl."

I whip around to find a man standing at his seat on the other side of the hall. He sits down and another man, maybe in his mid-twenties stands up in his place.

"I never made it to Acceptance. The Cardinal sent me to the PIT when I was twelve for selling contraband liquor to help feed my family." He sits and a woman next to him puts a comforting arm around his shoulder.

The woman sitting next to Liam, Ana, who gave the PE report, stands up. "I was put in the PIT because every essay I wrote for grammar school was about wanting to be more than just a mother and a wife."

"And you are." Liam puts his arm around her and plants a kiss on her forehead. "You are so much more."

I'm frozen. Marcus told us there were others, but I didn't really stop to think about what that meant. There are other Rejects living out here and several of them live in this village.

"We would never put you on display to hurt you." Liam focuses back on me. "This community survives because we trust each other. And that trust starts with trusting us with the part of you that you most want to keep hidden."

I nod at him and pull Daniel back to the front of the room.

"My name is Rebecca Collins."

A soft murmur travels around the room. Liam takes a step closer, his eyes wide. "Are you the Rebecca who made the video that ruined the Acceptance ceremony?"

I nod in shock. "Did you see it?"

"No, we don't keep a connection to the Territory feed, but it doesn't take long for word about something that big to travel around the villages." Liam makes a little bow. "Please, continue."

"My name is Rebecca and the Cardinal Rejected me because I think his policies are unfair." I rub my thumb against the smooth knot of my necklace and smile at Daniel. "And apparently I have a hard time keeping my mouth shut."

Any tension still in the room vanishes, and everyone bursts into laughter and calls of encouragement. The knot that's been swirling in my gut slowly untangles. I was wrong. This isn't a public shunning, it's an initiation.

The others line up behind me, and one by one we all share our Rejection stories, while the people of Allmore laugh and cheer us along. Patrice gets a good laugh out of everyone when she explains the Cardinal Rejected her because, "apparently Rebecca has a hard time keeping her mouth shut."

Eric is last, and the only one who doesn't look relieved to finally make claim to the false charges that sent us careening on a path to right here. "My name is Eric." I can barely hear him over the silence of the room. Several villagers shout out for him to speak up. "My name is Eric, and the Cardinal Rejected me because I deserved to go to the PIT. Because I didn't understand the importance of loyalty or family."

Liam stretches out a hand to Eric. "But you do now?"

Eric nods, but won't look Liam in the eyes.

"Now, what say you?" Liam spreads his arms out to the room, his face beaming. "Will we welcome these brave souls, or send them away to fend for themselves?"

"Welcome! Welcome!" Shouts fill the room, bouncing against the walls until the sound drowns out even my own heartbeat.

"The people have spoken. Welcome to Allmore, where all are welcome and more!" Another round of applause finishes his words, and a warmth spreads through my arms. I grab Daniel's hand and he grabs Constance's next to him. The others are holding hands as well. I catch Elizabeth's eye. A few tears track down her face, but her smile is beaming. I nod at her; we don't need words. Molly would have loved this. Actually, she would have hated everyone staring at her and clapping. But this embrace, as if we're instantly part of the family. This she would have loved.

"I'm sure you have more questions, but they will hold until tomorrow. The sun is set and the day is done. Until the morning's rise, friends, sleep well."

The entire room responds with a chorus of, "Sleep well." Villagers group up and move about the room, sharing hugs and brief greetings with friends. Several stop by to share a hug with us or to welcome us again. Slowly, the room thins out as others head out the door into the village.

"Well, that was fun." Liam leans against the table, a smile stretched across his face. "I'm afraid we weren't expecting new arrivals, so we don't have the best accommodations to offer. Greg has already let me know his group will get to work on new housing right away. For tonight, we'll put you up above the medical building since there are actual beds there."

He waves at the last few stragglers to leave the building then stands to stretch.

"Ready?" Without waiting for an answer, Liam spins around and marches out the door. "Allmore is fairly safe, but we encourage everyone not to walk alone at night. We share the forest with plenty of animals, not all of them friendly. We've not had an attack in forever, but better safe than sorry." He looks over his shoulder without missing a step and flashes a smile at us. Is he joking? Maybe, but I'm okay with the buddy system.

A few buildings down, Liam pushes open a door with a sign hanging to the side reading 'Infirmary.' He pauses just inside and waves at the wall. Instantly, the room is flooded with soft artificial light.

I'm aware of my mouth dropping open, but there's nothing I can do to stop it. "Well, that's fancy." I grin when I catch Daniel rolling his eyes at me. "And unexpected."

"Our infrastructure team has solar panels hooked up to all our main buildings. We've got most of the private houses set up as well. All except the most recently built. We're hoping to be fully set up before winter sets in." Liam gestures to a staircase. "There are spare beds upstairs. Not much privacy, I'm afraid, but we'll work on it."

We all walk up, and Liam waves the lights on in a wide open space with nothing but two rows of beds and rolling racks with hanging sheets that serve as the only privacy. Ana walks into the room with a huge bag and plants a kiss on Liam's cheek.

"Thanks, love. May I present my beautiful, amazing, patient wife, Ana."

Ana slaps him on the arm, but there's no ill will behind it. "You forgot level-headed. If not for me, you'd have these poor souls sleeping in the clothes they walked up in." She hands the bag over to me.

"Thank you. I'm Rebecca. This is Daniel, Elizabeth, Eric, Constance, Thomas, and Patrice." I point to the others and they nod at their name.

"Well, I'm never going to remember that in the morning, so don't be shy about reminding me." Ana wraps her arm through Liam's. "There are plenty of pajamas in there, so hopefully we've got something to fit everyone. We'll work on getting you some clean clothes in the morning. For now, you can hand your dirty ones over to me after you change, and I'll make sure they get added to the wash."

With her olive-toned skin and dark hair, Ana is stunning. Her plain clothes do nothing to diminish her beauty, and the simple green shirt she wears brings out golden flecks in her eyes. Back home, a woman this beautiful would be married to an important man, too. The difference, of course, that back home, that woman would never lower herself to fetch clothes and do laundry for a bunch of strangers. It could be easy to become friends with Ana. "Thank you, again. For everything. Honestly, it's a little overwhelming."

"Don't mention it. You've been through enough." She tugs on Liam's arm and leads him to the door, suppressing a yawn. "You wait downstairs, and I'll be down in just a moment."

Everyone digs through the bag for pajamas, checking to see which of the light cotton pants or shirts will fit. Such simple clothes, but it feels like our collective birthday. For the first time in forever, we are safe and fed. It almost feels normal.

Night clothes sorted out, the others move about the room, rearranging the beds and privacy sheets. Daniel pushes two beds together and grabs several of the rolling curtains to create a little bit of privacy for us. I step behind one of the sheets and my heart rate soars faster than an Airtrain. This is the first time Daniel and I have been anything close to alone since before the Acceptance ceremony. Our last night in the PIT together flashes into my head. We made promises, vows.

He's my husband. But every moment since that night has been focused on staying alive. There wasn't time to think about the two of us when I had so many other people depending on me. But they're fine now, tucked safely in their own beds with full bellies and clean clothes. Right here it's just me and Daniel, and I have no idea what I'm doing.

"I hope the pajamas fit," Ana's chirpy voice calls from the other side of the curtain. "Just pass out your dirty clothes once you're changed."

Daniel smiles at me and pulls his dirt-encrusted shirt over his head.

My eyes follow the smooth curve of muscle across his chest, spreading to his shoulders and on down his arms. My fingers itch to run along the edges and soak in the heat of his skin.

Daniel catches me staring at him and smiles in the way that attempts to liquefy my bones. With one step he's right in front of me, his hand cupping the side of my face.

He leans down and whispers, his lips brushing against my ear and sending shivers coursing through my body. "You are beautiful."

His mouth finds mine and I'm lost in him. The whole world falls away and nothing exists but his warm lips on mine and his hands testing, exploring. My fingers grip his waist. I can't get close enough to him.

Daniel pulls back and, with one swift motion, my shirt is off and tossed to the floor. He pulls me back to him and the heat of skin meeting skin threatens to scorch us both. Flames flare everywhere his hands touch me until there's nothing left of me but ashes.

"Ah-hem." Ana clears her throat no more than a foot on the other side of the thin piece of fabric separating us from the rest of the room. A giggle follows that I'm pretty sure belongs to Constance.

Apparently these curtains are more sheer than they look. A year ago I would have been embarrassed, but not now. I love this man with his arms wrapped around me and I don't care who knows it. Daniel smiles down at me and places one more soft kiss on my lips.

We untangle our arms and finish getting changed so Ana can take our clothes. After she leaves, the room settles around us, and the whispered conversations die off. Daniel and I snuggle into bed, my back pressed against the hard planes of his chest.

I close my eyes and enjoy the sheer perfection of the moment. We are full, safe, and warm, tucked away in a village that even the Cardinal himself can't control. Right here, right now, we have nothing to worry about.

But the moment doesn't last long.

Flashes of the PIT fill my mind. All those innocent people still in the PIT, still struggling to eke out some kind of existence with empty bellies and the constant threat of danger. Those women who thought they were getting out, but got left behind. I'll never forget the hurt of being that close to freedom only to have it snatched away. I can't forget them. Soon, it will be time to bring them to safety, too. But tonight, at least for one night, I'll sleep in peace.

Fifteen

My eyes pop open and I bolt upright, my pulse racing. It's pitch black, but a second later my eyes adjust. I'm safe. I shake my head to dispel the remnants of the nightmare that broke my sleep. Daniel stirs next to me, but doesn't wake. I could lie back down, but I'll never get back to sleep and will probably only wake him up with me.

I scoot out of the bed, careful not to disturb Daniel, and wrap one of the blankets around my shoulders. Soft snores fill the room. Everyone else is still tucked away in dreams that aren't filled with shouting guards and the Cardinal, laughing maniacally while I'm dragged in front of a rioting crowd.

I tiptoe from behind the sheet separating us from the rest of the room. At one end is the doorway leading back downstairs, but there's another door at the other end of the room. Might as well use these last few hours before dawn to check out our new home.

The door opens to an old-looking staircase. I wrap the blanket tighter so I don't trip and walk up into the dark. I push open a door at the top of the stairs and step out onto the roof. Cool night air blows around me and whips away the last ounces of sleep from my eyes. A hunched figure perches at the edge of the roof. Eric.

Shutting the door softly behind me, I crunch across the loose rock of the roof to where he's sitting, his own blanket wrapped around his shoulders.

"Looks like I'm not the only one who couldn't sleep. Mind if I join you?"

Eric nods without looking up. "The stars are the same here. And the moon, it looks just like the moon of the PIT. But there aren't any waves. The night is too quiet without them."

I sit down, purposefully leaving space between us. He's right. The night sounds wrong without the waves. Of course, it's also missing the screams and shouts and angry guards, but I don't miss that at all. The forest around us has its own sounds. Frogs and crickets and the wind through the trees and a river somewhere not too far away.

"Why did you save us?" The words blurt out before I have a chance to think about them first.

Eric is silent for minute. Nothing answers me except the unfamiliar sounds of this new kind of night. "You needed rescuing."

"I may not know you as well as I once thought, but even I know that's not the truth."

Eric stiffens like a guard hit him with a shock stick.

"I'm not saying you didn't want us to escape. Last year was more about saving yourself than stopping us. But there is more to it, isn't there?"

Eric glances over at me. His eyes stare at my face, but he's seeing something far away.

"When I…when I joined the guards, the Cardinal had to give me a new identity. I kept my name since it's common enough, but everything else changed. My background, where I came from, who my family was…my birth date."

I wrap my arms tighter around my blanket. I've never given much thought to what happened to Eric after he turned traitor, sabotaged our escape mission, and joined up with the Cardinal. At the time, I figured anything better than rotting in a fiery hole was too good for him.

"I had to be old enough to go through Assignment. He made me almost twenty, which means, according to the official Cardinal record, I'm almost twenty-one."

I nod, understanding instantly what comes next. "How many months until your Compulsory?"

"Three."

If he had stayed, Eric would have been forced into a Compulsory marriage in only three months, four years ahead of his actual birthday. A Compulsory used to be my greatest fear, back when the PIT was nothing more than my mother's threat to keep me under her thumb. I shake my head at how much everything has changed since then.

"I couldn't keep living the lie anymore." Eric stands up and buries his face in his hands for a minute. "It's not so much the marriage. That would have been just one more layer of facade the Cardinal made me wear. It was the finality of it. I kept pretending that the guard's uniform was a costume I put on. A role I played to survive. But the marriage would have changed that. I didn't think I could keep pretending and I didn't want to be that man anymore. When you hacked the feed and got thrown back in Quarantine, I knew it was now or never."

Cold seeps into my pants from the night-chilled rocks, so I stand up and stomp my feet a bit, working to put heat back into my legs.

"It's kinda funny, you know."

"No, Eric. None of it sounds funny to me."

"Really?" He turns to me. His eyes are bloodshot and every feature of his face sags. He hasn't slept at all tonight. "Out of all of us, I'm the only one the Machine Rejected for the right reasons. The rest of you were in there because of how special you are, because the Cardinal can't stand that. I'm the one who's evil."

"You're not evil."

"Really?" Eric spits the words out. "Because even helping you came about for selfish reasons."

We both stare out into the inky black sky in silence. What can I say to that? He did help us, but would he have done it if he wasn't facing a Compulsory marriage?

"I will say this." Eric's voice breaks through the quiet sounds of the night. "I meant what I said that day before the ceremony. If I could go back and change what I did, I'd do it in a heartbeat. I regretted what happened pretty much from the minute it was too late to stop it. I know that doesn't change anything, but it's the only reason I have to think I might deserve this second chance."

Cardinal help me with what I'm about to do. "You were young and afraid and put in an impossible situation." I take a deep breath. I can do this. "I'm not going to say I agree with what you did or that I'd do the same, because obviously I didn't. But, I understand why you turned us in." I can do this. "I forgive you."

Eric blinks, his face unreadable. "Why?"

"Maybe forgiving you is easier than trying to hold on to all the anger." I shrug the blanket higher up on my shoulders.

Eric shakes his head and turns away, staring deeper into the forest. "I just don't understand…you, of everyone here, have the most reason to hate me."

He's right. Eric convinced me he loved me and made promises about our future once we escaped the PIT. I didn't love him, but I was determined to marry him and make the most of our lives. I was ready to deny my true feelings so we could all find freedom. And then he betrayed us.

"I can't keep hating you, but that doesn't mean I'm ready to trust you. You got us out of the PIT, but our escape was as much to help you as it was us." He looks back at me in the darkness. "You'll have to earn that trust, and it won't be done easily."

"Of course."

"You understand I don't speak for the group." I don't say it, but we both know Elizabeth will be the hardest sell. Eric isn't the one who killed Molly, but his actions made it possible.

Eric nods. His face is solemn, but it reads more like determination than defeat.

To our east, the very lightest edge of pink highlights the forest. "I'm going to try to get a bit more sleep before breakfast. You coming?"

"I'll be there in a bit. I just want to..."

I nod and head downstairs. Back in bed, I snuggle under the covers and welcome Daniel's warm arm around me as I drift off for another hour of sleep.

Sixteen

Ana leads us to breakfast like a mother duck, all of us following behind in our freshly laundered clothes. The street is busy with men and women moving from building to building. Even though everyone acts like they have somewhere to be, the morning is filled with calls of greeting and laughter. The whole village feels alive.

In the dining hall, the cheerful atmosphere continues, with the last few folks grabbing some food and sharing laughs before starting the day. Whatever the food is, it smells amazing. Warm and nutty and spicy and nothing at all like the PIT. With enough meals like this, I might stop looking like a living skeleton.

"Bowls and spoons are here," Ana says, pointing at a long table in the front of the room. "Breakfast and lunch are buffet style since everyone has such different schedules with their jobs around the village. That's why dinner is such a festive event. It's the only time during the day when we can all be together."

Ana grabs a bowl and ladles a heap of perfectly cooked oatmeal into it. "The oats are seasoned so you can eat them plain, but feel free to add on some apples or toasted walnuts. Sorry to say, we don't get any meat for breakfast."

Is she kidding? As if I would be disappointed with this feast. Real apples! My stomach growls, and none of us wastes any time loading up our bowls with a little bit of everything. I'd almost feel bad except Ana is smiling and keeps pointing out the toppings to make sure we all get some. We grab cups of cool, clean water and dig in.

Liam joins us as we're all finishing up, an adorable little girl tagging along behind him. "Nellie and I thought we'd join you for the official tour."

"Hi, Mama." Nellie dashes into Ana's embrace and wraps chubby little arms around her neck. She pulls back and flashes all of us a toothy grin that lights up her whole face. "Hi, I'm Nellie. I'm three years old, and mama says I'm a handful."

Nellie laughs right along with the rest of us. "I bet you are." Constance leans down closer to her as if she's going to tell her a secret. "My mommy use to tell me the same thing."

Nellie's warm brown eyes grow wide before she bursts into a fit a giggles. "You're funny."

"I think someone found a new best friend." Liam ruffles the top of Nellie's hair. "Are you all ready to see the rest of the village?"

It takes a minute to clear our bowls and get Nellie settled. She insists on holding Constance's hand, but doesn't want Ana to be too far away either.

"You've seen the dining hall. There's a cellar underneath we use for storage, but it's not much to look at." Liam gestures toward the door. "Let's start with Doc's office since you stayed there last night."

Outside there are fewer people about, but the street doesn't feel deserted. Even with the buildings in need of repair, little touches make the village feel welcoming. Clean curtains hanging in a window, pots of flowers on a porch, and white chalk drawings on the cracked asphalt all add to the sense that Allmore isn't just a hiding place in the woods. It's a real home.

"Most of the buildings here on the main street serve a public function, though there are a few homes, like ours." Liam points to several buildings along the way. "Beside the dining hall and kitchen, we have storage buildings for supplies. Though we store most of our bulk food items in the storage rooms under the dining hall. Then we have the schoolhouse, the bakery, and PE building, the tannery and the craftsman houses."

"What are the craftsman houses?" My head zips from one side of the street to the other, trying to take in everything at once.

"Some things we have to trade for, but we try to make as much of what we need as possible." Ana points to a squat building that might have been yellow once upon a time. "We have artisans in there that use the raw fabric we get to keep everyone in clothes that fit. We've been experimenting with growing a few specialty plants to spin our own fibers, too."

"What else?" Daniel's face is lit up like a child in a candy store. "Who handles the technology?"

"That's an area where we're lagging behind a bit." Liam looks apologetic, as if we'll be disappointed. "We're still a fairly new village, just settled ten years ago and Frank is pretty much a one man show when it comes to gadgets. Do you have an interest there?"

"Are you kidding?" Elizabeth calls from behind us. "Daniel would give up his left leg if you let him play with tech all day."

"No need for an amputation." Liam chuckles at his own joke. "Frank would be thrilled with some knowledgeable help. We can head there after Doc's office."

Daniel stops Liam with a hand to his shoulder. "Wait. Are you saying we get to pick what we want to do?"

"Pretty much." Liam shrugs as if this is no big deal. "If we have tasks that no one wants to do we take turns and rotate them around the village for a month at a time. Other than that, everyone pretty much does what they're best at."

"And the women, too?" Elizabeth sounds like she just found her own candy store.

"The Cardinal doesn't let women contribute outside the home because he thinks we're incompetent. It's just an easy way to control half the population." Fire blazes in Ana's eyes. This is exactly why she was Rejected. "That's the difference here. We aren't trying to control anyone.

Plus, we need everyone's help to keep this place running smoothly."

"And what if we don't want jobs?" Of course Patrice would ask if she actually has to work.

"No one is going to force you to do anything." Ana raises her eyebrows at Patrice. "But this isn't the Capitol. We don't have country clubs and afternoon tea. Without a job, you're going to get pretty bored."

"We can talk about job assignments later." Liam pushes open the door to Doc's office. "Let's start the real tour."

Liam leads us past the lobby with the staircase up to where we slept and straight to the back rooms. We find Doc in one of the exam rooms. Or at least, it's probably an exam room. It has all the same equipment as the doctor's office back home, but every surface is covered with boxes and bins of...everything.

"Liam." Doc steps out of the midst of a stack of small towels. "I didn't realize you were stopping by. If I had known I would have...well I wouldn't have cleaned up, but I would have shut the door and met you in the lobby."

"Nah." Liam shakes his outstretched hand. "The clutter is starting to grow on me. Is this still an unpacked box from when you moved here?"

"Don't judge me. One man is not enough to take care of this village. Especially since we keep growing."

"I know it's hard on you, but you'll never hear me complain that more people want to be a part of what we're doing here." Ana looks through an almost empty box. "Are you good on supplies for now?"

"So how exactly did all of this work?" Elizabeth interrupts as only she can. "You said the village is still pretty new and Doc still hasn't unpacked. Can anybody just run off, find some abandoned buildings, and start their own village?"

"I guess you could," Liam flashes her a crooked smile, "though I wouldn't recommend it. Most of us used to live in Arbor Glen, but Alan, the leader there, won't allow PIT runaways to stay."

"Yeah," Daniel snaps out. "We noticed."

"Well, some of us disagreed. When Ana showed up, and was promptly tossed out, it was the last straw. We packed up and headed here since we already knew there were abandoned buildings." Liam flexes his fingers in and out of a fist while he speaks. "It was miserable at first, but then more people started hearing about what we were doing. Doc found us about a year later and we haven't been able to get rid of him since."

"Yeah, yeah," he says, walking around a few boxes. He gestures to my shoulder. "Mind if I take a look at those stitches? We can't be too careful with infections out here. The Cardinal doesn't exactly share his medicine with us."

I lift my sleeve, and Doc takes a quick look before moving to the others.

"Ana." I move over to where she stands so Doc has more room. "How did you get out without setting off your capsule?"

"I didn't." Ana rolls her sleeve up to reveal a long, ugly scar across her upper arm. "I used to sleep up on the roofs to avoid attacks in the middle of the night. Sometimes

I would see people scurry past the fence. I would watch them for as far as I could, and without fail, each of them would hit around a similar distance and fall down dead. It was the same distance, but always a different place, so I figured it had to be something internal. I didn't know it was poison, but that detail didn't matter."

"So you got your capsule out. But how?"

"I found a dirty nail and gouged at the lump on my arm until I got it out. Almost bled to death first, but I figured that was better than sticking around in the PIT. By the time I made it to Arbor Glen I was close to death. They let me stay a week to recuperate, and that's how I met Alan." She runs a hand over her arm. "My arm's as ugly as the Cardinal, but it was worth it."

"Alright," Doc says, stepping over another box. "All their stitches look good. Now get out of here so I can get back to work." He winks at Ana and she leads us all back outside.

Ana and Liam take us all over the village, stopping at a few other places. As promised, we meet Frank, and Daniel decides to pass on the rest of the tour so he can stay and talk about all the ideas always swimming in his brain. I'm amazed at just how much they've done here in ten years. Everything would be considered primitive by Territory standards, but it works for Allmore like a well-oiled machine.

"Mama, I want to show Constance the flowers." Nellie pulls at Constance's arm, forcing her to follow her new shadow.

Ana looks exhausted, but smiles warmly at the little girl who clearly holds her heart. "Okay, last stop before lunch."

Ana leads us all to the outer edge of the village and through a copse of trees, into a sunny glade. Yellow dandelions fill the space as far as the eye can see.

"See, Constance." Little Nellie jumps up and down in front of her, throwing in the occasional spin to mark her excitement. "Aren't the flowers pretty?"

"They sure are." Constance squats down next to her and listens intently as Nellie gives her a mini-lesson of some kind.

I shoot a questioning look at Ana and she just laughs. "This is our dandelion patch and tending it might be the most important job we have here."

"How is that?" Elizabeth questions.

"Our biggest export is a dandelion ale that many have tried to duplicate, but can't get quite right. Several other villages have tried to include beer and spirits into the trade routes, but they don't come close to our ale. When you're the only game in town, you can pretty much name your price. This ale ensures we can always get exactly what we need."

Such a powerful little flower. It reminds me of another powerful dandelion. The one Eric found growing at the corner of Constance's bunkhouse. Searching for another led to finding Constance's rope. How different my life would be if she hadn't caught us trying to take it.

I walk down a little dirt path running between the flowers and tilt my head back. Is it weird that I have happy memories from the PIT? Constance laughs at something Nellie says, and the tinkling music is contagious. Ana sweeps her daughter up into her arms and spins her around. No, it's not weird. The PIT wasn't all bad if it brought me these amazing people. It made me a better, stronger person. Living through the PIT gave me the courage I'll need to leave this patch of paradise to go back and help the innocent people still suffering at the Cardinal's hand.

* * *

"I tell you." Elizabeth lounges back against a stack of pillows on her bed. "A girl could get used to sleeping on a full belly."

With dinner over and the village settling in for the night, the seven of us have some time to ourselves. I'm exhausted, but everyone has their curtains pulled back. After everything we learned and saw today, no one seems quite ready for sleep yet.

"I sat next to Doc at dinner. He said these meals are pretty standard. Not even the best they have." Eric sits at the edge of his bed wearing the biggest smile I've seen from him in ages. "And he said I can be his apprentice. I get to start learning everything tomorrow and eventually I can be a doctor, just like I always wanted."

"That's great!" Constance snuggles tighter into Thomas's side. "I want to work with the kids. I mean how adorable is Nellie, right? What is everyone else going to do?"

"Greg said I could help with getting the houses ready for us." Thomas smiles with the healthy side of his face. "When they don't need more housing, there are always repairs and updates. They have a shop with tons of tools, some of them I've never even seen."

"We'll probably get to work together quite a bit." Daniel stands and stretches his arms above his head. "Frank and I have about a million ideas between us, but we'll probably need someone a bit more handy to put them into reality."

"You got it. As soon as the houses are done, consider me your right hand man." Thomas turns his attention to me. "What about you, Rebecca? Anything catch your interest today?"

I set down the stack of clothes from Ana I've been folding. "I haven't decided yet."

Thomas and the others stare at me, expecting more, but that's all I can say. I haven't picked a job because I'm not planning to be here long enough to need one. With the conversation cut short, everyone calls it a night and moves the curtains back into place.

The second I have our sheets set, Daniel pulls me to the bed. "Want to tell me why you're so quiet tonight? What's going on in that unpredictable head of yours?"

"We can't stay here."

"Wanna run that one by me again? Because it sounded an awful lot like you want us to leave the place that has offered us the only safety we could possibly hope for."

I turn to him and grab his hands. "This place is amazing, and I can't wait to spend the rest of forever here with you."

"So we are staying?"

"As soon as we get all those people who helped us out of the PIT. You promised."

Daniel tightens his grip on my hands and lines pop up between his eyebrows. "I would have told you anything to save your life. No way are we going back there."

I throw his hands back at him. "I'm not asking your permission, Daniel. If you won't come, then I'll go alone. They could all be dead by now, but I have to go back in case they're still alive."

"That sounds like just about the dumbest idea you've ever had, and if you think I'm going to watch you march out of here on a suicide mission, you've completely lost your mind."

I twist the leather bracelet around my wrist and take a deep breath to calm the anger festering in my core. I don't want to fight with him. "Then don't watch me."

"Oh, I'll be watching you every second of every day." Daniel stands and wipes his hands over his face. "And if by some chance you happen to sneak by me, I'll lead the charge to go get you. I'll carry you back slung over my shoulder if I have to."

"You're an ass."

"And you're stuck with me."

Desperation and fury boil up in my gut and spread out to the tips of my fingers. I stand up and stomp as far from him as I can in our little curtained off corner of the room. "Maybe there's nothing I can do for them, but I can't stay here and carry around the guilt of leaving them behind. We just left them, minutes after promising to get them out. They don't even know about the poison capsules. Now we do and we can go back and get them out, just like Eric did for us."

"Some of us are trying to sleep." Patrice's haughty tone is unmistakable.

I push past our privacy sheet without waiting to see if Daniel is following. Taking the same stairs as last night, I march out onto the roof. Daniel is right on my heels and slams the door behind us.

"What do you want, Rebecca?"

"What do I want?" I throw my hands in the air. Shouldn't it be obvious? "I want the life I was supposed to have. I want to go home and check on my father. I want to sit with Cheryl and not worry about anything more important than finishing school. I want to go back to a few weeks ago and never make that video so Patrice wouldn't be here and all those innocent people in the PIT would be safe. Or at least as safe as they were before I messed everything up."

Daniel pulls me into his arms, but I resist the urge to snuggle into him. I don't deserve his comfort. "I'm sorry, love. I can't give any of those things to you."

"I'm not asking you to." I push away, and the night air instantly cools my heated face. "I can't undo my past, but I'm in complete control of the future. That's why I'm going back to the PIT. My father and Cheryl are outside my reach, but there is something I can do about those people back in the PIT."

"Like what?" Daniel takes my hand and squeezes a little too hard. "What is your master plan for helping those people? Are you going to start a riot and break them out, too?"

I snatch my hand out of his. "I don't know, alright. I can figure it out on the way there. But I can't stay here and do nothing."

"Rebecca," Daniel rubs his hands over his face. "Think about this. You can't possibly want to go back there."

"You think I want to go back!" I spin away from him and let out a scream into the night air. "Of course I don't want to go back. I'd have to be insane to want to leave this place. But this isn't about what I want. Those people trusted us. We told them we were all getting out, and you promised me we could go back for them. Those people deserve Allmore, too."

The PIT always felt like such a dark place, but I was wrong. Sure there were bad people there. But there was also good. People like us who were thrown away, but trying to make the best of a rotten situation. I assumed we were a minority in a cesspool of criminals, but what if it was the other way around? What if only a tiny portion made the PIT miserable for the rest of us?

That old man I met my first week in the PIT. He tried to help me, tell me that not everyone in the PIT was a lost soul. But he was old and scary, so I discounted his words. The truth was there right from the start and I ignored it because I still believed the Cardinal's lies.

The door to the roof opens, and Elizabeth saunters out like the cat who caught the canary.

"Go away, Elizabeth." I practically spit the words at her.

"Whoa, don't shoot the messenger." She holds her hands out at her side. "I just came up here to let you know that your private conversation is so loud, half the village has probably heard. Including Liam and Ana who live right next door. You might want to keep it down."

"This conversation is none of your business."

"Look, princess. I couldn't care less if you want to pack it up and run a solo death march back to the PIT. But then you might mess up. Maybe give away the location of this cushy new paradise, and I can't have that."

"Not everything is about you, Elizabeth."

"And the rest of the people who live here?" Daniel takes a hesitant step toward me. "Are you willing to put all of them in danger? What about sweet, little Nellie?"

"I…" I hadn't even thought about it. I spin away from him and let out my frustration in a deep growl that comes all the way from my toes. How can I possibly measure one life against another?

"Let's make a deal." Daniel waits until I give him my full attention. "Thirty days. Thirty days to live here. To get healthy, rest our bodies, learn what we can about life outside of the Territories. Thirty days to think about this and plan it out. After that, we can talk about this again." He stops my protest with a raised hand. "I'm not making any other promises, Rebecca."

I turn away from him and kick a loose piece of gravel across the roof.

"You know I'm right about this. Going off without a plan will only be a fast death."

Of course he's right. Daniel always has a logical answer to everything. But I don't want to be rational or be soothed. I want to tighten my fist around the anger boiling over in my belly and charge into it full speed.

"Fine." I shove past him to the door without looking him in the eye. "Thirty days."

"Perfect," Elizabeth claps her hands together. "Now let's get some sleep."

I march down the stairs, through the curtains, and climb into bed, pulling the covers up over my head. Daniel joins me a minute later, but I pretend to already be asleep.

Part of me is burning with anger at being stopped. But mostly I'm relieved. Grateful that I have another thirty days to live here with all of them. Thirty days with Daniel, even if I am furious with him right now. And that fuels my anger at myself. If I were as strong as Daniel seems to think I am, I would have fought harder. But the truth is I don't have the courage to leave.

Seventeen

Breakfast is a silent affair, and everyone but Daniel and I eat quickly before moving out into the village to start their new jobs. Patrice sticks around a bit longer before heading out, I guess going back to our room above Doc's office. Daniel taps his foot in a spastic pattern on the floor. He has to be itching to get over to Frank's office, but no way is he going to leave me alone.

Liam and Ana glide into the dining hall like fairytale royalty, sharing warm smiles and greetings with the people still finishing their meals. It takes a few minutes, but eventually they make their way over to us.

"Daniel." Liam holds his hand out to shake Daniel's. "After yesterday I figured you'd already be half-deep into some crazy scheme with Frank."

"I...," he meets my gaze so I know his words are mostly for me. "I wanted to make sure Rebecca found the right job first."

"I think I have the solution to that." Ana holds a hand out to me. "We'll make sure she finds the right place here."

The three of them all stare at me expectantly. I don't have any other options. I grab Ana's hand and allow her to pull me up. Liam nods, and tension I didn't realize was there slips off Daniel's face.

"I'll see you at lunch." He drops a brief kiss on my cheek then pushes out into the bright sunlight.

"Let's walk." Ana tucks my arm into hers and the three of us walk outside.

The main street is still bustling with activity as the village launches into another day. To our left, Frank has already found Daniel and the two of them amble down the street, engaged in an animated conversation. Ana tugs my arm to the right and we head in the opposite direction.

"Do you know what I admire about you, Rebecca? It's your passion." Ana pats my arm. "And not just your passion, but the way you express it. You've got a way with words, which incidentally, I suspect had a role in your Rejection. But that's also why I think I have the perfect job for you."

Liam holds open a door, and Ana bounces in, tugging me along with her. Inside, the intoxicating aroma of baking bread soaks into my pores. Ana pulls me deeper into the bakery, but Liam hangs back at the door. Everything inside is coated in a thin dusting of flour, including a full wall of shelves holding bread pans filled with rising balls of dough. All the yeast, sugar, and flour mix together to make my mouth water despite the fact that I just finished breakfast.

"Morning Carol, do I smell raisins?" Ana coughs a bit and waves her hand in front of her face to shoo away the flour that seems to float in the air.

"Keep it a secret, dear. We got a nice supply in the last load so I thought I'd whip up some bread pudding as a special treat in honor of our new arrivals." Carol nods her head of curly gray hair in my direction, and my chest fills with warmth. This place really is a little slice of perfection.

"My lips are sealed." Ana turns to me and pulls me over to the table where Carol is kneading another roll of dough. "Carol, Rebecca. Rebecca, Carol. This is the lady responsible for all the puddles of drool on my desk. Speaking of, time to get to work."

Carol is easily the oldest person I've seen so far. In addition to her gray hair, wrinkles branch out from her smiling eyes and crease her forehead. My fingers worry at my necklace, and I smile at the memory of my own grandmother baking sweet treats.

Ana walks back toward the door where Liam is leaning against the wall watching our interactions with his arms crossed and a little smile on his face. "You can head off and do all your important leader duties." She lifts up onto her toes and plants a kiss on his cheek. "I'll take it from here."

"Alright, try not to scare her off on her first day."

Ana pushes him gently out the door and adds a quick tickle to his ribs. "You do your job and let me do mine." She closes the door behind him, but immediately opens it back up, leaning her head out. "See you at lunch." She closes the door and turns back to me. "Now, time to get to work."

"Listen, this might not be the right place for me. I don't know anything about baking bread."

Ana laughs like a small child full of giddy delight. Carol booms with a deep belly laugh from behind me. "As if Carol would ever let anyone else even come close to her bread. No, I'm hoping you'll be much more interested in what I have in my office. Come on."

She gives Carol a wave and heads upstairs, pulling me behind her. The space is open just like the room above Doc's office. But where we have bare walls and sparse beds, Ana has one huge open room without an inch of free space anywhere. Everywhere I look are maps, lists of all kinds, sheets with strings of numbers, and so many items I can't identify.

Ana bounces over to an over-sized table and pulls out two chairs. "Come. Sit. Learn."

I pull my eyes away from the walls and wander over to the table where she's moving stacks of paper and folders from one place to another. I've never seen so much paper in my life. Back in the Territories, everything was on our Noteboards and paper was scarce, only used for the most important documents or special items, like our dance cards.

"Don't you have a Noteboard?"

"Yeah, there's one over there." She flicks her wrist at the corner where a Noteboard in pristine condition rests precariously on a table overflowing with paper. "I tried it, but I like my system better." She lifts away a completely scrawled over calendar to reveal a huge map that covers the entire table.

"Your system? What is this place?"

"Neat, huh?" Anna grins at me like a kid on her birthday. Her excitement is infectious and spurs a bubbly feeling in my stomach. "I like to call it my command center."

"What do you command?"

Anna rubs her hands together with unrestrained glee. "Everything."

"You lost me. Can we start over?"

"Okay, you sit, I'll talk?"

I move a thick folder to the floor and sit in one of the chairs, my eyes floating from one end of the room to the other.

Ana spreads her hands across the map in a presentation style. "Now, tell me if this looks familiar to you."

I lean over the table and try to make sense of the different colors, lines, and symbols. "It kinda looks like a map of the United Territories. Except it's bigger and the labels are all wrong."

"Good, good." She grabs a purple marker and marks off an area inside the map. "So this part inside is what we know as the United Territories. And before we were the Territories, we were the states. That's what you see in this map, along with Canada and Mexico. You with me?"

I nod. "We learned in school that the Territories used to be the states, but the name was changed after the government dissolved and the original Cardinal took over."

"Yeah, well, like most things they teach in the Territories, that's more of a half-truth."

I trace my finger around the purple lines she just added. "So what's the whole truth?"

"The history books start out right. The states were completely out of control. Violence was so commonplace that infrastructure shut down. Farmers let their fields go empty, and factories shut down. The combination of violence and lack of resources created a drastic drop in population."

"Right, that's when people abandoned the small towns and moved to the few cities that still had food and power."

Ana taps the map with a little more force than needed. "Except we were taught that everyone moved. The rest of the country was left empty as the citizens flocked to the safety that the Cardinal promised everyone."

I shrug my shoulders. "He did make them safer. Then the Machine was invented and the current Cardinal pretty much eliminated violence."

"Along with personal freedom and the ability to be anything other than exactly what the Cardinal ordered. But not everyone bought into all the promises he was selling."

I nod. "The Freemen."

Ana nods back. "The Cardinal set up the Territories around the country's most essential natural resources and then abandoned everything in-between. That left the

Freemen alone to create their own society. With the old money system worthless, they reverted to a trade system and that's what I do here."

"Trade? You mean with Arbor Glen."

"No, not with them." She holds her hands up to stave off my questions. "That's Liam's story to tell. This," she taps a little flag on the map, "is where we are, in what used to be Virginia."

"What are all the rest of the flags?"

"Those are known Freemen villages."

"What? All of them?" My eyes fly over the map. "There must be dozens."

"One hundred forty-two known villages, to be exact, spread out throughout all of what used to be the United States. And that's where this office comes in."

She bounces over to one of the walls and gestures to several of the lists pinned to the wall. "Right here I have the latitude and longitude coordinates for each village we know about. The ones marked in green are active traders and the ones in orange like to keep to themselves." She moves over to another section. "Here is a list of village-specific specialties. These are the items that are only available through one or two villages and might require an extra-long trip or coordination with another village to collect similar supplies."

She looks around her wall and bites her lip, then rushes over to a table and unearths a folder. "In here are the names and locations for each of the coordinators at the other villages."

I should be saying something, but my brain is temporarily disconnected from my mouth.

She stares at my face like an inspector. "Tell me what you're thinking."

I focus on Ana's face. The way her dark hair curls around the smooth line of her jaw. The little lines between her eyebrows that match Daniel's when he gets upset. One hundred forty-two. Not a handful or even a dozen. One hundred forty-two villages just like this one filled with people who live by their own decisions and never worry about how some Machine will judge them. One hundred forty-two perfect examples of everything that is wrong with everything I've ever known. One hundred forty-two Cardinal lies I accepted, just like everyone else.

Light hands rest on my shoulders. "You're looking a little shell shocked. I may have even worn myself out with all that." Ana sinks into the chair next to me and rests her head back over the edge.

"I just thought." I take a deep breath and stare at the world laid out in front of me pinned to the walls. "In a hundred years, I never would have imagined all of this. I'm not even sure what to say."

Ana sits up and surveys the room. "Yeah, sorry. I guess this is a bit overwhelming. After I escaped, I was so afraid by the time I found people out here, they could have told me they were advanced life forms from outer space and I would have been okay with that."

"And the Cardinal? He has to know you exist."

"Oh he knows." A wicked smile turns up the edges of Ana's lips. "He just doesn't know exactly where we are.

There are thousands of abandoned cities throughout the country. Plus, some villages have several locations that they rotate through to keep the Cardinal off their trail. We stay away from the Territories and he tends to leave us alone. Every couple of years or so he sends some guards out to look for us. None have ever gotten close enough to be an issue."

"And if they did?"

Ana stands up taller and looks me dead in the eyes. "This isn't a game of hide-and-go-seek. The Cardinal would not hesitate to destroy us and take down every Freemen village he could get his hands on. Out here, we do what we have to in order to survive."

I should be upset. In not so many words, she just admitted that the village is willing to kill in order to keep their secret safe. Even just thinking about taking someone's life would be enough for the Machine to grant a one-way ticket to the PIT. But I'm not upset. I'm grateful I can sleep tonight feeling safe. I'm a monster and couldn't possibly care any less.

"So what do you think?"

I look around the room, taking my time to really see it. Paper everywhere and maps that should be a foreign language, but actually might make sense to me. There's a beauty in the chaos. Like the huge puzzles my grandmother used to work on at the kitchen table. I would sit on her lap and watch as she seemed to always know which of the identical pieces went into the right space.

Ana bounces on her toes, clutching her hands in front of her like a child waiting for their teacher's approval.

I clutch at the knotted necklace that's been with me since the beginning of this crazy journey. "It's the most amazing thing I've ever seen. Tell me everything."

Ana's eyes light up like fireworks on the Cardinal's birthday. "The village map is only the beginning." Her hands rub together as if we're about to be co-conspirators in a nefarious scheme. "Let me tell you about the Pony Express."

* * *

I stagger into the medical building and give Doc a nod on my way to our upstairs room. I can't wave with the huge stack of blankets and new clothes piled in my arms. Ana was able to switch around some of our trades so we could all have more than one spare set of clothes. She insisted it was no big deal, but after only a week of helping her in the PE, I know just how much a single change can impact as many as a half-dozen other routes. I'm guessing by her request for a pre-lunch nap, she pulled more than one all-nighter to make it happen.

The door at the top of the stairs is closed, so I have to set everything down to open it. At this time of day, everyone else will be out working or getting ready for lunch. I reach for the doorknob, but freeze as shouting pours through the thin wooden door.

"What has gotten into you? You've changed completely." Daniel's voice is unmistakable, even with the muffled shouting.

"Well, you haven't changed at all," Patrice yells back at him. "Back at home, you were perfect little Daniel. The doting son that did whatever Dad told you. You do the same thing out here except Rebecca is the one calling the shots."

Great. Patrice still hates me just as much as ever.

"Leave Rebecca out of it. This is between you and me and your bad attitude."

"Are you kidding me? You think you're so in love you can't even see what's going on?"

"Then explain it to me."

"She makes all the decisions around here and you just run around trying like crazy to make her happy."

"Of course, I want her to be happy." There's a pause, and I can picture Daniel rubbing his hands over his face the way he does when he's too frustrated to speak. "I love Rebecca. She's my wife."

"And I'm your sister. That used to mean something."

This isn't a conversation I should hear, but I can't leave. I need Patrice to stop hating me, and maybe this will clue me in on how to make that happen.

"Cardinal on a cracker, Patrice. We got out of the PIT and found a safe place to live. While the rest of us work to make this place a home, you sit up here pouting, and I haven't said a single word about it. What more do you want from me?"

The springs of a bed creak. "I want you to figure out a way to let me go home."

"That's not going to happen." Daniel's voice is loud enough now that even Doc can probably hear it.

"And whose fault is that?" Patrice's voice lifts up to near hysterical levels. "Rebecca. The perfect one who can do no wrong."

"You have no idea what Rebecca has done."

"I know it was her genius idea to hack the ceremony feed, and that means it's her fault I'm stuck out here."

"Everyone we ever met back in the Territories was willing to sacrifice the world if it meant getting ahead, but Rebecca is willing to sacrifice herself for the world. If you'd stop living in a world of self-pity and hate, you'd see that."

"And maybe if you stopped staring at Rebecca like she hung the moon, you'd see that I'm here, too."

Footsteps pound across the room and the door jerks open before I can move. Patrice stares at me through the doorway.

"Patrice, I—"

"Save it for someone who cares what you have to say." Patrice pushes past me on the stairs and stomps down through Doc's lobby and out the door.

Daniel replaces her in the doorway, his mouth droopy with defeat. Who knows how long they've been up here arguing.

"Here, let me get these." He reaches down and easily grabs the stack of blankets and clothes. Back in the room he dumps them in a very non-Daniel manner on an empty bed.

"Wanna talk about it?"

"Not much to say." He clomps over to our pushed together beds and collapses across the width of them face down. "She's right. I did everything my father told me to do. Including keeping quiet about the information I found about who really gets sent to the PIT."

I sink to the mattress next to him. "So what? I did everything my mother told me."

"This is different." He sits up, but doesn't look at me. "My father was grooming me to replace him on the Cardinal's council someday. I didn't just follow his instructions. I was a Cardinal fanatic. I memorized everything he said and took every word of it to heart. Every morning, I would recite bits of his speeches to myself in the mirror. There wasn't an ounce of doubt in my mind that the Cardinal was responsible for every ounce of happiness in my life."

"He fooled everyone." I grab his hand and run my fingers over the hard calluses on his palm. "Myself included."

"But am I doing it again? We get here and I never once stopped to question any of it. Liam asks me for something and I work to make it happen. You have to know that I'd move mountains to make you happy."

"And you call me out on my crazy whenever I go over the deep-end."

"But I—"

"No." I shush him with my hand. "Patrice is wrong on this one. You don't follow me blindly. You support me and love me and challenge me to be better. You were the one that showed me I'm more than a series of disappointments to my mother."

I slide off the bed and kneel in front of Daniel, grabbing his face with both hands so he's forced to look me in the eye.

"We were all different people before the Rejection. You are not that person who parroted the words of the Cardinal. I don't know that Daniel. The Daniel I know is careful with his words so he doesn't cause hurt in others, but isn't afraid to speak up when he knows he's right. My Daniel didn't hide away with knowledge that could make a difference. You stood in front of the camera when you didn't have to."

Daniel pulls me up until I'm sitting in his lap, his strong arms wrapped around me.

"We are all different people now. Patrice included. We had the PIT, and as awful as it was, it forced me to see the world for more than the fake piece of perfection the Cardinal is trying to hold on to. Patrice will have her moment of realization, too. It just might take longer because she isn't starving or fighting off attackers. And that's a good thing.

"You were patient with me when I kept insisting I could be happy living a lie as Eric's pretend wife. You need to be patient with Patrice, too. She'll come around."

Daniel kisses my forehead. "When did you get so wise?"

"Probably around the same time I admitted to being in love with you."

"Very wise indeed."

"Shut up and kiss me."

"Now, there's a demand I'll follow blindly any day."

Eighteen

"Perfect." I add Constance's order for the schoolhouse into my Noteboard. "Let me know if you need any other supplies for the summer apprenticeships."

Constance picks Nellie up and swings her onto her hip like she's been taking care of children her whole life. "That should do it. Do we need anything else, Nellie?" Constance tickles her belly and the miniature Ana lets out a stream of infectious giggles.

"Okay, I'll see you at dinner." I push out of the schoolhouse, still laughing. Outside, the spring sun warms my face. It won't be too much longer before summer arrives. Hard to believe we've been here three weeks already.

Strong arms snake around my waist. "Just the lady I wanted to see." Daniel nuzzles against my ear before spinning me around to face him. "I have a present for you."

"Well, I can't say no to that."

Daniel pulls a Noteboard out of his bag, a huge grin on his face.

"Not to sound ungrateful, but I already have one of these." I shake my own Noteboard just for emphasis.

"Oh no, you don't have this," he says, pushing the power button. "And trust me when I say you'll definitely want it."

The screen lights up, but doesn't have the normal menu screen I'm accustomed to seeing at boot up. Instead, the screen has several boxes with the names of Territory cities, all of them in fairly close proximity to Allmore. Daniel smiles at me again before tapping one of the boxes.

The screen flashes a few times before a live news broadcast pops onto the screen. I reach for the power button to cut off the signal, but Daniel pulls the Noteboard out of reach. "Daniel, you have to turn it off. The Cardinal could pick up on our signal and track us down."

"No, he can't." He pulls the screen back down to where I can see it. "I was able to disable the outgoing signal. Well, I couldn't disable it completely, but it's so scrambled they'll never be able to track it. But now we can pick up the news broadcast."

He taps a button on the side and the nasally voice of the host pulses from the Noteboard. "I figured you and Ana could use it to keep track of planned guard movements in order to keep your riders out of trouble."

"This is amazing." I lift up on my tip toes to reward him with a kiss. "Why don't you come back to the Pony Express office with me so you can show Ana?"

"I'd love to, but I need to take one of these treasures over to Liam, and then Thomas wants me to come have a look at the wiring for the house they're working on. I'll see you at dinner." Daniel leans down to return my kiss and then runs off into the spring sunshine.

* * *

"Hey, lady. Back so soon?" Ana nods up at me from her spot on the floor, surrounded by half a dozen piles of paper. "Thanks for going out for me. I just don't have the energy today. This cold is kicking my butt and I'm not sleeping well at all."

"No problem, you rest up all you need to get back to one hundred percent." I pull my Noteboard out and hand it over. "Here are the lists from Frank and Greg. Constance will let me know if she needs anything else soon."

Ana takes a look and then hands it back to me. "Perfect. Before you add those to the trade route, can you show me what you did with the southwest run? These routes are completely different than what we've been doing."

I sit down on the floor where she's comparing the trade route I drew up with the old route. "We don't have to change it, but if we go through Willow Creek instead of Canyon Vista we can shave two days off the travel time. Then instead of getting cornmeal from Canyon Vista, we can get it from Independence when we do our biannual stop for vanilla. Carol said the cornmeal will keep fine if we get a six month supply all at once."

Ana stares at the map for another second then claps her hands, a huge smile on her face. "How'd you do that? We've been running this old route for at least six years and this never even crossed my mind."

"I don't know, but all of this," I wave my hands at the stacks of maps and trade lists, "just makes sense. It's like how Daniel can pick up a new piece of technology and figure out how it works and ten ways to make it better without even trying. He's tried to show me how the Noteboards work and none of it ever sank in." I twist the leather bracelet around my wrist like it can keep me from jinxing myself. "Everything about this room feels right to me."

Ana smiles at me with watery eyes that may or may not be from the spring cold she can't seem to shake. "Having you here feels right to me, too."

A knock at the door interrupts our conversation.

"Hello?"

"Come in." Ana's voice comes out thin and weak.

Patrice inches into the room, a Noteboard pressed to her chest. Her eyes widen as she takes it in and we all wait in silence for several minutes while she gets her first look at the PE office.

"What can we help you with, Patrice?" I don't mean to be curt, but I don't have time to hear a list of items Patrice thinks she can't live without.

"No need to be snippy, Rebecca." Patrice hands the Noteboard over while her eyes continue to sweep the room. "I'm here for Doc."

"Ah, see I told you eventually you'd get bored and want a job." Ana is beaming despite the flush of her face.

"It's not a job." Patrice finally stops her investigation and faces us. "I was just there and he asked me to bring this over for him."

"Just there, huh? So this has nothing to do with spending weeks as an anti-social hermit without anyone to talk to except during meals." Ana coughs, but it comes out more like a laugh. "You aren't even in the least bit bored?"

"I haven't been a hermit. Eric's been letting me hang out—"

Patrice stops cold, her brown eyes as wide as saucers and her mouth drawn up in an O. So miss-priss hasn't been holed up alone all day. She's been slipping downstairs to spend the day with Eric. Interesting.

"I have to go." She uncrosses her arms and holds out a hand. "If you have the list, I'll need the Noteboard back."

"Sure thing." I hold it out and she snatches it from my hand. "But wait just a second and I have something else for you." I grab the Noteboard Daniel just gave me and hand it to Patrice. "While you're lounging around in bed, not being bored, you can use this to keep an eye on the news stations. Let us know if there is any discussion of guard movement or anything weather related that might impact trade routes."

"What is this?" Ana stands to check out the Noteboard over Patrice's shoulder.

"Daniel managed to scramble the outgoing signal so we can spy on the Cardinal. Or at least, what the Cardinal puts on the airwaves."

Patrice taps the screen a few times. "So, to be clear, you're saying it can be my job to sit in our room all day and watch the newsfeed?"

"Unless, of course, you found something else to do. I'm sure Elizabeth would love a hand taking care of the herd." I clap my hands as if I've just thought of the best idea ever. "Or you could go apprentice under Daniel! I'm sure he'd absolutely love to teach you everything he knows."

"I don't think so." She stacks the Noteboards on top of each other and heads toward the door, her eyes already glued to the screen.

"Don't forget to take Doc's Noteboard back," Ana calls to her as she leaves.

"And tell Eric we say hello."

Patrice freezes and pulls the Noteboards closer to her chest before rushing down the stairs.

Ana erupts into a fit of giggles.

I manage to hold it in until I hear Carol call out a goodbye and the front door downstairs slams closed. Then I lie down and laugh until tears stream down my cheeks.

Ana chokes back her laughter and clears her throat. "I think we're growing on her. First a job. Now we just need to find her a husband."

"Don't let Daniel hear you say that." I grab a clipboard and pen and head over to the supply wall. "Can I ask you a question?"

"Ask away." Ana stares back at her map.

"I was actually wondering about getting married. Or rather, how to get married?"

"I thought you and Daniel were already married?"

"We were, are." I set my pen down and shake out my fingers. I'm not off to a stellar start. "I was just curious about any wedding traditions you have here."

Ana stands up and pulls out a chair near where I'm working. "When Liam and I got married, everything was perfect." She sits down and a goofy grin slides over her face. "The whole village took the day off so everyone could be a part of our special day. We managed to get some gorgeous satin from a village that trades frequently with Mexico and the team here made me a dress. It was like a princess fairytale."

"So...just like a wedding in the Territories?"

"Kinda." Ana bursts into a hacking cough and needs several minutes to get some water down and her breathing under control.

I take the glass of water back from her. "Okay?"

"Yeah, sorry about that." She leans back into the chair. "Guess I'm a little sicker than I thought. Might be time to stop back over at Doc's office."

"You might want to give Patrice a minute first, because I'm pretty sure she hates both of us now instead of just me."

"Nah. You know, she became a part of this village the minute she walked out of the forest. You all did. Oh sure, you had to confess." She holds up her fingers to make quote marks in the air. "And the village voted, but that was more a formality than anything else. Just a ceremony, really. Because you joined us the minute you decided you wanted to stay and we accepted you long before that. It's what's in your heart that makes you who you are, not any formal declaration."

"Are we still talking about Patrice?"

Ana winks at me, but keeps a straight face. "Ceremony has its place and it can help us to reconcile what we know inside with the world around us. But it's the promises we make without any pomp and circumstance that take root in our souls."

"You're either the wisest woman I know," I squeeze her arm, "or that fever has finally gone to your head. How about we get you over to Doc's to get you checked out and see if we can drive Patrice crazy?"

"Oh, you're evil." Ana pushes off the back of the chair and stands up next to me. "I like it."

Nineteen

"Ethan, those are all really great ideas and I've got them all recorded." I set my Noteboard down on the overly crowded desk. "I'm completely swamped right now trying to get the Northern trade ride set on my own, but as soon as Ana gets back, I promise we'll go over all your ideas together."

"I know it's a lot of changes, but I promise they'll make a big difference." He turns away from where I've finally got him near the door. "Are you sure you don't need me to go over the wagon upgrade design again?"

I open the door and angle my body so the only place to go is out. "Nope, you were really thorough in your description. I feel like I could build it myself."

"Ha, you're a funny girl, Rebecca." Ethan takes a few steps down the stairs, but pauses to look back again. "I can see why Ana likes you so much."

"Thanks, Ethan. I'm a pretty big Ana fan myself." I take several steps down so Ethan either has to keep moving or get uncomfortably too close to me. After what feels like the world's most awkward dance, we finally make it all the way down to the bakery.

"So, just let me know if you want me to come back over and explain any of that once Ana gets back." Ethan has both feet out the door, but his head and torso stuck inside keep me from shutting it. "I really don't mind and it gives me something productive to do between rides. Guard duty is a little too solitary for me."

"I can see why." I glance back at Carol behind the desk. She isn't looking at me, but there's a definite smirk in her smile. "I'm sure Ana would love to have you in as soon as she's back on her feet."

"Great." Ethan pulls his head back, but then ducks inside again. "Maybe I should leave her a note."

"No," I practically shout before calming my voice. "No need to make yourself late for lunch. I promise I'll let her know about your visit next time I see her."

"Okay. I'd better get over to the dining hall. I've got some ideas to run by Liam, too. See you later. Bye, Carol."

"Bye, Dear." Carol waves him off with a flour-coated hand.

I shut the door with maybe a little too much force the second Ethan is all the way on the other side and lean my back against the old wood.

"I know Ethan is our best rider, but he's exhausting."

Carol giggles like a woman half her age. "Ethan is a bit like rich chocolate cake. A wonderful treat best consumed in small portions."

"You're telling me. That's his third drop-by this week." I peek out the window to make sure Ethan is moving down the street. "I don't know how Ana ever managed this on her own."

"She's been at it a lot longer than you. Don't worry, you'll get there."

"It just feels like I should be doing more." I move away from the door and slide onto a stool by Carol's counter. "I need to prove to everyone here that I'm worth the second chance they are giving me."

Carol dusts her hands together and then wipes them against her apron. "Have I ever told you about why I came to Allmore?"

"I don't think so. Didn't you come with the others?"

"No, I didn't come until a few years later, and I'm all for treating people fairly, but that didn't have anything do to with my move." Carol grabs a plate from the shelf and scoops a gooey pastry onto it. "Honey bun?"

"Thanks. So why did you come?"

"My husband died."

"Oh, Carol, I'm so sorry."

"No worries, dear." She pats the hand I laid on her arm. "It's been almost fifteen years now. We lived in a village to the south of here. I stayed for a while but there were just too many memories of him there. Everywhere I went was another reminder of Jimmy."

"That must have been hard."

"It was, but not for the reason you think." She pinches off a piece of my bun and works it around in her mouth for a bit. "Jimmy was the love of my life and I don't regret a single moment together. Having memories of him was a blessing. But I'm not the kind to wallow in my own self-pity. I needed to keep living, and I know Jimmy would feel the same. But everyone there saw me as just Jimmy's poor widow. I couldn't move on or work through my grief and that's no way to live."

"So you left?"

"I heard about the people forming Allmore and decided it was my best option. I still miss him and I'll always love him. That many years of memories don't just go away. But just because something awful happens in your past doesn't mean you aren't allowed to enjoy your future."

We both sit in silence for several minutes, taking turns tearing off bits of honey bun. By the time it's gone, I feel better. I still want to do my best, but not because I have to keep proving myself. I want to make this work while Ana is out because I want to see this village thrive.

"You know, you give pretty good advice, Carol."

"Who, me?" Carol takes the empty plate and sets it in the sink. "I'm just the lady who bakes the bread."

"Sure, just the bread." I get up and wipe my sticky fingers on a towel. "I'm heading over for lunch now. Want to join me?"

"Naw, I'm gonna finish up here, then go get cleaned up. I'll be finding honey in places it shouldn't be for days unless I get a good soak."

I head out the door with a laugh. A good, genuine laugh. The kind that wouldn't have been possible only a short month ago. Everything about this place makes it easier to be happy.

* * *

In the dining hall, Daniel is already sitting down, though he's barely picking at his meal. Across from him, Patrice is chatting a mile a minute about who knows what. For as quiet as Daniel can be, his sister more than makes up for it.

I grab a bowl of vegetable soup and a thick slice of Carol's bread and slide in next to them. Patrice stops talking the minute I sit down.

Daniel sets his spoon down and grabs both of my hands, forcing me to turn toward him. His mouth pulls down at the edges, but he flashes me a brief smile that he can't seem to hold on to. "Rebecca, there's something we need to tell you."

Patrice points her spoon at Daniel, bouncing it with each word. "Hey, leave me out of it. I was just watching the news feed like I was told."

Daniel stares at her until she picks up her bowl, leaving us somewhat alone with everyone else enjoying their lunch.

"Whatever it is, you can tell me anything."

Daniel nods before leaning in to plant a kiss on my forehead. He won't look me in the eye and keeps staring at our joined hands. "Patrice was listening to the news feed today when the broadcasters made an announcement from Cardinal City."

"Spit it out, Daniel. You're scaring me."

"They're gone." He closes his eyes and sucks in a deep breath. "The Cardinal killed all of them."

"What? Who?" I throw a leg over the bench like I can run it to stop whatever has happened.

"They announced that the ring leaders for last month's sabotage of the Acceptance ceremony are still loose in the PIT. But the others have all been found and eliminated."

I pull my hands out of Daniel's and stand, stumbling back a few steps. "No. No no no no no no." I shake my head and stare around the room. How can everyone just sit there? The Cardinal just murdered a dozen innocent people.

"Rebecca." Daniel reaches for my hands, but I step away from him. I was supposed to go back and save them. I said I would. Has it even been thirty days? I stopped keeping track; forgot all about them. We left them there and now they're dead.

"Rebecca!" Liam rushes down the room toward us. "Thank goodness I found you."

I can't talk yet, but manage to stare into Liam's panic-stricken eyes.

"We need your help. Now." He doesn't wait for my response and takes off back out of the room.

Daniel walks over to me. "Whatever it is—"

I shove past him, grab my Noteboard off the table, and head toward the door. "Liam needs me." And I'm not going to wait again.

Liam waits for me right outside. "We need to go back to my house."

I follow him, struggling to keep up with his pace. "Liam, what's going on?"

"It's Ana," he calls over his shoulder and keeps walking. It's clear that's all the information I'm going to get until we get back to his place.

In a few minutes we're pushing through the front door. An aura of sickness hangs in the air, a mix of crushed herbs and soap that can't quite cover the odor. Liam leads us to the back bedroom. Ana lies in bed covered in blankets, her face sunken in like a person who hasn't eaten in weeks. Doc and Eric are at her side, checking her vitals, but looking completely helpless.

I drop my bag and sit on the small stool next to her bed. Her hand is cold and the skin is papery against mine. "Hey there, pretty lady."

Ana smiles weakly and opens her mouth to respond, but her body takes over, shaking violently in a coughing fit. I jump back out of the way and Doc and Eric rush in to lift her torso up and wipe a cloth against her forehead. When the coughing dies down, they rest her back on the mountain of pillows and force her to take a few sips of something that smells like moldy leaves.

"What is this? What can I do?"

Liam takes her thin hand and gives it a soft squeeze. "We can't be one hundred percent sure—"

"It's cancer." Ana cuts him off, her voice stronger than she looks. "Can we just stop pretending like it's not? Doc, that's what the blood work says, right?"

"I don't have the machines needed to give a proper diagnosis of this type. I have no idea how much there is, where it is, or where it might have spread." Doc holds up a hand to Liam who opens his mouth. "But I've run the blood work four times. I had Eric run it a fifth time just to be sure I wasn't making a mistake. I wish I was."

This is why I'm here. Ana needs me. "I can have a new rider out of here first thing in the morning."

"Without knowing exactly what we're dealing with, most treatments are going to be a shot in the dark." Doc sinks down onto a chair by the bed, the stress of the situation aging him by the minute. "But there is one therapy out there that has excellent results treating several types of cancer. It's our best shot."

I already have my Noteboard out and ready to take down the information.

"It's called Paclitaxel Anastrozole Methotrexate, or PAM. It's a Territory product. I can't imagine what the trade will cost us."

"Just let me take care of that, Doc. We can all tighten our belts for the winter if that's what it takes to get Ana better." I type in the name, my brain already whirling with supply lists of what we can do without this winter. "Ana, any idea on who might have this?"

"No one that we regularly trade with—" Deep coughs wrack her body, and I stand by, useless, while the others hold her torso up until the hacking stops. She takes the smallest sips of water before lying back down. "There is another option."

I'm already crossing several items off the list. We can wait until spring for system upgrades.

"There was some chatter last year about a village down in the southwest getting a drug like this from Mexico. They called it Dador de Vida."

"What do you say, Doc?"

"That may be our best bet. I don't like the idea of how long it's going to take to get a supply run from that far, but we're not likely to find something better any closer."

"What about Arbor Glen?" I turn to Liam. "I know we don't trade with them and I don't need to know why, but is there a chance they have this and we don't have to go so far?"

"I doubt it, but it's worth a shot." Liam runs a shaky hand through his hair.

I tuck the Noteboard back in my bag and grab Ana's hand. "You just hang in there and do whatever Doc says, including drink whatever died in that cup. I am going to get this medicine and you'll be fine. I promise."

"I believe in you." Ana squeezes my hand, though the pressure is so light I barely notice.

I turn to leave, but Eric's hand on my shoulder stops me. "If they make this drug in the Territories, why not just go there to get it?"

He stares at me, a strange mix of determination and desperation in his eyes. I want to say yes, but I can't.

"It's one of the few rules we have. No trading with the Territories. It's the first thing Ana taught me."

"But—"

"No, Eric." Ana's voice is barely a whisper, but there's force behind it. "We can't put everyone at risk." Her eyelids flutter shut and in seconds she's asleep.

We all step into the kitchen so Ana can get some much-needed rest.

"Liam, you could make an exception." Eric ignores Doc and me as if we aren't even in the room. "You know they have PAM. I can get it for Ana and enough to have on hand for next time."

Liam collapses into a chair, his torso falling over onto the table.

"Please, Liam."

It's wrong, so wrong. Everything Ana said is true. The Cardinal would love to shut down the Freemen, and finding one would be just the first step to finding all of us. But it's Ana, and I can't lose any more people.

"No." Liam's voice is muffled from where his head rests on his arms. "Ana's right. It's too dangerous. Rebecca, promise me you won't let any of the riders go anywhere near the Territories."

I don't want to make that promise. "I promise." But I have to.

Eric storms out of the kitchen, through the house, and bangs out the front door.

"I'll talk to him. Don't worry about it." Doc pats Liam's shoulder on his way out. "Call me if there are any changes. For now, at least I can make her comfortable."

Doc leaves and I stand motionless in the kitchen. All those people in the PIT are dead. I didn't go back for them, and now they are gone. But Ana is still alive, and I'll do anything I can to keep her that way.

Ana breaks out into another coughing fit I can hear all the way in the kitchen. "We're going to get the medicine, Liam. Don't give up hope yet."

His hand jerks out and grabs my wrist. "I can't lose her."

"I'm not going to let that happen."

Twenty

I leave Liam sitting alone in his kitchen. There are a million tasks to take care of. I need to call in all the available riders, and maybe ask for volunteers, and I've got to set up routes to maximize the number of villages we can hit. But my brain won't stop whirling around the scene in Ana's room. Her frail body propped against the pillows and the slight touch of her papery hand in mine.

She's dying, and it's all happening so fast. Right now, our best hope is the southwest villages, but by the time our riders get down there and back again, she might be gone. But what if we could get PAM from the Territories? The others in the PIT are gone, but Ana still has a chance if I can figure out a way to get the medicine in time. I stand in the middle of the main road, my eyes closed tight, and wait for the afternoon sun to give me an answer.

"Are you okay?"

Thomas stares down at me when I open my eyes. He must think I've completely lost what was left of my mind.

"Most likely not, but there's nothing I can do about it." I shift the Noteboard in my hand. Thomas and I aren't exactly close, but Constance thinks he hung the moon. "Can I ask you a question?"

"You can, but I can't promise an answer."

Always so straightforward. Thomas wasn't the answer I was looking for, but he might be exactly the help I need.

"What would you do if Constance was really sick, and you had a way to help her, but if you did it, it could mean a lot of trouble for everyone else?"

"It *could* mean trouble?" Thomas wipes his forehead with a handkerchief. "'Cause the way I figure, if Constance dies it definitely would mean trouble and pain for me. So you've got the choice between something that could make trouble and something that would definitely make trouble. I'd say that 'could' is looking pretty favorable."

"Thanks, Thomas." I reach up on tiptoes to kiss his spoiled cheek. "Constance is lucky to have such a wise husband."

"Do me a favor," he says, walking away, "and remind her of that next time you see her."

I run off for the Pony Express office, reinvigorated by the decision to do something.

I'm almost to the PE office before I hear Eric calling my name. He runs up to my side, but I don't stop.

"Don't say a word. Not out in the open where others can hear."

We both practically sprint through the bakery, only giving Carol a cursory hello before taking the steps two at a time and locking the door behind us.

Eric grabs my arm. "We both know the Doc can't do anything for Ana without this medicine. We also know she might not last until the riders can get back from traveling all the way to the southern villages. That's why I need to get what we need from the Territory."

"I know."

Eric opens his mouth and then shuts it again, tilting his head as if he's seeing me for the first time. "What did you say?"

"We don't have time for theatrics if we're going to save Ana." I march to the desk and shove papers out of the way. "Come take a look at this map if you still want to go."

"Yes."

"I need to know one thing first." I wait until I'm sure he's completely listening. "This is the most dangerous stunt we've ever pulled. Bigger by far than escaping from the PIT. The likelihood you end up dead or leading the Cardinal right to us is higher than I'd like to admit. I want to know why you're doing this."

"I need this."

I shove my finger into his chest. "What do you mean you need this? You need this to save Ana or you need to be the hero so Elizabeth and Daniel will stop looking at you like the village leper?"

"Both."

I nod. Good enough for me. "I'm going to send Ethan with you. He's our best rider and the most likely to keep you alive. But he has to wait outside the Territory border. Two of you will be too suspicious, so once you're inside the city, you'll be on your own. Ethan will get you there safely and make sure you aren't followed in or out."

"Thank you."

"Don't thank me yet. You might want to wait until you come back in one piece." I grab a scrap of paper and scribble a quick note. "Do me a favor. Find Ethan, give him this, and tell him to rally all the riders for a meeting in the stables in thirty minutes."

Eric grabs my hand and squeezes tightly. It's not a romantic gesture, but it feels more intimate than any of his gentle touches back in the PIT. For the first time, we are working in sync. "Ana is going to be fine. Ethan and I can get this medicine."

I squeeze his hand back. "You'd better. When you're done talking to Ethan, go get some rest. You'll leave at sunrise."

Eric takes off down the stairs. I stare at the door for a minute, my brain whirling with a nervous buzz in my head. If something happens to him, I'll be the one responsible. I'm willing to risk his life to save Ana's and I don't even feel guilty about it.

Two minutes later, the door to the office bangs open without so much as a cursory knock. Liam rushes in, his bloodshot eyes scanning the office as if danger lurks in every corner. Satisfied we're alone, he collapses into Ana's empty chair.

"We're going to lose her." His head falls onto the desk and silent sobs wrack his torso. "She gets weaker by the hour. It's going to take weeks for riders to get down to the southwest villages and back, and there's no guarantee they'll find the medicine she needs."

But less than half that time for Eric to get it. I just can't tell Liam that I defied his order. Better to ask for forgiveness after we have the medicine and Ana is on the mend. "I've already got our plan in motion. These riders aren't going to rest until we have what we need."

"It'll be too little, too late."

"We don't know that."

"I know it." He sits up, pulls my hands together, and grips them so tight I almost fall over on top of him. "You have to send Eric to the Territories."

"But you said it's too dangerous."

"I don't care anymore." The haunted expression on his face will haunt me until the day I die. "Going to the city is the only chance we have to save her."

"Then it's a good thing I lied when I promised not to let him go."

Liam stands, his hands squeezing even tighter. He opens his mouth, but only more sobs escape.

"Eric is delivering a message to Ethan right now that the two of them will go on a secret run to the Territory to our south first thing in the morning."

Liam pulls me into a hug so tight my ribs dig into my skin. "Thank you, Rebecca. I just…thank you."

I squeeze him back, the full reality of the situation smacking me in the face. I may have only known her for a month, but Ana is already a huge part of my life. She's everything I'm trying to be, and I still need her here to help me be better, stronger. For Liam, she's so much more.

I pull back and nod, the lump in my throat making conversation impossible. Liam rushes out of the office, probably to sit at Ana's bedside until someone forces him to eat or sleep. I'll have to let someone else worry about him for now. There's so much to do and it needs to happen before the riders can leave in the morning.

Twenty-One

I drop my plate on the table and slump onto the bench across from Daniel. I'm not the least bit hungry. I take a bite of baked potato anyway because I need to keep up my energy if I'm going to figure out a way to save Ana.

"Where have you been all day?" Daniel asks between bites of his potato.

How is it possible so much has changed since lunch and everything else just goes on? "It's Ana. She sick, really sick."

"But Doc is taking care of her, right?" Constance leans across the table so she can hear better over the joyful noises of dinner. "Yesterday Eric told me she probably has a really bad flu."

I shake my head and set my fork down. "It isn't the flu, and Doc is pretty much helpless right now."

Thomas wraps an arm around Constance while Patrice and Elizabeth stare off in their own worlds.

"So now what?"

"I'm coordinating every rider in town, along with a few volunteers. They leave tomorrow morning to hunt down some medicine that might save her. But it's really rare. There's a chance…"

"Is Eric with Doc at Ana's house? Neither of them were in the office all afternoon." For all her insistence that she doesn't care about any of us, Patrice actually looks concerned.

"Doc is there now. Eric is at the stables." I squeeze Daniel's hand. "He's one of the volunteer riders."

Patrice jumps up, leaving half a potato behind, and doesn't say a word before dashing out of the room.

"With that many riders out, they have to find the medicine, right?" Constance has tears in her eyes.

"There are so many villages and we have no idea who might have the medicine or know where we can find some." I push my plate away. "I'm basically guessing at where to send the riders."

"I'm sure you'll figure it out."

"And what if I don't?" Daniel meant to be encouraging, but his words are empty. Everyone has so much faith in me, but can't they see that I have no idea what I'm doing?

"Hey." Daniel waits until I look him in the eyes. "You have to stop being so hard on yourself. You can do this."

"No, seriously. When have any of my plans ever worked out?" The room is suddenly way too hot and loud. I have to get out of here before I lose my mind. I push away Daniel's offered hug and follow Patrice's path into the night air. Carol told me I'm allowed to be happy here. How in the world am I supposed to find happiness when I can't help the people I care about the most?

Strong Daniel arms wrap around me, but I push out of them. I don't need comfort right now; I need someone to give me the answer.

"Are we going to talk about what happened earlier today?"

"What's the point?" I grab the wooden railing and squeeze until my knuckles turn white. "The people we left in the PIT are dead and there's nothing else I can do about it."

"Okay." Daniel drags the word out like he's trying to talk down an irrational toddler. "So tell me what it is that you want here, Rebecca?"

"I don't know what I want, okay? Here I am, free, something I never thought would really happen. And we have an amazing community that accepts us for who we are. And what could I possibly have to complain about? But those people died in there, alone and afraid. No one came rushing in to save them. We agreed to thirty days." I pace across the porch of the dining hall, too much energy pulsing through my exhausted body. "Thirty days and we'd come up with a plan for how to get them out. But there was never a plan. There wasn't even part of a plan. Instead I let myself get sucked into this life here with Ana and the others. And now Ana needs me and I'm just as useless to her as I was to all those people stuck back at the PIT. So what am I doing? What am I doing with my second chance?"

"Living, Rebecca. That's what you're doing." Daniel rubs his hands over his face in a move that's become all too common lately. "You have to let go of this idea that you are responsible for saving the world. You already put your neck on the line to try to save everyone and almost got yourself killed. Isn't that enough?"

"Yes…no…how am I supposed to know? I mean, is it? Is it enough that I tried? Do I get a gold star on my citizenship chart because I gave a lot of thought to helping people?"

"There's nothing you could have done for those people."

"Are you sure about that? What if we had waited five more minutes?" I put my head in my hands and try to block out the sickening feeling in my stomach.

"And then we all might be dead."

"Even if you're right. Even if we couldn't save them, I'm just supposed to forget about them? I used them, Daniel. I used them to make my stupid point and then just left them. I'm just like my mother, willing to walk over whoever I need in order to get my way."

"Rebecca." Daniel takes my hands and folds them in his, halting my frantic pacing. "You didn't use them. Those people came willingly, because they believed in the same things you do. I'd be willing to bet some of them felt more relief that day than they had in years. You gave them a voice and a chance to tell their own truth."

"And that's enough?"

"We got out, and I'm grateful every day. But that's not what we thought would happen. I was ready to die that day." He holds up a hand to stop my interruption. "And not because you asked me to, though I would do anything for you. I was willing to forfeit my life because it was the right thing to do. Because I believed in you, too."

"Doing the right thing doesn't always make things right."

"No, but sometimes it does." He wraps me up in his strong arms. "There are no guarantees in life, and imagine how boring it would be if there were."

"I just wish I didn't feel so helpless."

"We all do, Rebecca." He loosens his hold to look me in the eye. "Don't you think I want to ride out tomorrow and get that medicine? Of course, I do. But we can't save everyone."

"Do you really mean that? Would you really go on a ride?"

"Of course."

A million ideas run through my head, but I need time to sort through them. "I need to get back to the office. There are still a few routes to plan."

"Rebecca, are you okay?"

"Not really, but I will be." I reach around for another hug. "Thank you."

"For what?"

"For being here." I squeeze my arms tighter and draw him as close to me as I can. "Sometimes it feels like I have the weight of everything on my head. But then there you are, reminding me with your presence that I'm not alone and I never have to be again."

"Never." Daniel kisses the top of my head. "I promise."

"That's good enough for me."

Twenty-Two

The village is quiet this early in the morning, but it won't be long before it's filled with the sounds of a new day. Carol will get the ovens ready to bake a new batch of bread while breakfast is set out for the earliest risers. It'll be just like any other day except every rider we have is out looking for the medicine that can save Ana's life. They left over an hour ago, and now it's our turn.

"Are you sure you want to do this?" Daniel stands at the ready next to his horse at the edge of the village.

I tighten the strap on my saddle and give the horse a soft pat on the neck. After staying up half the night to put together a strategy for our riders to hit the most villages, I would much rather be back in bed. But that doesn't get us the medicine for Ana. "It makes sense. Arbor Glen is the only Freemen village to our east so another rider team would have to backtrack to Allmore before going to check the next village on their run."

Daniel steps away from his horse and wraps me in a hug. "That's not what I meant and you know it."

"Of course I don't want to do this. Alan treated us like hardened criminals the last time we were there." I pull back so I can look Daniel in the eyes. "But I can't just sit around here and wait for the riders to get back. I need this to keep my mind off Ana getting sicker and Eric and Ethan walking into disaster in the Territories."

"Then we go." Daniel kisses my forehead and helps me onto my horse. "Ready?"

I give my pack a final check, then turn back to Daniel and nod.

"Wait. Wait for me."

From down the street, Patrice comes racing to where we sit outside of the stables. One of the packs we brought with us from Eric's apartment is strapped to her back and her brows are furrowed.

"Son of a…" Daniel dismounts, but doesn't take any steps toward Patrice.

She gets to us a half minute later, out of breath, but smiling.

"What are you doing here, Patrice?"

"Don't fight me on this." She holds up a finger so she can suck in another breath. "I've done everything you asked of me and I haven't complained."

Daniel shoots her a doubtful look.

"Okay, I haven't complained much. I promise I won't slow you down and I won't say a word in Arbor Glen. It'll be like I'm not even there."

"It'll be exactly like you aren't even there, because you aren't going."

"Please, Daniel." Patrice tosses her pack on the ground and reaches out for Daniel's hands. "I'm going to go crazy just sitting here. I can't stare at the Noteboard feed all day worrying I'm going to hear a report that you guys or Eric have been captured."

"Patrice, you can't—"

"She can come."

Patrice and Daniel whip their heads toward me.

"Rebecca…"

I hold a hand up to stop Daniel's protest. How can I possibly tell Patrice she has to stay here when her reasons for going are exactly the same as mine?

"We have the last two horses." Daniel crosses his arms and stares me down.

I stare back at him. "She can ride double with me."

"This isn't a day trip." Daniel rubs his hands over his face. It's going to take us two days to get there, who knows how long to negotiate a possible trade, and two more days to get back."

"I have food and extra clothes packed and ready to go. We can leave right now." Patrice glances back and forth between me and Daniel.

Daniel can be mad at me all he wants. I'm not going to leave Patrice here. I can't force her to stay, knowing what waiting for all of us to get back safely will do to her. I hold my hand down and help her mount up behind me. We're snug in the saddle, but it will work.

Patrice lets out a slow breath and puts a hand on the back of my elbow. "Thank you." Her words whisper against my ear and hold a tiny hint of the desperation she must have been feeling.

"Don't I get a say in this?"

"No, but you can have a vote." I shield my hands against the first rays of sun filtering through the trees. "All in favor of Patrice going with us?"

Patrice and I raise our hands in unison.

"All opposed?"

Daniel throws both of his hands up in defeat. "This is ridiculous."

"It's just a quick supply run. We should be there and back in four days. She's just as safe with us as she would be waiting back here."

Daniel doesn't say a word and refuses to look me in the eye as he mounts back up. He's mad, and that's fine. He still sees Patrice as the little sister he left at home all those years ago. But she's no more a helpless flower than I am.

I use the reins to turn our horse east.

* * *

It's mid-afternoon when we stop at the top of a tree-covered hill. Below us, Arbor Glen is stretched out like a long serpent. It looks smaller. That first time we marched into the village everything seemed so much larger than life. Funny how a little time can change my perspective so much. The main street is a bustle of activity with most everyone heading toward one central building. Probably the dining hall.

"So how are we going to do this? Just ride down there and demand to speak to Alan?"

After a day and a half of non-stop suggestions and questions from Patrice, I'm beginning to second guess my vote to let her come.

"I'm guessing if they don't know we're here yet, we won't have to get much closer before they see us." I scan the forest around us for signs of guards, but they're either too well-hidden or not there. "Let's just make our way toward the boulders where they led us out of town. And remember, I'll do the talking."

Daniel gives me a smile of encouragement. He got over his anger pretty quickly when he realized Patrice would talk my ear off for the whole trip. He muttered something to the effect of 'you get what you ask for' before we all fell asleep last night.

True, it won't go down in history as my favorite day ever, but I'll take Patrice's constant chatter to her sullen sarcasm any day.

We only travel another fifty yards when a piercing whistle echoes through the trees.

"Well, there's a face I didn't expect to see any time soon."

"Mary." I slide down out of the saddle and rush over to the only person I was actually looking forward to seeing here.

"You've still got the bracelet, I see." She shakes my hand and waves back at Daniel and Patrice. "What are you doing here? How are things in Allmore? Tell me everything."

In another lifetime, Mary and I would be good friends, but some things aren't meant to be. "I'd love to catch up, but time is a luxury we don't have. I need to speak to Alan, now if possible."

"Let's go then. If we hurry, we can catch him at home before he leaves for lunch." She takes off for the village without waiting on us.

Patrice stays on the saddle, but Daniel jumps down and takes his reins in one hand and my hand with his other. "How are you holding up?"

I take my time to walk over a log before responding. "Honestly, I don't know." I squeeze Daniel's hand and keep walking. "I've been trying to focus on just traveling safely, but now that we're here, I'm terrified."

"I don't think Alan would actually hurt us."

"Not that." I walk in silence for a minute to put my thoughts together. The closer we get to the village, the more the sounds of the forest fade and give way to human sounds. If I closed my eyes, we could be back in Allmore and that only makes me miss the people back there more. It's our home now and one of our family members needs us.

"I don't know why, but there's bad blood between our villages. I need to choose my words carefully if we stand any chance of getting this medicine." I kick a rock out of my path. "They probably don't have it anyway."

"We don't know that," Daniel says almost before I can finish my sentence. "We haven't traded with them in years."

"I know, but it would be a miracle for any of these villages to have PAM. And yet, I can't help getting my hopes up, which scares me for how much it's going to hurt if they say they don't have it."

The forest floor gives way to the broken roadway that leads into town. Daniel stops just before stepping on and forces me to look at him. "Never stop hoping. Even when the chances are slim to none. Your ability to hold onto hope in the face of almost certain defeat is one of the best parts about you."

"Thank you."

"Hey, I thought you guys were in a hurry." Mary calls back to us from several buildings down where she waits outside of the cottage I recognize as Alan's.

Daniel helps Patrice dismount, and the three of us hurry over to Mary.

"You can leave the horses here with me. I checked, and he's still here. You can go on in to see him."

I give her a nod of thanks and head inside. Alan and Margaret are both waiting in the living room, seated side by side on a couch that has seen better days.

"Come in and shut the door behind you." Alan's voice is calm, but it's clear he's less than pleased to see us again.

"Alan, thank you for seeing us on such short notice." I march over and cut right to the chase. "We're here to see if we can make a trade."

"A trade?" Alan leans back and smiles as if he's enjoying a show. "Riders from Allmore haven't made a trade here in over a decade. The situation must be getting pretty bad over there if Liam is desperate enough to try trading here. Is the whole village falling apart?"

"No, nothing like that." I shake my head and force my voice to stay calm. Daniel places a hand on my shoulder, and that helps me keep the frustration from leaking in.

"Then why did he send you here to beg me to trade?"

"We need some medicine, you big—"

I jerk Patrice's wrist and startle her into silence. Alan is infuriating, but we can't risk ticking him off.

"One of our villagers has cancer. We're looking for PAM or Dador de Vida."

Alan stands up and Margaret mirrors his action. "We don't have it."

His words wrap in a fist around my heart and squeeze until it stops pumping. I tried not to get my hopes up, but I failed. And now I've failed Ana, too.

Daniel squeezes my shoulder and steps forward a bit. "Maybe we could check with Marcus. It's possible he has some stashed away and you just don't realize it."

"I would know if we had a Territory product laying around our storage shelves. We don't have it, and even if we did, I'm not sure I would trade you for it."

Patrice makes an indistinguishable sound next to me. Something between a squeak and growl.

"Liam made his choice when he left. We're done here." Alan marches over to the door and walks out without even looking back.

Margaret follows him halfway to the door, but stops to look back, her face riddled with a mixture of emotions. "How is Liam? Is he…is he the one who's sick?"

My voice has deserted me so I shake my head back and forth. How could I possibly explain to her that even though Liam isn't the one who's dying, a part of him will be lost forever if we can't save Ana?

Margaret nods and follows Alan out of the house.

And just like that, we're back at square one.

There's nothing left to do now but go back home and wait with everyone else.

Twenty-Three

Two weeks gone. Two weeks since we got back from Arbor Glen empty-handed. Two weeks of Ana getting weaker without the medicine she needs. Two weeks of practically sleeping in the PE office because in here I don't have to see the panicked and hopeful faces of everyone waiting for the riders to return. I don't have to see Liam.

A sharp knock on the door disturbs my study of the Noteboard listing our next supply run. I rub my hand across the back of my neck. "Come in."

Daniel slides the rest of the way into the room and leans against the chair where Ana should be sitting. We both stare at the empty seat. I turn away and refocus on the list.

"So you are alive. I wasn't really sure since I haven't seen you in ages." Daniel smiles. Not a little grin, but the full-face smile that lights up his rich brown eyes and makes my heart beat a little faster.

"I know. Staying busy is the only thing keeping me sane. I'm re-routing our next supply runs to account for the lost time to search for Ana's medicine. I have to make sure we don't come up short of supplies once winter hits. There's so much to do, and this stupid hunk of rock keeps going on the fritz and deleting my work so I have to start over." I toss the Noteboard onto the desk and lean back in my creaky chair.

Daniel taps on the screen, but the old batteries revolt. Undeterred, Daniel opens up the charging port and blows a few puffs of air into the machine. Another few taps and he has it up and running. "Probably just lack of sunlight messing with the power supply since you haven't been outside in forever. I could juice this up for you if you want."

"You have more important things to do," I say, taking the Noteboard back. "Now, if you could just create a network that works between the villages, but stays hidden from the network the Territories use, you'd be my hero."

"I'll get right on that," he spins my chair around to face him, "but first you need a break."

"No, I don't." I tap the maps on the table. "Ana is counting on me to keep this place running until she gets better." She has to get better.

"Rebecca," Daniel reaches over and takes my hands in his, "you've done everything you can to help her. You have every rider and a half dozen volunteers out there looking. Plus, Eric."

"Plus, Eric? Are you coming around on him?"

"We're not best friends, but I guess he's not the worst guy on the planet."

"Aren't you full of surprises."

"Come on, you can bring the Noteboard on a walk and let it recharge for a bit."

I stare at our joined hands. We've done so much together. "Okay, a minute."

Daniel pulls me out of my seat, down the stairs, and past a chipper Carol out into the street. The sun is high in the sky, heating my cheeks, and a warm breeze ruffles the blond hair that is finally growing out. I've spent so much time inside the trade office, looking for an answer to getting Ana her medicine, I didn't notice the turn in the weather. Spring is over, and summer is in full force.

Constance is out in front of the children's building playing a game with the younger children. I don't recognize it, but there's lots of running and laughing. Nellie is among the kids, laughing along with the rest, too young to understand how sick her mom really is.

We move down the main street, and other signs of summer stand out. The colors are brilliant. None of the tame spring flowers, unsure if they should emerge from winter hiding. Flowers bloom in boxes hanging in front of almost all the windows. Despite the humid heat, the grass taking root wherever the roadway has given up is bright green and calls out for someone to run around barefoot.

Allmore may not be as well kept as the Territories, but it's better in almost every other way. If we were there, the children wouldn't be allowed to play outside in front of the building. They would be tucked away playing some orderly game where their laughter wouldn't be a nuisance. And there wouldn't be so much variety in all the flower boxes. Not because the Cardinal ordered everyone to be the same, but because no one ever wanted to stand out. I didn't understand it before the PIT, but everyone is the Cardinal's prisoner. Even if they don't realize it.

Daniel leads me off the main road and down several side streets into the area that has more houses and fewer offices and store rooms. "Are you ready to tell me where we're going?"

"We're there." Daniel stops in front of one of the older buildings.

The door is missing, but a new one is resting to the side. The brick walls look sturdy, and the siding is in good shape, but in desperate need of some paint. Daniel climbs the stairs of the porch, and I follow him up and into the front room. Dust covers the floor except in a few places where footprints have disturbed the thick layer of grime.

"The building crew has been working on this place ever since they finished Thomas and Constance's place. They had to repair some of the walls and the floor was in pretty bad shape. There's still more work to be done, and then Frank and I will come in and get it all wired up." He walks over to the hole that should be a window, and the sunlight paints his dark skin in shades of shadow and gold. "Thomas and Constance live right next door."

I turn in a slow circle to take in the room. It's small, but a fireplace on the far wall makes it feel homey. In the corner, there's a dusty chandelier that could one day be gorgeous. The wood mantle is mostly intact, and I run a hand over the top.

"Does this thing actually work?"

"It's just for looks. These were all converted to solar furnaces before the town was abandoned." Daniel pulls back a faux brick to reveal a small panel of buttons. "Everything is controlled here, but there's no power yet. Besides, Thomas said they have to clear out the ducts to each house when they renovate or the whole place will fill with smoke."

I nod and walk out of the small room and down the hall. There's a kitchen to the left, just the right size for a little table to sit and go over trading orders. The bedrooms are bare, but I can imagine them with some simple furniture and cheerful curtains. I stare out the window hole and imagine sitting on the porch watching the sunset like two perfectly normal people, living a perfectly normal life.

"So what do you think?"

"It's amazing."

Daniel leaves the window and stands with me in the hallway. "Can you live here? Or, I mean, do you want to live here…with me?"

I stare up into Daniel's warm, brown eyes. Everything about coming here has been difficult for us. Cramped living quarters, getting adjusted to a new way of living, and then, with Ana sick, me spending all my time in the PE office. But this is what we deserve. A place for us, just us. Because Daniel was right. We have to live our lives.

"I love you, Daniel Whedon." I grab his arms and pull into him, my head nuzzled into the little hollow of his chest that fits me perfectly.

"And I love you, Rebecca Collins." He pulls back. "Though, I was thinking, maybe it's time to ditch the Collins. I take the vows we made back in the PIT seriously, but that was the best we could do then. We can do better now."

"What do you mean?"

Daniel gets down on his knee and takes my hands. "Let's get married. Here, with our friends and everyone we love. Let's have a ceremony and cake and all of it."

He lets go with one hand and reaches into the pocket of his jacket. When he pulls his hand back out he unfurls his fingers in front of me to reveal a small orange.

"Back in the PIT, you told me that growing up you loved standing at the Airtrain station waiting for the shipment of oranges to come in. That smell of fresh citrus announcing the train was your favorite memory of home. But I want this to be your home and for this moment right here to be your new favorite memory."

Of course Daniel would remember something so simple. Only a brief moment, no more than a few minutes of conversation when I was nothing more than the girl who was set to pretend-marry Eric. But he remembers.

I can't talk through the tears, so I just nod over and over again like a small child. This man, this beautiful man is everything I could never possibly deserve. He stands up again, and we stand in the front room of our future house, arms wrapped tightly around each other. Neither of us speaks, but it's not uncomfortable. We both know exactly what the other is thinking, so we don't need words right now. The orange scent reaches around to tickle my nose, and I squeeze my eyes tight to lock in this minute. I want this to be my new favorite memory, too.

The door bangs open and Constance rushes in, her wispy hair plastered to her head. "Rebecca, come quick."

"What's going on?"

"It's Eric." She leans against the door frame to catch her breath. "He's back."

Twenty-Four

I fling open the door to the infirmary and have to pull up short to avoid running into Doc. "Where?" I grab Doc's arm, squeezing tighter than I intended. "Where are they?"

"Eric and Ethan are upstairs."

I shout a 'thank you' over my shoulder and dash for the door that leads to our temporary housing. Several voices float down the stairs, but I can't make out the words over Daniel and me running up the treads two steps at a time. In the dorm, the curtains are pulled completely back from the beds and Eric lies side by side with Ethan. Elizabeth and Patrice are there and turn at the sound of our hurried steps. It's clear from their grim faces that the news isn't good.

Eric sits up in bed, though he's slumped back against a small mountain of pillows. His face is a mask of gashes and purple bruises. Patrice fills a glass with water and shoves it under his nose. "One more glass. Doc says we need to get as much fluid in you as possible."

Eric takes several large gulps and lets his head rest back against the pillows. Next to him, Ethan looks just as bad, but his eyes are closed and his chest rises and falls in the steady rhythm of sleep.

I slide up next to Elizabeth and flinch a bit when she grabs my hand. I haven't seen her face so pale since we lost Molly.

"E, stop looking at me like I'm a dead man walking." He shakes his head at Patrice's offer of another sip of water. "Doc says I'm just a little dehydrated and beat up. Nothing a bit of rest and water won't fix."

"What he said was you're both lucky to be alive and we have to watch for organ failure and internal bleeding, so can it with your 'I'm just fine' speech."

"Fine. Why don't you go sweet talk the kitchen staff with your sunny disposition into getting me some broth while I catch up on my sleep?"

"Fine. I will. Don't die while I'm gone." Elizabeth lets go of my hand and reaches out to squeeze her brother's leg.

Patrice sets the water down and gives him an identical squeeze on the arm. "I'll go with you. Just in case you need help with the sunny disposition part."

Elizabeth rolls her eyes at me and heads toward the stairs. Patrice steps around the bed, but pauses, placing a gentle hand on my arm. "I want you to know that I don't blame you anymore for my Rejection."

"What?" I glance at the guys, and Daniel is staring at Patrice, his mouth hanging open. But Eric is smiling at her, nodding his encouragement. I'd bet my best wall map that this little apology is Eric-orchestrated.

"I've been a pain for the past few months, but I know now that the Cardinal is the one I should blame. I hope you can forgive me and the two of us can start over. If Daniel loves you, then you can't be all bad."

"Of course."

Patrice nods and follows Elizabeth downstairs.

"Well, that was interesting." Daniel is still in a bit of shock.

"It sure was." I catch Eric's eye while Daniel is still staring off into space and wink. "I wonder what caused her change of heart?"

"I wonder." Eric yawns, and I get a glimpse of more bruises reaching down under his shirt.

"We'll go, too. You need your rest."

"You guys stay." Eric leans forward and I help him move the pillows around so he can sit up better. "We need to talk."

He needs sleep, but I'm dying to know what happened on their ride. I hesitate for a second, but curiosity wins out. Daniel and I move around to the head of the bed. "Eric, what happened? Did the Cardinal do this?"

"No, the plan went off without a hitch. I sneaked into the border where the contraband shops are and set up a meeting with a man that could get me several vials of PAM. I was able to get them for several bottles of dandelion ale. That stuff really is a hot commodity, by the way. I guess some of the other villages trade what they get from us with the Territories. This guy knew exactly what I was offering."

"So you got it. Then what?"

"Not much really. We got the meds. Ethan didn't run into any trouble, so we got the horses saddled and put some serious distance between us and the Cardinal's precious city."

"But your face looks like you had a run-in with a den of wild animals?"

I shoot Daniel a look, my eyes squinted. He's not helping.

"We were almost back to Allmore when we were attacked."

"Cardinal guards?" Goosebumps lift on my arms at the thought of his guards getting so close to our home.

"Vagrants." Ethan speaks up from his bed, his eyes now wide open.

"What do you mean by vagrants?"

"Back when everyone moved to the cities to form the Territories, the Freemen stayed behind and formed our own society."

"Right." I fidget with the leather braid around my wrist. "Ana told me all about it."

"Except some people didn't choose either of those options." Ethan coughs, and Daniel rushes over to help him with some water. "We call them vagrants, but I have no idea if they call themselves anything different. Some of them formed into small communities, never more than a dozen people altogether. And they're mostly nomadic, moving from place to place and making them harder to track. They live on the fringe and consider themselves to be some advanced society, rejecting all of our society's norms."

"So they are the ones who beat you up?"

Ethan nods. "They usually aren't so violent, though sometimes they will stun a guard in order to break into a village's storehouse. But these groups survive by stealing what they need, and they could tell we were hiding something. This was a bigger group, and they beat us until they found it."

"PAM." Ethan and Eric's faces fall at the word. "Were you able to keep it safe?"

"I tried. I tried so hard." Ethan's jaw clenches in pain.

My knees give out, and I slump down into the chair next to Eric's bed. All of this for nothing. There are still other riders out there, but this was our best hope for getting the medicine in time for Ana.

"I'm so sorry, Rebecca." Eric winces as he leans up on one elbow. "We can try again. We know where to go now, and a second ride won't take as long."

"No." I force myself up and help Eric ease back onto the pillows. "I can't send you back out there again, even if you were in any kind of condition to go. I'm sorry Liam and I agreed to send you in the first place."

"I'm not." Ethan's voice cuts across my personal pity party. "And if you asked, I'd do it all again. I would do anything for Ana, and I don't have to ask them to know the other riders would do the same."

I nod at Ethan, but don't say a word. He just nods back and rolls over to get some more sleep. I pull the curtain up next to his bed so he has a bit more privacy.

"Not to put the kibosh on this tender moment, but we've got a lot more to discuss, and it really shouldn't wait." Eric winces as he shifts on the bed. "So what do you want first? The bad news, or the really bad news?"

I meet Daniel's eyes. None of it. I don't want to hear any of it. Can we just go back to twenty minutes ago when Daniel and I were alone in our home and happily planning a future that didn't involve any bad news?

Eric sucks in a deep breath and lets it go in a hacking cough. I grab the water glass and shove it at his mouth. He gulps down half the glass and closes his eyes while we wait for his breathing to get back under control.

Daniel paces beside the bed. "Should I go get Doc? Elizabeth made it sound like there could be a serious problem."

"I'll be fine. Doc knows the score and there's not much more he can do than give us pain meds. My sister can get a little over-protective at times."

"Not so long ago she was ready to feed you to hungry bears." I twirl the glass between my hands. "See, I told you she'd come around."

"You were right, as usual." Eric's forced half-smile falls apart. "You were right about the Cardinal, too."

"What are you talking about?"

"That's the bad news. The Cardinal is stepping up his efforts to export the Machine to several European countries. It was all over the news in the city. Everyone is talking about the Cardinal taking steps toward world peace."

"More like world domination," Daniel says.

"I imagine that's what your father thought, too."

Daniel stiffens next to me. "You saw my father?"

"No," Eric says, shaking his head. "That's the problem. No one has. Seems he disappeared right after Patrice was Rejected."

Daniel grips my hand to the point of pain, and I squeeze back. My pain is nothing compared to his right now.

"I'll drum up some more volunteer riders and go with them myself. I can have a group out searching by tomorrow. He's probably still in the city or at least close by."

"NO!" Both Daniel and Eric shout the word at me together.

"Rebecca, you can't go anywhere near the cities. Ever."

"Eric, don't be ridiculous. We can't leave his father out there."

"He's not out there." Daniel slumps down on the edge of Eric's bed. "No one in the Territories simply disappears. The Cardinal doesn't tolerate threats to his absolute power. If my father questioned him, the Cardinal could never let that stand. Eventually they'll find him, and it will look every bit like an accident."

"No, we aren't going to let that happen." I grab his chin so he has to look at me. "I am not abandoning any more people."

"If you step one foot inside the Territories, you're as good as dead." Eric's voice is resigned in defeat.

I stand back up. "You did it."

"Yes, but my face isn't plastered all over every building alerting the public to my status as a traitor."

"So what?" They all think I'm still in the PIT. "They won't expect to see me walking their streets."

Eric rocks his head from side to side. "The Cardinal told them you escaped."

"I don't…why would he do that?" I grab Daniel's hand for strength. "That's the whole point of the PIT; no one ever escapes. Or at least that's what they tell everyone. Why ruin that now?"

"When your apology video never aired, the European countries started making noise, questioning the effectiveness of the Machine. Without you there to admit to lying, the Cardinal had no choice but to double down and show them just how dangerous you are. Because only a traitorous criminal mastermind would stage a riot and escape from the PIT."

"It's genius."

I crane my neck around to see if Daniel is joking. He's not.

"He's right." Eric points at Daniel. "You go from being a huge liability to the poster child of the Machine."

"But as far as everyone out there knows, no one has ever escaped from the PIT. They have to be in panic mode."

"Well, they aren't happy that such a dangerous criminal is running loose." Eric winks at me and Daniel squeezes a bit tighter. "But the Cardinal assured them he's tripled the security of the PIT and won't rest until you're found and brought back to justice."

"Wait." I stare at Daniel. "If the Cardinal has been making all of these announcements, shouldn't Patrice have seen them on the news feed? This would be a major story."

Daniel closes his eyes and rubs his hands over his face. "You have so much stress already. I didn't want to worry you."

"So you knew." Ethan stirs behind his curtain, so I drop my voice down to a harsh whisper. "You knew all this time that the Cardinal has everyone in the United Territories looking for me and you didn't tell me."

"What good would it have done?" He grabs hold of my shoulders. "I was just trying to protect you."

I push his hands away. "I'm not a child, Daniel. You can't shield me from everything. You want to be my husband, but you keep secrets from me? That's not how it works."

"You're right." He takes a deep breath and stares at his shoes. "You're right, and I'm sorry. I should have told you."

"No more secrets."

"None."

He just wants to protect me, but I don't want to live my life faking perfection.

"That goes for Patrice, too." I include Eric in my scornful look. "She isn't some delicate flower that needs shielded from reality. She deserves to know what's going on with her dad."

"I'll tell her." Daniel squeezes my arms. "It's going to break my heart to hurt her, but she should know."

I give Eric a pat on the arm. "Why don't you get some sleep? I'm going to go check on Ana." I turn away, and then turn back before Eric can close his eyes. "Thank you. You didn't have to do this."

"We both know I did have to, but you're welcome anyway."

I head downstairs with Daniel close behind me. Eric understands. Sometimes you have to do something, even if you know it's going to hurt.

Twenty-Five

I push open the door of the dining hall. My hair is a mess of curls, and I'm not even close to decent with only a light sweater thrown over my nightgown. But it's the best I could manage in the middle of the night. Daniel shuffles in behind me. He's not looking so great either, but he absolutely refused to listen when I told him to stay in bed.

Of course, I can't blame him. This is our last set of riders to return. Our last chance to save Ana.

At one of the long tables, Jeremy and Richard sit slumped on the bench shoving some of the bread left over from dinner into their mouths as fast as they can. Neither of them looks as if they've seen a bath or a bed in weeks. Jeremy's hair is normally a shade of red that every girl in the village would love to have, but tonight it's as dark as Daniel's with so much grime rubbed in. Please let it all be worth it.

"Welcome back, guys." I rush over and give Richard a hug. Dirt puffs off his shirt and dusts both of us in a fine mist of filth. Over a month traveling across the country would do that. "Daniel, can you get them both some milk to wash that bread down?" Anything to delay asking about the medicine. As long as I don't know, there's still hope.

Jeremy nods his head at Daniel. "That would be great, thanks man. My legs are so tired, I could barely walk over here."

"You guys made amazing time. Did you even stop to sleep?"

"Barely." Richard pushes his bread aside and lays his head down right on the table. "But that doesn't matter, because it was worth it. Rebecca, we got it."

Richard pulls a box out of his bag and holds it up just as Doc bursts through the door.

"Is that it?" He rushes into the room and grabs the box from Richard. "Did you find PAM?"

"We got as many doses as they'd give us." Jeremy can barely hold his head up, but his face is lit up like a fireworks display.

"You did it!" I don't even try to hold back my joy. My body jolts like I've been hit by lightning. I grab Doc around his elbows, and we end up in a strange dance/hug spin that is zero parts coordination and one hundred percent joy.

"I'm going to get this over to Ana and start the dosage tonight." Doc spins on the riders and gives both Jeremy and Richard a huge bear hug, sending more dirt spiraling into the air. With a grin on his face and tears in his eyes, Doc runs out the door.

"You guys are amazing." I repeat Doc's hugs, not even caring that I'm now covered in dirt. Daniel is right behind me shaking their hands. "You're the last riders to make it back and everyone else struck out finding PAM. I don't even want to think about next steps if you couldn't get it."

"Now you don't have anything to worry about." Jeremy drains the glass of milk Daniel brought him in one gulp. "I needed that."

"Now, you need bed. Go home and sleep as late as you want. We can go over the details of your trip when you've had a chance to recuperate."

"Sounds good." Jeremy pokes Richard in the arm. "Listen, you need to know before you send any more riders out. There's something going on out there."

"What do you mean?"

"We stopped at a lot of villages on the way down to the Mexico border and most of them were wonderful." Jeremy stands and grabs Richard's arm so he'll follow suit. "But some of the villages closest to Allmore refused to trade with us."

"Wait, what do you mean they wouldn't trade?"

"Some of them wouldn't even let us in to rest, so I had no idea what they're up to, but the rest of them told us exactly why they're willing to give up trade with us. They were asked not to."

"Who?" Daniel grips the edge of the table. "Who told them not to deal with us?"

"Alan."

I stare at Jeremy's eyes, but he won't match my gaze. "Alan from Arbor Glen? But why? Why would he do that?" I pace between the tables, my mind running a mile a minute. "I thought the Freemen villages worked together? We have to work together. It's the only way we can survive and stay clear of the Cardinal. Why would he want the other villages to cut us off? What does he have against us?"

"None of them would really spell it out for us, but I got a real uneasy feeling about the whole thing. I think it's because we keep allowing PIT escapees to live here."

I share a look with Daniel. Jeremy isn't the only one with an uneasy feeling.

"Thanks for telling me. I'll get more details tomorrow, but for now, I'm ordering you both to bed."

"Yes, ma'am." They shuffle out, leaving a stuffy silence behind them.

Daniel sits down and pulls me with him.

"When do we get to stop being PIT Rejects?" I pick at the bread Jeremy left behind, shredding the piece into tiny crumbs. "It's not bad enough that we're shunned everywhere, but now the people of Allmore are at risk of losing resources because of us."

"No. Because of the Cardinal." Daniel grabs my hands to keep me from destroying another piece of bread. "Because of who he's convinced everyone we are."

"I—"

"Hey, I'm serious. You can't control how other people see you, and you can't change your past." He tucks a loose curl behind my ear. "I personally think it's a good thing that the PIT can't be erased. I wouldn't want to miss meeting you."

"Those are lovely words, but it doesn't get us the supplies we need to survive the winter and it doesn't help the next time someone gets seriously ill." I push away and stand, too wound up to sit still.

"It's the middle of the night, Rebecca. Can this wait for morning? Sleep on it a bit?"

No, I don't want to sleep on it. It's unlikely I'll get any sleep for the rest of the night. But the rest of the village is asleep, and there really isn't anything I can do right now.

"Tomorrow, I'm sending riders out. We need to know who is still going to trade with us so we can plan our next routes. Ana is going to want to know about all this, too."

Daniel stands and wraps me up in his arms. His heart beating slow and steady against mine calms me down. "I'll go with you if that helps."

"Now there's an offer I can't pass up." I snuggle deeper into his arms and close my eyes. I'm not the helpless little girl that stumbled into the PIT last year. I don't have to depend on Daniel to take care of me. But that doesn't mean I can't borrow some of his strength.

"Better?" His deep voice vibrates through me, sending chills up my arms.

"Mmmmhmmm."

In a single fluid motion, Daniel lifts me up so one arm is cushioning my back and the other holds my legs under the knees. Up this high, I can see right into his eyes, and the emotion I find there takes my breath away. This man would do anything for me.

I tilt his face toward me and kiss him softly. The spark is immediate. Daniel's mouth pushes back against mine while his arms pull me in even closer. I lean in, needing more, wanting to forget about The Cardinal and missing villages and cancer. Wrapping my arms around his neck, I deepen the kiss until I'm lost in a tangle of arms and lips.

Daniel swings me around and I wrap my legs around his waist, my nightgown sliding up to expose my legs to the cool night air. He holds me up, fingers kneading into my thighs, and backs us up until I'm resting on the table. The second I touch down, his hands are moving, exploring the edge of my nightgown and the sensitive skin on the small of my back. Every touch sends little shock waves of pleasure up my spine, and I wrap my legs tighter around him.

His mouth moves to my cheek and then down to my jaw, leaving a trail of fiery kisses across my hot skin. I tilt my head up to give him more room to explore and clench my fists in the thin shirt around his shoulders. His hands move farther up my back and all I want is more. But I have to stop us now before we end up indecent in front of the breakfast crew.

"Daniel." His name comes out breathy with his lips against my throat.

He groans and drops his head down onto my shoulder. "I love you."

"So much." I drop his shirt and pull him into a hug. "More and more every day."

"Does that mean you'll still love me tomorrow if I whisk you away right now and make you get some sleep?"

I cradle his face in my hands and take a moment to appreciate the amazing man in front of me. "Even if we fight and I call you a pig-headed bull and you call me an overreacting numbskull. Even then, I will always love you."

Daniel hoists me off the table and drapes a strong arm around my shoulders. "Good, but just for the record, I would never call you a numbskull."

"No?"

"You're more of a hothead."

* * *

"Where have you been all day, princess?" Elizabeth grins at me over the plate of roasted veggies and potatoes we're having for dinner. "It clearly wasn't the beauty shop."

"Oh, hardy-har-har. You're a non-stop laugh factory tonight." I contemplate flicking a carrot at her, but I'm too hungry to waste it.

"Seriously though, I haven't seen you since breakfast."

"I know. Carol let me sneak some bread for lunch so I didn't have to leave the office. It's a mess up there." I shove a bit of potato in my mouth and don't even care that I'm talking with my mouth full. "Two teams of riders came back today with updates on our trading partners. Plus, both teams came back with trade requests that we aren't ready for. Though I guess that's a good problem to have."

Daniel gives my shoulder a quick squeeze. "It's a good thing that we aren't ready?"

"It's a good thing that there are still villages willing to trade with us." I shove more food in. "I guess Alan didn't convince everyone. I spent all day tracking down half the program heads in town to figure out how much we can spare for the moment. I still need to rework the routes to account for the villages that are cutting us off and send out riders to check on the villages to the west. And I never even made it over to look in on Ana."

Daniel pushes a glass of milk in front of me and adds what's left from his plate to mine. "And if you get sick from overworking yourself, we won't have anyone to work the PE office, and we'll all starve this winter."

"Daniel's right," Eric adds from across the table. Doc gave him clearance this morning to leave his bed and eat with the rest of us. "You won't be doing anyone any favors if you work yourself to the point of exhaustion."

"Okay, I get it." I take another bite of food to prove my point. "But until Ana is up and feeling better, I'm the only one."

"You know, Rebecca," Constance chimes in from a few seats down. "I'm sure they could spare me from the child center for a while if you could use another set of hands."

"Really? 'Cause that would be amazing. But you love it over there."

"I do, but with the older kids off on their summer apprenticeships, there isn't as much to do right now. Plus, those little ones are a handful. I could use a little break."

"It's true," Thomas says, nudging her with his elbow. "She came home so tired yesterday she would have slept through dinner if I hadn't tickled her awake."

"And I still haven't forgiven you for that." She drops her fork and attacks Thomas's ribcage.

I take another bite of perfectly cooked carrot and sit back enjoying the moment. Daniel pulls me close into a one-arm hug, and everyone laughs as Thomas tries to avoid Constance, who is fast like lightning in finding all of his ticklish spots.

The Cardinal is hunting me down, and our trading partners are dropping like flies, but here inside this village, life goes on. And it's a good life. Not perfect and certainly not what I ever predicted, but sometimes we get what we never thought to ask for.

"Can I have everyone's attention?" Doc's commanding voice breaks in over the chatter from the head of the room. I haven't seen him since last night, and his face has aged a hundred years in those few hours. A tightness builds around my chest. Nothing about this feels good.

The noise around the room dies down, and Doc takes a deep breath before continuing. "I am deeply saddened tonight to report…" A sob lets out of his throat, and it takes several heartbeats for him to calm down. "Our dear friend, Ana, has moved on to true freedom."

An icy blast drops into my core and spreads out to every inch of my body, freezing me to my spot on the bench. Gasps echo around the room. Constance bursts into tears, and even Elizabeth has watery eyes. At the other end of our table, several men and women cry openly, and a crowd floods around Doc. I'm too numb to move.

Doc's voice is raw as he calls out over the distress in the room. "Liam is obviously devastated, but has asked that we hold the release ceremony tonight. Please finish your meals and join us in the square. Anyone who's done eating, please help us with the platform."

Several people stand and follow Doc outside, including Thomas and Eric. Daniel moves to stand, but I grab the front of his shirt so tight he's stuck to the bench. Everything around me swirls into a mash of colors, like that toy kaleidoscope I had as a child. But I don't need a toy now to see the light show. The room twists and turns until it's nothing more than a blur of dizzying color and sound.

I was supposed to go see her today. Last night I told Daniel that was my first stop. Instead I slept in to make up for last night and then spent the whole day dealing with everything else. Who was with her? Was Liam in the room holding her hand when she took her last breath? Did little Nellie get to come in and say goodbye to her mommy?

"Rebecca?"

"I should have gone, but I didn't make the time to see her."

"Hey now, this is not your fault." Daniel wraps both arms around me and squeezes so tight I can barely feel my shaking arms. "There's no way you could have known.

She was sick and even with the meds, Doc wasn't sure she would get better."

I swallow the lump lodged at the base of my neck. "All the more reason I should have gone over there first thing like I had planned."

"Rebecca, you can't do that." Elizabeth reaches across the table for my hand, but I'm afraid if I move I might punch her instead. "You were doing what you were supposed to be doing, making sure we all have what we need to survive."

"Paperwork?" My voice is a panicked, high-pitch squeal that draws several stares. I don't care. "You think paperwork is more important than Ana's life?"

"That's not—"

"She was one of us, Elizabeth. You could at least pretend to care about someone other than yourself for a change."

I expect a fight. I want one. A fight will let me feel something other than this festering guilt threatening to empty my stomach. Instead, she calmly stands up and walks outside with the others.

"Rebecca…"

"What?" I snap at Daniel's tight-lipped stare. "Do you hate me now, too?"

Daniel smooths hair out of my face. "No one hates you."

"Well," Patrice says, spearing a piece of potato. "Elizabeth might."

"Patrice!"

"Right. I'll just go outside." Patrice stands and pinches off one last bite of bread. "Come on, Constance. Let's go see how we can help."

By the time they leave, most of the cafeteria is empty. We should get up, too. I don't know what the release ceremony is, but from the looks of it, the whole village is involved. I should find Liam. Poor Liam, who loved Ana so much that he created a new village where she wouldn't be judged. Oh, sweet Nellie. Who is watching her? Holding her hand? I should go help. Do anything other than sit here on this bench and stare at the wall.

I lean forward to stand, but Daniel pushes me back down.

"You barely ate half your food. You need to eat."

"I can't." I shake my head at the offer of more milk, my stomach churning at the thought. "Tomorrow you can force feed me until you're sure I won't die of starvation, but tonight I can't. I'm just...done."

Daniel nods and offers a hand to help me stand. I sway a bit on my feet, but stay upright. Too many thoughts are running through my head to isolate a single strand. My feet move one in front of the other, but more from instinct than a decision on my part to move.

"I'm done."

Twenty-Six

Outside, the night air is hot and humid. Others around me pick at damp shirts and fan themselves with their hands. My body stopped feeling the minute Doc started talking.

The center of the village is filled with movement, but it lacks its usual joy. Everyone is working, but it's clear no one wants to be. Several members have built a small wooden platform with mountains of kindling and several bundles covered in black tar. Everyone seems to have a job to do, and they are all moving about, getting it done in almost silence. I can't decide if it's reverent or mournful or just methodical.

We arrive at the platform and most of the activity around us comes to a halt. From down the street, a small group moves toward us, several light sticks bobbing in the dark. It's not until they are closer that I can see who it is.

Doc is there with a few other men and women. Carol holds poor Nellie in her arms. All of them form a semi-circle around Liam, who is carrying Ana in his arms, the same way Daniel carried me last night.

Was it really just last night that we sat in the cafeteria and argued over trade routes and then made up in spectacular fashion? Last night when Ana was alive, and it was just a simple matter of walking over to her house to ask some questions.

The silence of the village is broken by the sounds of mourning. Soft cries and loud sobs echo around the wooden platform. Even in the dim evening light, I can tell that there isn't a single person here who doesn't feel the enormity of Ana's death.

The group approaches the platform and helps Liam lift Ana up onto the top. She's wearing a plain pair of slacks and the simple green shirt she wore the day we met. It would probably still bring out the golden flecks in her brown eyes if they weren't closed. She could be sleeping.

Liam holds on to her, even after she's been lain down and her arms and legs arranged just so. He leans down and whispers something in her ear. I'm glad we aren't close enough to hear. Watching is breaking my heart.

He pushes her hair away from her face and plants a kiss on her forehead. I can't watch anymore. Daniel wraps his arms around me as I bury my head into his chest. Pressure builds up behind my eyes and my head weighs a hundred pounds. This isn't right.

"Thank you all so much for coming out and putting this all together so quickly." Liam's voice breaks through the silence, and I dig deeper into Daniel's hold.

"Ana loved everything about her life here with all of you. It would have been easy to dismiss her or make her an outcast because of her past."

The silence returns, and I turn in Daniel's arms to see what's going on. Liam still commands everyone's attention, but he's done speaking.

On his knees, his head buried in his hands, silent sobs wrack his body.

"My husband and I never had children of our own." Carol steps forward a bit, her face still spotted with flour. "When he passed on, I came here so I could find a new life. I never imagined I'd find Ana. The daughter I always wished for. She brought me friendship every morning and helped to heal this old lady's broken heart. Ana will live on in me."

Carol steps back into the swell of the crowd and another woman steps forward, sharing a silly story of her and Ana getting caught naked when their clothes fell in the river on a swimming trip. Everyone laughs at the image of them scurrying back to town with nothing but leaves covering their lady bits. Like Carol, she ends her story with 'Ana will live on in me.'

One by one, various members of the village step forward and share a favorite memory or a time when Ana touched their lives. The night fills with an endless chorus of tender moments.

Daniel squeezes me, and I know he's asking if I want to speak. And I do, but I can't. What could I possibly say in a few short words to sum up how much Ana meant to me? She's the first person who made me feel like starting over here was possible. She helped give me a purpose and let me be more than just someone the Cardinal Rejected. Now that she's gone, there's a huge hole inside, and I don't see how it ever gets better.

Eventually, the stories slow, and Liam steps forward again, his face still drawn, but collected.

"Ana was a special soul who touched the lives of everyone she met. This world was a better place with her in it, and she will be missed. And now it's our job to continue to give her life purpose, by remembering to be kind to one another and finding value in every gift. We release her from this world and the suffering she endured, but we capture her light and hold it close to our hearts always. Ana will live on in me."

At his final words, two torches on either side of the group light up into flames. As one, they lower to the black tar bundles underneath and it instantly catches fire. In seconds, the whole structure is a swirling mass of white and blue so thick I can't see the body lying on top.

The crowd moves around the burning pyramid, embracing. Sharing hugs and smiles. It's too much. I pull out of Daniel's grasp and walk back toward the dining hall. He's only a few steps behind me, but for once his closeness is too much.

I stop and hold out a hand to him. "I need a few minutes alone."

His expression is unreadable with the light of the fire flowing out behind him. He nods and pauses the tiniest second before heading back toward the crowd.

* * *

Inside the dining hall, everything is exactly where we all left it after Doc's announcement. Mostly empty plates and cups line the tables. Except for all the missing people, it could be any other night, any other dinner.

Except it's not, because Ana isn't in here joking around and trying to steal extra pieces of bread. She's out there, lying dead on a huge funeral pyre, and I can't pretend like that's okay.

I grab the nearest thing to me and hurl it at the wall. The last few sips of water spray out of the wooden cup seconds before it smashes against the wall, splitting in half.

It's not fair. Not fair that Ana should get sick. Not fair that Eric and Ethan almost died trying to get her medicine. Not fair that we finally got some and it still didn't work. I pick up a plate and fling it against the wall, too. It explodes against the wood panels and splinters into a hundred tiny pieces flying in every direction.

Why do we get to live here safe and sound while Molly never even got close to her freedom? My fingers curl around the edge of another plate and pull it back over my shoulder. The door slams open seconds before I'm about to catapult it to destruction.

"Keep that up and we'll all be eating off the floor." Elizabeth edges into the room, a burlap bag slung over one shoulder. "Of course, this food is so much better than what we got in the PIT, I'd be the first down on my knees with a fork in hand."

"Are you seriously joking right now?" I throw the plate down on the table, scattering the remnants of a few dinners. "What is wrong with you? Ana is dead. Molly is dead. For all I know, all those people we left behind in the PIT are dead, and you want to joke about the food!"

"It's better than throwing plates or moping in a corner."

"Horse shit!"

Elizabeth sinks down onto a bench. "You're upset so I'm going to let that slide." She pats the bench next to her. "Come sit down for a minute."

"I don't want to sit down. I don't want to be calm and rational. I want to throw stuff and scream and rage in the street." I jump up and down, shaking out my fingers, trying to get rid of the all the extra energy surging through my body. "Why is everyone out there pretending like this is just okay? It's not okay. It's not. It's so far from okay and I don't…I don't…" I sink to the floor right where I stand. "I can't make it stop hurting."

Elizabeth walks over and lifts me up onto the bench. We sit in silence for several minutes while I get my choking sobs under control and find my breath again.

"I could lie and tell you it gets easier, but it doesn't ever really stop hurting." Elizabeth stares at a spot on the wall. "After Molly died, I just wanted to crawl up into a ball and wait for my own life to be over. It hurt so much, and it still does."

Elizabeth reaches into her bag and pulls out five smooth, white stones. Molly's memorial cairn from the PIT. So that's what she took out of the PIT. "I think about her every day. About how much she would have loved this place. She was always such a peacemaker, she would have fit in anywhere, but would have gladly worked wherever they needed her the most."

She turns one of the stones over and over in her hand. "Sometimes I think that she should be here instead of me. But that's not the way it works, and I have to let go of that."

"How?"

"Death has to be an accepted part of life if we are going to gladly take all the rest of it." She sets the stone down and turns to face me completely. "There are so many joys we get to experience. Love, family, friendship. We can't welcome those without also allowing that death is an inevitable fate for all of us. But it only hurts because of how much we value life."

"Then maybe I should stop caring so much."

"No, princess. That is not the answer. That's the Cardinal's take. He doesn't value life, and look at him. We stay out here and live this new life to the fullest. That's our way of defying everything he stands for."

"And you just stop being angry?"

"Maybe." Elizabeth stares off across the room. "At least, I let go of the rage. I had to do that or go insane. But I'll never stop loving Molly or wanting justice for her. I can be patient, but some day the Cardinal will pay for what he did to her."

I wipe back a few more tears. "You sound like you've been talking to Daniel."

"Yeah, well, everyone once in a while he stops talking about how amazing you are and says something that isn't completely stupid."

I laugh, though my heart isn't really in it. "Thanks."

"You don't have to thank me."

"I mean it. Thank you." I stand up and wipe my clammy hands against my pants. "But we need to stop saving these little heart to hearts until someone dies."

"Deal." Elizabeth stands and gives me a short one-armed squeeze. "Speaking of which, I was thinking maybe you'd want to help me find a new home for these." She gives the bag with Molly's stones a little shake. "It's time."

"I'd be honored."

Twenty-Seven

We push through the dining hall doors, and the atmosphere outside has changed completely. The fire died down some and the crowd shifted a bit farther into the square. On the edge of the crowd, Ana's body burns in peace.

"Goodnight." Patrice waves at us as she heads off to our room, but it doesn't look like anyone else is going to be calling it a night for quite a while.

At the heart of the square, dozens of lights are strung up from trees and porch roofs, giving the space a party feel. Liam has taken up residence on one of the porches with a huge barrel. In small groups, villagers come to him to share a hug and get a cup of whatever he's passing out.

"What in the world?"

"Rebecca. Elizabeth. Over here," Liam calls over to us, his face split into a wide grin.

"Liam, what's going on?" I spread my hands out at the crowd as several guitars strike into an upbeat melody. "It looks like a party out here."

"That's exactly what it is." He fills a mug from the barrel and hands it to me. "It's okay to feel sadness and pain over losing Ana, but tonight we celebrate her life and the lasting legacy she has on all of us."

I take a sip from the mug. It's simultaneously sweet and bitter. "What is this?"

"Village specialty. Dandelion beer." Liam hands a mug over to Elizabeth and grabs his own. "To Ana."

"To Ana." I take another sip and let the creamy warmth spread down my throat. All those hours my father spent in the yard trying in vain to rid our yard of dandelions. My mother ordering him back out when he missed them. "If the people back in the Territories had known what these weeds could make, they might not have worked so hard to eliminate them."

Liam tilts his mug, and his eyes take on serious gaze. "Some people are so worried about achieving an unrealistic perfection that they miss out on something unique and special."

Tears well up at the bottom of his eyelids as he stares at the fire in the distance.

We step away from the porch as others line up for a drink to toast a beautiful woman. The music kicks into high gear as a violin joins into the tune. Those without a mug move along with the music, skipping about without any sort of pattern. So different than the waltzes, gavotte, and cotillions Cheryl and I used to practice in our rare moments of freedom.

The energy is contagious. Even with my hands full, my toes tap along to the sailing melody. A celebration is exactly what I'd call this.

"I was wondering where two of my favorite ladies wondered off to." Daniel walks up behind us and puts an arm over each of our shoulders. "I see you wasted no time in finding the refreshments. Though, Rebecca," his voice takes on a tone of mock horror, "I'm shocked to see you with a beer in your hand. What would your mother say?"

"Before or after she fainted from pure humiliation? And how many mugs have you raised tonight?"

Daniel grabs my cup, hands it to Elizabeth and pulls me by both hands into the growing group of dancers. "Enough that I want to embarrass myself with the woman of my dreams."

"You're crazy," I shout above the swelling music. "And possibly tipsy."

"Crazy in love," he shouts back, spinning me around and pulling me in close.

The music soaks into my clothes and through my skin to sit on my heart. The tempo picks up and my feet move along with it, spinning and jumping like a child. It should feel wrong to be this joyful, but it doesn't. The sadness is still there, sitting just below the surface, but this is right. If Ana were here she'd be right in the middle of the crowd, grabbing anyone who got too close to be her next dance partner. She lived life with abandon, taking advantage of every day of freedom given to her.

"I have to stop." There's a brief pause in the music long enough that I don't have to shout at Daniel.

"Okay, we can sit for a bit."

"No, no I don't mean stop dancing." I grab his shoulders and his hands wrap tighter around my waist. "I have to stop spending so much time worrying about what-ifs and could-haves. I don't have to stop caring about everyone else out there, but I can't let that concern stop me from living this life."

Daniel pulls me in until not even the wind could pass between us. "You deserve to be happy."

"I think I finally believe you."

"Announcement, gather round. Constance has an announcement." One of the women playing the guitar hops down off her chair and offers a hand to Constance to climb up.

The noise fades away, but not the kind of silence as during Ana's release. This is the kind filled with unspoken promises.

"Okay." Constance wipes her hands on the side of her skirt. "I hadn't quite thought this through."

Thomas pulls another chair over to her and hops up on it to hold her hand.

"Right, well, since this is a celebration of life, I thought it might be a good time to let everyone know." She looks at Thomas and breaks into a huge grin. She's giddy with love for him. "Thomas and I are having a baby."

Cheers erupt from the gathered crowd and the musicians launch into a cheery tune to celebrate the good news. I rush forward with Daniel into the sea of well-wishers.

"Constance!" She pulls me into a huge hug the second we get close enough. "What? How! I thought you couldn't have children."

"Well, that makes two of us." Excitement pours out of her, and she can't even stand still. "I made Doc give me the test three times. Turns out Dr. Harold was wrong about how much damage there is."

"I can't believe it." I pull her into another hug, and happy tears fill my eyes. "Congratulations. You are going to be a wonderful mother."

"Thank you," she whispers, so softly I can barely hear her over the music. "Thank you for everything."

I pull back and flash her a wicked grin. "Rebecca is a lovely name for a girl."

The guys are shaking hands and slapping backs. For a second I can imagine this scene completely different, with all of us gathered in the backyard of a typical house in the MidWest Territory. Instead of this amazing, eclectic celebration, we're having a spring garden party complete with fresh lemonade and orchestral music pumping through the sound system.

It's the perfect image of everything I ever wanted. And it looks horribly boring. How in the world did I ever think that kind of life was right for me? Would I really have been happy living the same planned out life as everyone else? Would I have pretended like my mother, but hated everything?

Thomas pulls Constance into a one-armed hug, his free hand falling to rest on her belly. Daniel wraps me in a hug from behind and all I feel is love. Thank the stars I'll never have to find out exactly how dull my life might have been.

"We have an announcement, too."

"Are you..." Constance smiles and lifts her eyebrows at me.

"No, but we are getting married." I squeeze Daniel's arms. "I know we already said we're married, but that was the PIT, and it was rushed and no one was there and it just...well, we want to do it the right way."

"This is wonderful." Constance waves Daniel off so she can give me another hug. "You have to let me make you a dress. Nothing as elaborate as a Territory dress, of course. But trust me, you'll be stunning."

"I'd love that."

"Oh, I'm so excited." Constance is squeezing my arms so tight she might actually cut off circulation.

"Hey, everybody." The people closest to us turn at her shouts. "Rebecca and Daniel are getting married."

Another swell of shouts lift up from the dancing melee and the excitement takes over. Everyone is shouting, hugging, and well-wishing. My heart might actually burst from an overabundance of love. It sounds cheesy just thinking it, but there's just so much joy it tingles along every inch of my skin. I may actually be getting everything I ever wanted.

The crowd thins around us as a new song kicks into gear. Daniel grabs my hand, spins me into him, and kisses me right there in front of everyone. It's quick and strong and leaves my head spinning when he pulls away.

"I love you, Rebecca Collins."

"You keep saying that, and I'm gonna make you marry me."

Daniel laughs so loud he almost drowns out the music. His hands fall to my waist and he picks me up, twirling us both around.

My head is spinning double time when my feet hit the ground. "Where is Patrice?"

"I think she was heading up to our floor to change her shirt or something. Why?"

"Because she's going to be my sister, and I want to ask her to stand with me at the wedding."

"You never cease to amaze me, you know that?"

"Then I'll make it my personal mission to keep you on your toes no matter how many years we're married." I lift up on my toes and return his kiss. "I'll be back."

Liam is still on Doc's porch, refilling mugs and sharing stories.

"Did I hear the news right? Are you and Daniel tying the knot?"

"We want to make it official, here with all of you." I pat his arm on my way to the door. "You're our home now."

"We're lucky to have you."

I push open the door and wipe at my eyes. I hate that Ana won't be there to see it, but I won't be sad. Seeing everyone so happy and full of life was all Ana ever wanted for any of us.

My feet are light as dandelion fuzz flying up the stairs. "Patrice, I need to talk to you."

I freeze less than a foot into the room. Patrice and Eric pull back from what seconds ago must have been a hot and heavy make-out session. They both stand, slightly awkward, only inches apart amid the gauzy white sheets that serve as our walls.

"I was going to say you're missing the party, but it looks like you're doing okay up here." I back up toward the door. "I'll just talk to you tomorrow."

"Wait," Patrice reaches out to me, her face desperate. "You can't tell Daniel."

It's not at all nice, but I can't help the laughter that bubbles up and out of me. "Oh trust me, Patrice, I have no intention of telling Daniel anything about this."

The relief is evident on both their faces. "Thanks, Rebecca." Eric takes her hand. Maybe I should feel a little twinge of envy. After all, last year it was me Eric was holding close. But I don't. All I feel is happiness.

"I really appreciate you keeping quiet about this," Patrice says.

"Maybe don't thank me yet," I say, taking another step toward the stairs and grabbing the door handle. "I'm not going to say anything." I wink at them both. "But you're going to have to."

I pull the door closed and skip down the stairs. Back outside, the party is going as strong as ever. I grab another mug from the table by Liam and let the slightly fruity ale fill me up.

In the crowd, Daniel dances with Elizabeth while Constance and Thomas clap to the music and shout encouragement from the sidelines. They look ridiculous and amazing. Arms and legs flying in a dozen different directions. Elizabeth could be the world's worst dancer if she wasn't in competition with Daniel for the title.

I finish the drink and nod at Liam on my way to the crowd. "Daniel, how about we give Elizabeth a break and show them all how it's done."

"Careful, princess," Elizabeth says as we trade places in the dance. "He gets a little wild with his leading foot."

I take Daniel's hands and turn him in an awkward spin. "Who said I'm going to let him lead?"

"Good call," Elizabeth yells over her shoulder. "I'm going to go check on Eric."

I watch Elizabeth thread her way through the crowd and straight to the building I just left. So much for not saying anything. No way Elizabeth doesn't come running back down here with a wicked grin on her face in less than five minutes.

I chuckle at a picture of the moment in my head.

"What are you laughing about? My dancing isn't really that bad, is it?"

I smile up at him. "To be fair, yes, it really is. But I wasn't laughing at you."

"So what were you laughing at?"

"Can't a girl laugh just because she's happy?" I pull in close until our noses are almost touching. "Because right now I am immensely happy."

"Me, too." Daniel nuzzles down into my neck, resting his cold nose in the warm skin where my neck and chin meet. "You make me happy."

Wild laughter flows out of Doc's office. Elizabeth is almost bent over, grabbing her stomach and working not to trip off the porch. A terrified Patrice and Eric appear at the doorway.

"Oh Daniel," Elizabeth calls out in a sing-song voice.

I wrap a hand over my mouth to keep from giggling. The scene is too much to hold in. Patrice looks ready to run at a moment's notice. Of course, it's not her that should be ready to bolt once Elizabeth spills the beans.

Elizabeth makes her way to us, still laughing, but holding it together a bit more. She hands Daniel a mug filled to the brim with ale. "Here, you're gonna need this."

I catch her eye, and the two of us are hopeless with laughter. I want to bottle this minute up and store it away in my pocket for those days when nothing seems to go right.

"So I was thinking," Elizabeth says between barely contained fits of laughter. "How'd you like to be kin?"

"What!"

Daniel looks up and stares right at Patrice and Eric. Everything freezes for a second, and then Eric takes off, running down the street.

Everyone breaks out into laughter, including Daniel. Well, everyone except Patrice, who looks torn between going after Eric and giving her brother a swift kick in the pants.

The expression on her face only makes me laugh more. Yep, a bottled-up little moment in time would make this just about perfect.

Daniel swings me around and kisses me again as if we're the only ones within a hundred miles. Never mind. Keep the bottle. I'll take this. Right here. Forever.

Twenty-Eight

"Knock, knock." Daniel pokes his head through the door, all smiles until he gets a look at the office.

With Constance helping for the past few weeks, I've been able to keep from completely sinking under the workload. But with taking time to explain the system and answer questions, at times it feels like we're working backward. The maps that used to line the walls have all come down so we can remark delivery paths and route the riders around the villages that won't trade with us anymore. Now maps cover more than half the floor.

Old folders filled with trade sheets are scattered on the desks. We've been trying to figure out where to get some of our essentials for this winter now that our trade partners have been cut in half. It's a tedious and, so far, unfruitful process. We need those villages. I've even got Ethan and some other riders delivering bottles of dandelion ale to soften them up.

From a quick glance, it looks like two imbeciles are in charge of trading for all of Allmore. It doesn't help that morning sickness has Constance running to the bathroom and scattering maps as she goes every few hours. Thank goodness Carol keeps her supplied with crackers or the poor girl would never have food in her belly.

"You might as well come in." I try to keep my tone light, but the strain of keeping up without Ana is wearing me down.

"Wow, I'm kinda afraid if I step in the wrong spot you'll end up with a trade for shoe leather instead of breakfast oats."

"You and your stomach will be pleased to know the food trade has been almost completely untouched."

"Oh no," Constance jumps up from her chair, but by the green shade of her face, she's not going to make it down the hall.

"Trash can." I point at the metal basket in the corner, and Daniel hands it to her just in time.

"Sorry," Constance says, wiping her mouth off. "I was doing okay until you started talking about breakfast."

"It's fine. In fact, today's been a little rough." I take the can and flash her a convincing smile. "Why don't you head home and get some rest. You and that baby need to take it easy."

"But we're supposed to research more of the villages this afternoon."

"It can wait. Your health is more important." I take her by the elbow and guide her toward the door. "I'll send word to Thomas so he can come keep an eye on you. I don't like the idea of you sick in that house all by yourself."

"Okay, I'll go," Constance still sounds unsure, but her face is already more relaxed. "I'll see you tomorrow. Bye, Daniel."

Constance makes her way down the stairs and I collapse into my chair, my head flopped back to stare at the ceiling.

"So I guess that answers the question of how are things going." Daniel plops down in the other chair, but promptly jumps back up, sets the sick-filled can on the stairs and closes the door. "That's better."

"I wish I could set all the rest of my problems on the stairs and they'd disappear."

Daniel walks behind me and uses his warm hands to massage out the tension in my shoulders. "Want to tell me about it?"

"It won't do any good." I lean forward so he can work at the knots in my back. "Doc has a list of items he needs to prep for Constance's delivery and I still have no idea where we're getting half of our winter supplies with so many villages cutting us off. Add to that a hormonal, pregnant woman who desperately wanted to make me a wedding dress for next week and coming up empty handed with any appropriate material."

"I don't care what you wear for the wedding." Daniel pushes his thumb into the tender muscles bordering my spine.

"But you will care when we run out of wool or canned fruit halfway through winter because I can't get the trade routes together."

"Everyone understands you are doing your best."

I let my head drop into my hands. "And everyone is counting on me to pull it together the way Ana always did."

"Rebecca," Daniel spins my chair around until I'm facing him and kneels down so we're eye to eye. "I know you. I know you can pull off miracles when you put your mind to it."

"And if I can't—"

"If there is something that you absolutely can't manage to get, obviously because it no longer exists, we'll all learn to live without it." He takes my hands and rubs soothing circles against my wrists.

"I just...these people here, they matter so much to me." I squeeze his hands and blink back hot tears stinging my eyes. "I don't want to let them down."

"That's not even a possibility." Daniel reaches into his pocket and pulls out a handkerchief.

It's one of Molly's. I can tell by the tiny flowers she embroidered using spare bits of thread she scavenged from the clothing donations.

Elizabeth and I went out the morning after Ana's funeral and found the perfect spot in the woods for Molly's stones. A small bed of moss, surrounded by purple and blue wildflowers. It exudes peace the way Molly did.

Several of the others saw our work and have built up cairns for their own loved ones. A half-dozen stacks of white stones decorate the little patch of forest, creating both a solemn and happy spot.

Elizabeth held it together until we were almost done before letting the tears fall again. But this time, they were happy tears. She told me Molly was finally at peace, resting among others who fought for their freedom.

The day brought relief for Elizabeth, but only filled me with more stress. I can't help but imagine how many more cairns will be added this winter if I can't manage to get all the supplies we need.

My heart rate kicks up just thinking about it. I hand the handkerchief back and straighten up in my chair. So much work to be done.

"I love you, but I've got a lot to do, so I'll see you at dinner."

"Nope." Daniel grabs my hands and pulls both of us to standing. "You need a break."

"There's no time."

"Doc's orders," Daniel says, tugging me over to the door. "He swears you'll end up with a vitamin deficiency if you spend every day stuck up here without any sunlight or fresh air. So let's go."

Daniel opens the door and we're both smacked in the face with the lingering odor from the trashcan. Daniel picks it up with one hand and holds it out as far from his body as possible. "Besides, we have to take care of this before Carol quits in protest."

"Fine, I'll give you ten minutes."

"Fifteen or the trashcan stays." Daniel swings it around to waft back into the office.

"Fifteen," I say, pushing him and the putrid can down the stairs.

* * *

Daniel threads my arm through his as we make our way through town. People who were strangers only a few months ago shout out greetings as we pass through the square. It's shocking to think about how much has changed in such a short period of time.

Less than six months ago, we were eking out an existence in the PIT, trying to cobble together makeshift furniture from cast off junk. Daniel, Elizabeth, and I were just barely getting by and focused on keeping the hopelessness of spending our lives in the PIT from dragging us into the dark places in our heads.

I barely recognize that scared little girl who couldn't be trusted walking down the alleys alone. Even with Daniel watching out for me, I wouldn't have survived in there much longer. Eventually, the despair would have won out and I would have quit trying.

Now we're walking down the middle of the street. Free from all the confined drudgery of the PIT and surrounded by kind, caring people who welcomed us like old friends. None of us are those old people anymore.

"So is there a destination for this walk or are we going to meander around a bit? These clouds are pretty dark so we could get rain any time now."

Just to prove my point, a sharp gust of unseasonably cool wind whips down the street, tossing my growing hair in a million directions.

"I thought we could walk over and check out progress on the house. Thomas said they've been working double time, but they don't think they'll have it ready by the wedding."

"I'll take it whenever they can be ready." I didn't mind all of us sleeping in the same room at first. It was so much like our cabin in the PIT, it was kind of comforting to have something familiar in the midst of all the changes. Several months in, and I'm dying for some privacy. Not just from each other, but from Doc and others randomly showing up to get supplies or collect laundry. It will be nice to have a place of our own, with a door.

Constance's house already has little touches of home. Paint is too hard to get in the trade routes, but she used some kind of berry dye to put their hand prints on the door. Constance says once the baby comes, she'll add their hand prints as well. The curtains in the front windows don't even come close to matching, but they still give her home that distinct lived-in feel.

Next door where we'll live, the house sits blank and forlorn like an empty soul. The work crew that would normally be pounding away at something has disappeared. Maybe they thought the rain was a given and decided to stay dry working on an indoor project.

Daniel clomps up the front stairs, pausing on the third one to bounce a bit on the new tread. "Must be getting close if they fixed the stairs already."

He winks at me and pushes open the door. My jaw about hits the floor with the transformation.

A month ago, this main room was filled with broken and dusty furniture and places on the ceiling that made me worry for my safety. Now, that's all been cleared out. The dusty chandelier from the corner glistens in the main room, revealing freshly plastered walls and ceiling.

Daniel reaches around the door and hits a button. The bulbs in the chandelier pop to life, filling the room with light and shining little glittery diamonds against the walls. I want to grab a blanket and move in.

"Surprise," Daniel shuts the door behind him, grinning ear to ear. "I might have under-promised on the house's progress."

I spin around and take in the beauty of the room, picturing the little details that will make it a home once Daniel and I move in. "So that's it. It's ready."

"Almost, there are just a few details to finish up, mostly on my end, and then getting the furniture in here." Daniel takes my hands and pulls me close. "Everyone worked overtime to get it ready for next week. It's our wedding gift from the whole village."

"It's amazing." I want to run through the rooms turning on every light in the place, but I can't pull my eyes away from this room. It's ours. The perfect little house I always dreamed of, but so much better because of the amazing people in my life. "You are beyond a doubt the best thing that has ever happened to me." I put my hands on the sides of his face and pull him in until our foreheads touch. "What did I ever do to deserve you?"

"Questioned the Cardinal and his policies, got yourself Rejected, and then staged a coup inside the PIT."

That smart mouth of his is going to get him in trouble, but right now all I want to do is kiss it. No tender, sweet kisses will do right now. I come in strong and Daniel is right there matching me with force and desperation. We're a tangled mess of arms and hands, each of us reaching for more. His hands slide up the edge of my shirt and I grip his to pull us closer. It's a good thing there isn't any furniture in the house or we might not come up for air until the wedding. We've had too few moments of privacy, but with this new house, that's about to change.

My back bumps up against the wall and pulls me out of the moment. Daniel places two more kisses on the side of my neck sending chills down my overheated body.

"Hot in here." I barely get the words out without moaning.

"I was able to salvage the ACS with a few new fuses in the motherboard and get it wired into the solar module much easier than I had previously thought." His thumb traces tiny circles where the collar of my shirt ends and my collar bones begin. "Thomas and his crew patched it into the ventilation ducts used for the furnace."

"I love it when you talk techy to me, but I have no idea what that means."

Daniel chuckles, his lips vibrating against my ear and making it nearly impossible to pay attention to what he's saying. "I have an artificial cooling system all ready to go as soon as we need it."

"If that kiss was any indication, we're definitely going to need it."

"Would you like to see it now?" His thumb dips lower, the circles expanding across the exposed skin on my chest toward the buttons.

"I think we had better find something else to keep your hands preoccupied." I kiss him slow and deep. "At least until the wedding."

He kisses me back and pushes off the wall. I feel better that he at least looks as flustered as I feel.

"Right, cooling things off." He walks over to the wall panel and rubs his hands over his face.

I walk behind him and wrap my arms around his waist, resting my cheek in the little crevice of his spine. Perfection.

The panel emits a few beeps and the system kicks on with a quiet purr. Daniel turns in my arms and drapes his hands over my shoulders. "It should only take a minute for the condenser coils to hit the right temp."

As if on cue, a puff of air pushes out of the vent by our feet. I close my eyes and bury into Daniel's chest. He smells like oil, pine, and dust. Dust?

I open my eyes as the pungent odor of dead leaves and old dirt fills my nose. Clouds of dust billow at our feet.

"Daniel?"

"Shit, the vents haven't been cleaned yet." He pulls a handkerchief out of his pocket and puts it over my mouth. In the few seconds it takes to do that, the dust-filled air climbs up around our knees. "Let's go."

I take Daniel's hand and run behind him as he leads me back toward the front door. We run out the door and down the stairs half-coughing, half-laughing.

"So that's what happens when a house sits empty for a century or so."

Daniel nods, clearing the last of the grit from his throat. "I'm thinking we might need a bit of spring cleaning before we move in."

Daniel grins, his golden brown eyes lit up with glee, and reaches around my waist to pull me close. His eyes turn from glee to passion in the space between heartbeats.

"No matter what obstacles you face or how impossible the future looks, I will always be there. I will always keep you safe." He dips me back and singes my lips with a deep kiss. "Always."

Twenty-Nine

"I shouldn't be nervous about this, right?" I stare out the window down at the group moving benches from inside the dining hall to the square. "I mean, what's to be nervous about? We already said our vows ages ago. And Daniel is…"

"Yeah, yeah," Elizabeth chimes in from her spot splayed out on one of the unmade beds of our bunk room. "If you start spouting a bunch of lovey-dovey stuff about Daniel being the perfect guy and finding your soul mate, I'm out of here."

"Ignore her, Rebecca." Constance sticks her tongue out at Elizabeth. "If a girl can't gush about the one she loves on her wedding day, when can she?"

She fingers the net veil made from some old fishing gear. Without the material to make a dress, it's the only part of the traditional bridal outfit I'll be wearing.

"I'm not sure why anyone would want to marry my brother, but I think it's romantic that you're nervous."

"Thanks, Patrice, but you should be careful speaking ill of marrying other people's brothers." I wink at her.

"I think part of me is nervous. But the other part is just excited." I march across the room and plop down on the bed with Elizabeth, forcing her to scoot over. "Ever since we left the PIT, it feels like the whole world has been in a state of flux. Even when we got here and the village voted us in, I still never felt settled.

"Maybe it was all the unknowns about living here, or it could have been the temporary housing. But having this ceremony, feels real. I can sink my feet into the soil and plant roots."

Constance walks over, and I reach out a hand to rest on the little bump of her belly. "Maybe have a family of our own. Can you imagine what it would be like to grow up and never have to worry about the Machine?"

"Our kids will never have to feel like they don't stack up." Constance smiles down at her growing baby.

Elizabeth sits up. "Your kids won't have to grow up knowing they can never fit the mold."

"They'll never feel targeted." Patrice joins our little group.

"I know in the grand scheme of it all, this is just another day. A flash of time. But I can't help but feel like this is the beginning of a fresh start. For all of us."

A sharp rap on the door pulls us all out of our moment of reverie. "Is everyone decent?"

"Liam." I rush to the door and throw it open. "What are you doing here?"

"Special delivery." He holds up a small suitcase that has definitely seen better days.

"Well, come on in."

Liam walks in, smiling hello at our little group. He sets the case down on a spare bed and we all gather round to see what's inside.

"I heard you couldn't get material to make a dress." He unlatches the two rusty hinges from the front of the case. "I know Ana would have wanted you to have this."

He pushes the lid open and pulls out a crisp white satin dress. He holds it out until I take it in my hands, the weight of the material making it feel even more important.

"I should have brought this to you weeks ago, but…" He stops and closes his eyes. "I wasn't sure I could handle seeing this dress come down the aisle again."

"Liam, you don't have to—"

"But then I heard Ana in my head, giving me a good talking to. 'Liam Weaver, that sweet girl deserves to have something beautiful to wear on her wedding day and you're just going to let that dress rot away in a box? Why don't you give it new life and let me be a part of her day.' And as usual, Ana is right."

I set the dress down carefully on the bed and pull him into a huge hug. "I would be honored to wear Ana's dress."

"She really was a beautiful bride." There's both pride and pain in his voice, and it's tearing me apart.

"Okay, enough," he says, stepping back and wiping at his eyes with the back of his hands. "You need to get changed before the ceremony starts without you."

"Thank you."

Liam doesn't say another word. Just sucks his lips in and nods at all of us. We watch him head out the door and close it behind himself. It's a full five count before any of us moves.

"Well, you heard the man, ladies." Constance claps her hands like she's calling to order a meeting of the ladies auxiliary. "Time to get this bride dressed for her big day."

* * *

With every step we take down the stairs, more excitement builds inside me. It started in my toes and worked its way up my legs, through my belly and down to my fingers. A soft buzz in my ears makes the conversation around me sound like it's happening under water.

I take a peek from behind the window curtain and gasp. The simple benches in the main square are transformed with layers of cushy moss and little bouquets of wildflowers attached to the ends. In front of the benches where everyone is currently staring, Daniel and Liam wait under an arch made of branches and ivy. Thomas and Eric stand right next to them, and all of them stare at the door to Doc's office.

They're all waiting on me.

Constance squeezes my hand. "Are you ready?"

Instantly the nerves fade away, only to be replaced by an excited energy. "Let's do this."

Constance adjusts my veil one last time and nods to Patrice, who's waiting with one hand on the door handle, ready to go. At Constance's signal, Patrice opens the door and walks out. Constance shoots us a wink and follows right behind.

"Thank you for doing this." I take Elizabeth's hand and squeeze it tight. "A bride's family usually walks her down the aisle, and you are my family. It took a while to convince you not to kill me, but I can't imagine being here or doing any of this without you."

"Alright, princess, don't go getting all overemotional on me. Just because you're all dolled up in satin and lace doesn't mean I can't drop kick you down to Daniel."

I squeeze her hand again. "I love you, too."

She pushes the door open and we march out into the mid-morning air.

At first, all I can take in are the rows and rows of benches. Everyone from the entire village is here. Even the crew who volunteered to make the special lunch for after the ceremony stopped to come watch our vows.

The musicians see our entrance and kick into a slow march that signals my arrival. Everyone stands, making it impossible to find Daniel. We walk along the back row until we get to the little walkway created by a split in the benches.

The second we turn the corner, my eyes fly to Daniel. No one owns a suit since they are completely impractical, but Daniel still looks stunning in dark gray slacks and a crisp white shirt. He found a bow tie somewhere and it's perfect.

His eyes flash a shock before they light up, his face going into full smile mode. I can't imagine what he's thinking right now. He expected me to come down the aisle in nothing more elegant than a simple skirt and blouse. Ana's dress is so much more.

The satin feels like silk against my suntanned skin. Thin straps hold the dress up over my shoulders, but leave my arms, neck, and upper chest bare. A delicate lace overlay adds dimension to the cream dress, and a silk ribbon around the waist creates a final finishing touch. I don't know what Constance would have created, but I can't see how it could have topped this.

Halfway down the aisle, Daniel catches my eye, winks, and smiles even wider, though I didn't think that was possible. Help me, that man could charm the Cardinal himself with that smile. Mere mortals like myself are completely helpless against it.

Elizabeth and I had been walking fairly slowly, in time to the beautiful music, but enough of that. I tug on her arm a bit and pick up the pace. No more waiting. I want the world to know that this man is the one I'll love forever.

At the end of the aisle, I'm breathless, but not from the quick walk. I will never get tired of staring into his dark eyes or seeing his face split in half with a smile that just can't be faked. Maybe for the first time ever, I fully understand just how wrong the Machine was when it

Rejected me. Because there's no way someone that bad could earn the love of a man this good.

Elizabeth drops my hand and pulls Daniel into a bone crunching hug. He doesn't hesitate a second to wrap those arms around her and love her back. They've been together through so much, and we're both lucky to have Elizabeth in our lives. Even if she does still call me princess. At this point, I kinda like it.

They pull apart, and Elizabeth takes my hand again. This time she sets it in Daniel's and cups our joined hands between both of hers. "I don't like a whole lot of people. I love even fewer." She pumps our hands once and deliberately avoids eye contact with either of us. "Be good to each other."

If I thought she wouldn't punch me, I'd pull her into a big hug of my own. But I've seen her right hook, so instead I nod and smile as she takes her seat in the front row.

Liam steps between our joined hands, and everyone on the benches takes their seat.

"Today is a happy day," Liam says in a strong voice that carries through the crowd. "Not just for Daniel and Rebecca, but for all of us."

A murmur of agreement ripples from the sea of people behind us, their heads nodding like the undulation of a wave. Back in the PIT, the ocean was supposed to be our ticket to freedom. I know better now, looking out over the ocean of love surrounding us on this special day. Freedom isn't found in a place; it's how you choose to live your life every day and the people who fill that life with you.

"I've had the pleasure of getting to know both of these amazing individuals over the past several months. I could stand here and tell you all about Daniel. He's the guy you have to thank for getting so many of the legacy systems back up and running around here. He's too modest to say anything about it, but thanks to his keen eye, he found and fixed a broken circuit board from last winter's storms that would have taken down the heating system in the dining room just as the weather turned cold."

Daniel shakes Liam's hand and the two of them share of moment.

"And then there's Rebecca, looking gorgeous as ever in Ana's wedding dress." Liam plasters a fake smile on his face, but I don't miss him wiping a tear away while everyone's attention is focused on the wedding gown. "Ana spoke often of you, always pointing out how determined you were to figure everything out. She was convinced that in the next ten years you'd have the Pony Express running so well it could run itself."

Everyone laughs, and Liam manages to smile off the melancholy that fell over his face for half a second.

"But I didn't need to spend more than a few minutes with you to know exactly how devoted you are to each other."

I turn my focus back to Daniel and the faces in the crowd blur into the background.

"In your short lives, you've faced more trials than most of us here could ever imagine. And while it would be understandable if those experiences had left you bitter or guarded; it's almost beyond comprehension to see the exact opposite. Where there could be fear, there is trust. Where there should be apathy, there is empathy. And where we might see anger, there is love. Love for each other and for the people you call family."

Liam holds one hand out to Patrice and the other to Thomas. They both hand him the simple bands that Thomas crafted from an alloy of bits of leftover wiring and parts from machines that couldn't be salvaged. Daniel wanted to find something fancier, but I actually prefer this.

My free hand wraps around the simple silver knot pendant that I still wear. I never wanted a life of pomp and splendor. My only desire was to find love, and I don't need a rare gemstone or elaborate design to confirm that Daniel is exactly what I always wanted.

"These rings will be an outward symbol of a dedication that you already hold in your hearts. A confirmation of the love you created long before arriving here."

He hands a ring to each of us. It weighs nothing in my hand, but it carries the weight of the whole world as far as I'm concerned.

"Daniel and Rebecca have chosen to recite their own vows. Daniel."

I stare into Daniel's eyes and my mind flashes back to the last time we recited vows. Everything around us was falling apart, but that night, none of it mattered.

This time, everything is exactly as it should be. The Cardinal is still out there, but he's not our problem. My only problem is keeping it together while I put into words just how much I love the amazing man standing in front of me.

"Rebecca," Daniel takes my hand and everyone around us disappears. "When I first met you, you were naive and completely uninitiated in the way the world really works. I worried that you wouldn't last a day in the PIT, let alone a lifetime."

I lift my eyebrows and give him a look I hope he reads as, 'You're pushing it.'

"Don't worry, I'm getting to the good part." He squeezes my hands and winks. "Since that day, I've seen you grow into the person you were always meant to be. You've learned what it is that you want, and you're willing to go after it. But even through those changes, you're still the girl who would give her only slice of bread to a hungry, little boy. You think of others in everything you do, even if it means putting yourself at risk. You make me want to be a better person, and I'll spend the rest of my life working to deserve you. I love you."

Daniel slips the little band of metal on my left hand. Such a simple action and yet it feels like everything right now. I glance out at the crowd, and there isn't a dry eye to be seen, including Elizabeth. For a brief moment, I wish Cheryl and my parents were here to see this. Or, at least my father. He would want to know that I'm happy. And I am. I really am.

"Your turn, Rebecca."

"Daniel—"

Several shouts ring out from the back of the group. A woman rides into the crowd on horseback, though she's slumped over the horse's neck and barely in control. A few men jump up and grab the reins to keep anyone from being trampled. Doc is there in an instant, pulling the woman down off the horse.

"Liam, get over here now."

The crowd splits down the middle, and Liam takes off for the back. Daniel and I both freeze for a second, but only a second, and then we are running on Liam's heels.

"Mary, what's going on?"

Liam kneels at the head of the woman lying on the ground. Someone hands her a glass of water and she gulps it greedily.

Mary...the woman who saw us off from Arbor Glen. It feels like another lifetime ago when she slipped the braided bracelet on my wrist and wished us luck. But what is she doing here?

"Liam," she hands the cup back and grabs at Liam's shirt. "You have to come back. We need your help. You have to come."

"Hey, slow down." Liam wraps his hands around her and gently pulls them down. "I'm here, and you're safe. Take some slow breaths, and then tell me what's going on."

"Cardinal guards attacked last night. They came into the village with guns and took all the men away. I managed to sneak out, but everyone else is back there in danger."

"Why did they come? They've never even come close to the villages before."

"They're looking for Rebecca Collins."

Every head turns in one fluid motion to find me as all the air is sucked out of the world. I choke trying to get air down my windpipe. Daniel grabs me around the waist and carries me over to a now empty bench.

The Cardinal is attacking people, and it's all my fault. I'll never breathe again.

"Rebecca," Daniel squats down in front of me. He pushes his hands against my face and forces me to look right into his eyes. "I need you to focus and breathe. You can't shut down on me. I need you."

Something inside my head snaps. I open my mouth and suck in a huge gasp of air. Daniel may think he needs me, but he doesn't. Those people back at Mary's village need me.

Mary sits up and grabs Liam's shirt again. "You have to help. Alan needs you."

"Our father made his choice when he refused to let Ana stay." Liam stands up and addresses the crowd. "Arbor Glen is under attack by guards looking for Rebecca. I need some volunteer riders to escort Rebecca out of here and to another village. When the guards realize she isn't there, they are going to come looking for her, and we need to keep her safe. The rest of you, get into the storage rooms under the dining hall. Take what you need and stay there until we get back."

Liam turns back to Mary, and everyone around us springs into action. Alan is Liam's father. Our hostile relationship with Arbor Glen makes so much sense now. But, he isn't going to help him and wants me to run and hide. While those people back at Arbor Glen are possibly losing their lives.

They don't deserve this. Arbor Glen wasn't the safe haven we hoped it would be, but they did help us. And they led us to Allmore.

"No." I stand up and then climb onto the bench so Liam can hear me. "We can't just run away while there are people out there who need our help."

"This isn't a time to play hero." Liam walks over and pulls me down off the bench. "I'm not going to let you risk your life."

"But you'll ask all those people to give theirs just because I spent a night there. And how long before someone tells them I passed through? How long before the guards come here and start killing them?" I throw my hands out at the crowd still gathered around us. "We waited to save the people in the PIT, and now they're dead. I'm not going to make the same mistake twice."

Daniel pulls me into a quick kiss and then puts an arm around my shoulder. "Still giving her bread away. Where she goes, I go."

"Sign me up, too." Thomas moves to join our conversation. "But Constance stays here."

"No way is the princess going to have all the fun on her own." Elizabeth walks over and puts her arm around my shoulders from the other side. "The Dunstans are absolutely going on this little party."

"This isn't a social call." Even I'm surprised at how steady my voice sounds. "We need as many bodies as we have horses. This is a rescue mission."

Liam stares at us, his mouth opening and closing with no sound. I stare into his eyes so he knows I'm as serious as they come. This is happening with or without his approval.

"Okay." He nods and the confidence seeps back into his words. "Okay, change of plans. Everyone willing and able, go get a horse and a weapon. We have a village to save."

A small cheer lifts up from the group, and everyone springs back into action.

"You might be the craziest woman I've ever met," Liam says, staring at me like he's really seeing me for the first time. "And I was married to Ana."

Married. "Wait." I grab Patrice and Thomas before they run off. "I know we've got to go, but I'm not leaving here until we finish what we started."

In the midst of swirling chaos, the people I love most in the world form a little circle around me and Daniel. The big crowd and fancy flowers were wonderful. And I'm sure the banquet that will now go mostly to waste would have been delicious. But this little ring of people is all I ever really needed.

"Daniel," I grab his hands and take a deep breath to calm the chaos from within and without. "You've been there for me from the beginning. At first, you saved me from myself when I was too foolish to know better. Then you allowed me to make my own mistakes and worked tirelessly for my happiness, even when that happiness didn't include you. You were a silent supporter through it all.

"It took me way too long to realize just how much I needed you in my life and I almost waited until too late to let you in. I'm grateful every day that I got another chance, and I'll spend every day from here until eternity loving you with everything I am. I spent the first sixteen years of my life doing everything in my power to avoid the PIT. Now I can say, going there was the best thing that ever happened because it brought me to you. I love you."

I slip the little band on Daniel's finger and even though nothing has really changed, I love him even more.

"Daniel and Rebecca, I now pronounce you husband and wife. You may kiss the bride."

Daniel pulls me in and kisses me hard and fast. Our arms pulling each other closer than should be possible. Much too soon, the kiss ends and for a second no one moves. And then we all move, because there is work to be done.

Just like last time, our wedding vow kiss is a prelude to battle with the Cardinal. But this time everything is different.

Last time it was just me and Daniel alone against the most powerful man in the United Territories. We had a plan, but fully expected complete failure. I never thought I'd live to be Daniel's wife.

This time, we are surrounded by a whole family of people who are willing to follow us into battle. This time there is no plan, but I'm counting on success.

Because this man here next to me is everything. This wasn't a ceremony because we didn't have anything better to do. I meant every word I said and I don't even have to wonder if Daniel did as well. I want to spend years loving him and that all starts here, with showing the Cardinal I'm not his pawn anymore.

I grab Daniel's hand, my husband's hand, and squeeze hard. "Let's go."

Thirty

In less than an hour, we have two dozen horses saddled and ready to go. Constance and the other villagers packed up the wedding feast and other supplies into the storage rooms under the dining hall. It won't be comfortable, but if the Cardinal attacks before we get back, at least they'll be safe.

"I think that's everything and everyone." Daniel cinches up the saddle on the last horse.

"Not everyone." Patrice runs over to the group loading up. "I don't have a horse yet."

"Patrice." Daniel grabs her hand and leads her back toward the dining hall. "We've been over this. You can't go with us."

She pulls out of his grasp and plants her feet in the loose dirt and gravel. "So you expect me to sit here and wait while one of the last members of my family runs out and gets himself killed."

"No," Eric catches up to us. "I expect you to wait for me so I can concentrate out there knowing you're safe."

"What do you care? I'm not your wife."

Eric pulls her into his arms and kisses her hard. I turn away to give them some privacy, but Daniel stands there staring open-mouthed. "Maybe we fix that when I get back."

"Now, wait just a minute—"

I grab Daniel's arm and pull him back toward the horses. "Let's save that battle for another day."

Daniel doesn't fight back. He helps me up onto my horse and gets situated on his own. Eric runs over, without Patrice, and saddles up. He won't meet Daniel's hard-mouthed glare and at least has the decency to look embarrassed. I use the reigns the way Daniel showed me to move my horse around to Elizabeth and find Thomas and Constance.

There's no argument here. Constance can't put herself or the baby at risk. The ride alone would be bad enough, but we have no idea what we'll face once we hit Arbor Glen.

The two of them stand inches apart, their eyes closed and foreheads touching. Thomas grips Constance's hands like they are his only source of air. They don't say anything, but the moment is so intimate I have to turn away.

Liam pulls his horse around so everyone can see him and all thoughts of kisses and promises disappear. Mary rides at his side, against Doc's orders. She rode into town only an hour ago completely exhausted, starving, and with early signs of dehydration. She could really use a full day of rest, but she threw a fit loud enough to raise the dead when Doc even suggested she stay with the rest of the villagers in the storage room. Liam finally stepped in and said she could go. He glances at her now as if he's regretting that decision.

"If we ride hard, we can get to Arbor Glen by nightfall. I have no idea what we'll find there. I'm trying to stay hopeful, but I can't help but fear for the worst. You all have my gratitude for this, and we'll be busting out the dandelion ale when we get back. So let's hurry up and do this."

I'm sure he meant for the speech to be inspiring, but I'm too *everything* for that. I'm a mixture of a million different emotions. Nerves about taking on the Cardinal. Fear of what we'll find. Excitement that we're finally taking action instead of running away. Gratitude that I don't have to do it alone. Everything bubbles around inside my head and it's all I can do to concentrate on not falling off my horse.

I've never been anywhere near a real battle. There was plenty of violence in the PIT. But that was always separate from me, like I didn't belong to that part of the PIT. This isn't separate. I can't pretend this is happening to someone else. It's real, and the people I love could die.

Mary rides up next to me, her body slumped over in exhaustion, but her face showing nothing but determination. "Thank you." She squeezes the reigns in both hands. "You don't owe anything to Arbor Glen." She doesn't elaborate, but we both know she's talking about the way they treated us like criminals and kicked us out.

I reach over and lay a hand on top of hers. "Once upon a time, a generous woman told me that out here there are no debts to pay, only favors to be forwarded."

She touches the leather bracelet on my wrist and nods. No more words need to be said.

Instead of riding out to a battle cry, we head to the east silent, with nothing but our fear and determination to point us forward.

* * *

By the time we reach Arbor Glen, the sun is long gone. I'm sore and hungry, though the ache in my stomach is from far worse than a missed meal.

We stop at Jacob's rocks, the place where Mary first found our group of PIT runaways. That day feels like a lifetime ago. Everyone dismounts and we tie off the horses as best we can in the dark.

Liam creeps up behind me and whispers, "What's the plan?"

I turn and everyone is gathered around us.

"I don't have a plan." I stare at Liam, but he's still looking at me, eyes wide with expectation. "Do you think I storm villages on a regular basis?"

"You're the one that wanted us all to ride up here and fight back."

"I know, but..." sometimes I open my mouth and say things without thinking because the alternative is to say nothing and regret it. Now what? It's like I waded into one of the animal pens without slop boots on. I can turn around and run back out, but I'll still be covered in dung up to my knees. But the longer I just stand here, the deeper I'll sink. "Okay, we can't do anything until we know what we're dealing with. We need to send a few scouts to get closer and try to see what's going on in there."

Several members of the group raise their hands. "Good. That should be enough. You'll need to stay far enough back that you aren't seen. Surprise is on our side. Just watch and try to get an idea of where everyone is and how many guards are in there. Also, look for any weapons."

Six heads nod in the dark, including Mary's.

"The rest of you should wait at Jacob's rocks so we can avoid any watchful eyes."

I nod back at Mary and she takes off with the other scouts deeper into the village.

"Everyone else, take a minute to get some water. Check your weapons and then rest a bit while we wait for the scouts."

The remaining riders split up, heading back to their horses. The minute they're all occupied, I grab Daniel's arm and march us out of earshot before anyone sees us and follows. I move around a large stone and retch into the dirt.

Daniel's strong hand rubs circles on my back as I choke up the small amount of food in my stomach.

"I'm going to get us all killed." I stand up and wipe my mouth off with the back of my hand. "What was I thinking? This is the Acceptance ceremony hack all over again. Any minute now the Cardinal guards will find us. Except there isn't a Quarantine to drag us off to out here."

"Rebecca, no one is getting killed tonight."

Daniel hands me a canteen of water. I take my time letting the cool water wash my mouth, but there's no escaping the sour taste of knowing this is all going to end in bloodshed. "And you know that because?"

"Look, this is what you do. You're the kind of person who runs into the burning building first and figures out how to deal with the smoke second."

"Not feeling better."

Daniel rubs his hands over his face. "I'm struggling here. I have no idea how this is going to work and I will admit that I wish you would think things out first. But that's not how your brain works. You do your best work in the heat of the moment."

"Why didn't you stop me?"

"Cardinal knows I wanted to." He takes the canteen back and stores it in his saddle pack. "I'd do anything to keep you safe. But I'm not going to cage you up like the Cardinal and pretend that we can make everything perfect if I can only hold you tight enough."

Daniel grabs my hands, and I wish I could see his face clearer in the dark. I'm sure he's trying to be comforting, but this is not working.

"This is why you're here. Not just because you had the gall to question the Cardinal and not just because you seem able to rally an army with a few sentences. Your biggest weapon is your brain. You see things most of us don't."

"Like what? I'm going to need some more concrete examples to feel better."

"Like the Pony Express. It was running fine under Ana. Then you came in and took a look at the system and knew intuitively how to make it run faster and smarter. You didn't need years to slowly tweak a system to run better. You immediately saw the bigger issues and how fixing them would make the smaller pieces work better.

"Like how you knew when we got here what to send everyone off to do, even though you yourself had no idea what you could do to help."

"This is not a map with some trading posts on it, Daniel." I pick up a rock and hurl it into the forest around us. "These are real people who are in real danger."

"And I'm not worried."

Voices drift over from the others. "Well, maybe we need Doc to check your head when we get back, because you are making some questionable decisions today. First you agree to marry me...again, and now you think I'm some wartime general from the history books."

Daniel grabs me around the waist and pulls me in to whisper in my ear. "Marrying you will go down in the history books as the smartest decision any man ever made."

He plants a light kiss on my forehead, then pulls back to look me right in the eyes. "This is exactly why the Cardinal sent you to the PIT in the first place. You have a moral compass that demands to be followed and an ability to find solutions where others only see problems. It's time you start seeing yourself as the completely capable woman who stole my heart and terrifies the most powerful man alive."

I nod and pull his arms around me. For just a minute, I let myself relax into his embrace and forget that we're standing in the middle of the forest about to attack a contingency of armed Cardinal guards. Daniel is right. And even if he's not, we're still here and these people still need our help.

"The scouts are back." Daniel and I create some distance between our joined bodies as Liam comes around the corner. "Sorry guys, I know this isn't exactly an ideal honeymoon, but we need you back with the group."

Liam heads back toward the waiting scouts, but Daniel pulls me in for one last kiss. He breaks it off, his forehead leaning against mine. "That will have to do for now, but when we get back I plan to show you just how history book-worthy this marriage can be."

Thirty-One

Ethan draws a crude map in the dirt with a twig. Liam holds a light stick down by the ground so we aren't seen and everyone crowds around to get a look. "Looks like they are holding everyone in the main building."

"That's the dining hall," Mary cuts in. She hasn't stopped bouncing on her toes since all the scouts returned.

"Right. We checked out the other buildings on the main street and they are all silent. There is one guard in front of the dining hall. We can't tell how many are inside."

"Was he armed?" Daniel asks from his spot next to me.

"He had a gun. So much for the Cardinal's assurance that they were all destroyed."

I turn to Eric. "Did you know about the guns?"

"No, we only had shock sticks. He must only let his personal guard have them."

"We'll just have to figure out a way around that." I can't let everyone get discouraged before we even get started. "What else did you see?"

Carrie, the scout who went with Ethan, takes over. "While we were there, another guard came from a building over here." She draws an X to the north of the dining hall. "He went inside the dining hall, and we could hear some shouting. A few minutes later, he came out with a man whose hands were tied behind his back and head hung down in front. The guard was kinda dragging him, so I think he was hurt pretty bad. They went into this building." She taps the X.

"The schoolhouse." Mary can't control her nerves. Her hands shake worse than a leaf in a thunderstorm.

"Right." Another scout, Thad, takes over from Carrie. "There was another guard outside the schoolhouse. No idea how many inside. We were able to get pretty close." He pauses and rubs his hands along his neck. This isn't going to be good news.

"From the screams, I'd guess they are torturing them in there. They keep shouting your name over and over." Thad looks up at me with pity.

Daniel pulls me closer and steps back a bit from the map so we can expand the circle. "We have to assume the men in the schoolhouse haven't given up any information on Rebecca and the rest of us. If they had, the guards wouldn't still be here. We also have to assume that eventually one of them will break, so we need to move fast. The question is, how do we go in there against guns?"

I squat down and study the miniature map of the village. The layout is straight forward and doesn't offer any extra camouflage for us to go in unseen. The dining hall backs up to the forest, but that doesn't do us any good. We can't run in there without knowing what we're up against and we don't stand a chance against their weapons.

What we need is a way to draw them out individually until we can gain the upper hand. There is a tipping point, we just have to find it.

"Thad," the scout moves over to the side of the circle where I stand with Daniel and Liam. "You know the traps you set out in the woods and around the chicken coops? The ones you use for the larger animals, pigs and such. Do you think you can build one of those here? Do you have what you need?"

"Rope and a knife. I've got both in my saddle pack. What are you thinking?"

"I'm thinking I might be crazy, but crazy could be just what we need."

"I'll go get them." Thad hustles off to his horse, and Liam and Daniel close in.

"What's going on in that brain of yours?"

"I'm thinking they have us outmatched with their weapons. We might outnumber them, but we can't tell, and that's not something we can risk. We can't go in there and overwhelm them with mass force."

"So what do we do?" Liam keeps his voice low, but it's tinted with fear.

"We have to take them out one at a time. If we can disarm enough of them, we take the upper hand."

"And you think we can do that with one of Thad's traps?"

"That's phase one." I step out of our little threesome and back over to the main group. "Alright, everyone listen up. We have a lot of work to do and we need to move quickly while we still have darkness on our side. I have a plan."

Thirty-Two

"Are you guys sure you want to do this?"

Daniel and Thomas stand in front of me, their arms filled with pine cones, acorns, and rocks.

"It's your plan and someone has to do it." Daniel nudges my foot with the toe of his shoe and tries to pass off a weak smile.

"But do you have to be the ones potentially getting shot at?"

"Don't worry so much." Thomas looks at me with complete confidence. "Your plan is a good one. Everything is going to be fine."

"It had better be. Constance will kill me if I don't bring you back completely intact." I give him a peck on the damaged side of his face, and he moves off into position.

"It really is going to be fine."

"Really, Daniel? Is it really? Because I can think of at least three dozen ways this all goes horribly wrong, and in each of those scenarios you end up shot."

"Hey now—"

"Just promise me you won't get shot, okay?"

"Okay, I promise I will not get shot. Good?"

"Not even close, but I'll have to live with it." I reach up and give him a much more personal kiss than the one I gave Thomas. "Remember, disarm and capture only. Stay safe."

"I love you, too."

Daniel jogs off to join Thomas, and I have to move. Everyone is waiting on me.

"Mary, is the building clear and ready?"

The storage building next to the dining hall is the perfect place to watch my plan in action. I'll be able to see everything going on from the second story window.

"All clear."

"Perfect, now you and your team get back to Jacob's rocks. We need everyone as far away from here as possible and all hands on deck to keep the horses calm if any shots are fired."

She hesitates a minute, her eyes glued to the back door of the dining hall.

"Mary, we have a plan, and it's our best shot to get everyone out of there alive."

She gives the back door one more glance and heads deeper into the forest.

"Where's Thad?"

"Right here," he says from behind me. "The trap is set and ready. So long as they can lead the guard through here," he uses his hand to slice through a section of darkness between the buildings, "the trap should spring."

"There are a lot of variables in there, but I guess that's the best we can ask for." I squeeze his shoulder. "Thank you. Now get back with others."

Thad nods and heads into the pitch black forest. For a half second I'm alone, then Ethan walks out of the tree line.

"You ready?" he asks.

"For what? To risk the lives of a hundred or so people in Arbor Glen along with my husband of less than twenty-four hours and our new family on one of the craziest plans ever cooked up?" I shrug my shoulders. "Sure, why not?"

"In that case," he pulls open the back door to the storage building, "after you."

We make our way silently up the stairs and find the eastern window. Without any lights from the village, everything below is a solid mass of shades of black.

I wait a few minutes to make sure Mary and Thad both have time to get back to the main group.

"This is crazy, right?" I stare out the pitch black window and try not to envision all the ways this goes south.

"Oh yeah, completely nuts."

"Big help, Ethan." I shake out my hands. "I'm terrified."

"So what?"

"You know, for the guy who normally can't stop talking, you're not really giving me much here."

Ethan grabs my shoulders so I face him, though I can barely make out his outline in the dark. "I could try to talk you out of your fear, but we both know that would be a colossal waste of breath. Go ahead and be afraid. There's a lot on the line here." He gives my shoulders a quick squeeze. "Just don't let that fear hold you back."

I nod, though he can't see me. "Okay, give the signal."

Ethan leans out the open window and cups his hands around his mouth. If I weren't standing right next to him I'd swear there was a caged bird standing next to me instead of Ethan.

Even though I can't see them, I picture Daniel and Thomas scooting closer to the guard at the front porch. I keep my eyes trained on the front of the building watching for signs of movement.

I can't see anything, but I can hear it. At first, it's just the quiet mutterings of an angry guard, but as the attack of acorns continues, his voice grows louder. I hold my breath until finally he knocks on the front door. The pounding on wood echoes through the still night.

Another guard opens the door and a flood of light pours out. Their silhouettes have a conversation, but we're too far away to hear any of it.

They both step off the porch and head in the direction of the flying acorns and rocks. Crap, crap, crap. One guard we could trap and disarm, but how in the world are they going to handle two? There's only one trap and that means another fully armed guard able to shoot Daniel or Thomas.

They move out of the light of the building, and I'm blind again. Every once in a while I think I might see movement, but everything blends together in shadows.

I can't see or hear anything other than the shallow breathing of Ethan next to me. I grab at his arm. There is no abort signal. Once the plan went into motion, there was no way to stop it. I can't even warn them that everything is completely off course. I'm powerless to do anything but wait for the inevitable.

Someone shouts and then the silence is instantly replaced with way too much noise. Shouting and snapping branches and a bang, followed by more shouting. Ethan and I jump for the stairs at the same time. He beats me down and out the back door, but only by seconds.

"Daniel," I whisper his name into the pitch black as loud as I can. "Daniel, where are you?"

"Rebecca." Daniel's voice is off to my right, somewhere between the buildings.

"Daniel," I run in his direction and trip on a branch, landing face-first in the dirt.

Strong arms grab me around my upper arms and push me into the ground. "Stay down." Daniel's voice is gruff in my ear.

Ethan is at my side in seconds, followed quickly by Liam, who obviously ignored my instructions to wait at the rocks.

Daniel's breathing is heavy next to my ear. "Someone needs to go to Thomas. He went to check the trap, but he's out there alone."

"On it." Liam doesn't stop to ask questions. He moves, hunched over into the darkness until we can't see him anymore.

I lean in closer to Daniel. "Why didn't you go with Thomas?"

"You need to stay quiet until we know what is going on."

Something isn't right, but this isn't the time. If the second guard is still armed, the darkness is our only defense out here.

Footsteps crunch through the grass right toward us and I can make out four figures marching in our direction. Two in the front with hands up and two in back. I just can't tell which pair is which.

"Daniel, are you okay?"

Thomas and Liam walk up with guns trained on the backs of the guards' heads.

"I'm fine."

"What is going on?" I jump up and offer Daniel a hand. He sits up, but doesn't stand. "Daniel Whedon, I am your wife and you will tell me why you are on the ground instead of up here."

"Because the stupid jerk shot me."

"What?" I'm back on the ground before the word leaves my lips. "Where are you hit? Why didn't you say something?"

"I'm fine." He lifts his hand away from a spot on his leg and it comes away shiny in the minimal moon light. "I think the bullet just grazed my leg."

I don't know if I should hug him or punch him. "What part of getting shot makes you fall into the 'fine' category of wellness?"

"Rebecca, we don't have time for this." Liam's voice is steady, though I don't know how. "We need to get out of sight and regroup."

He's right. I bend down and force Daniel to put his arm around my shoulders. Using his good leg, we leverage up until he's mostly standing. "We're right behind you."

Liam and Thomas take the lead, pushing their captured guards back toward the rest of our group waiting by the horses. Ethan and I follow with Daniel hobbling between us to keep from putting pressure on his injured leg.

Back with the group, two guys jump up and tie the guards as soon as it's clear what happened. Ethan and I maneuver Daniel over to a clear spot beside a boulder and ease him down to the forest floor. "Ethan, can you get some water?"

"I'll be right back."

"Elizabeth."

"Right here." She kneels down next to us. "What happened?"

"We need a med kit."

"On it."

She runs off, and I turn my attention back to Daniel. In the dim glow of a light stick, I get my first look at the wound. There's so much blood I can't even see it. I swallow to keep the panic from my voice.

"Alright, tough guy. These pants have to come off."

"Is it too soon to make an anxious bride honeymoon joke?"

I give him the best glare I can muster. "I suggest you keep that to yourself unless you want a matching hole in your other leg."

"Yeah, too soon."

Elizabeth comes back with Eric just as I get Daniel's pants down around his ankles.

"Just couldn't wait—"

"Don't make me kill you while my husband lies bleeding on the ground."

"Right." Elizabeth has the decency to look slightly remorseful.

"Let's take a look." Eric comes around her with the medical kit in hand.

He takes the small light stick and dumps a whole canteen of water on Daniel's leg. The wound seeps blood as soon as he stops pouring. Eric moves the skin a bit with his thumb and Daniel lets out a sharp hiss.

"It's not good." Eric reaches into the kit and moves a few things around. "The bullet is still in there. It needs to come out, but if I try to do it out here without the right tools I might cause more damage. Best I can do is clean it and stitch it until this is over and I can get you on a real operating table."

"What can I do?" My eyes never leave the little hole in his leg, still flowing with blood.

"Go unhitch some of the reins from the horses. Three would be good."

"I'll help." Elizabeth lifts me up by my shoulders.

Once I'm on my feet, my brain clicks on again, and we rush to the horses. It'll take too long to undo all the ties and buckles. I grab a knife out of my saddle bag and slash through the straps. Elizabeth does the same and we have what we need in only a few minutes.

Back where Daniel lies bleeding, Thomas holds several light sticks strategically over Daniel's leg while Eric preps his equipment.

Eric grabs one of the leather straps and ties it around Daniel's thigh above the wound. Daniel jerks against the pain, but the flow of blood from the bullet slows down immediately.

"Thomas, can you loop one of these around that branch there?" Eric points to a thick limb above Daniel's head. "Test it to see if it can handle your weight." He takes the last strap and cuts a piece about six inches long.

"Are you sure about this?" Now that I'm standing still again, panic creeps back into my chest.

"Nope, but it's the best I can do out here." He turns back to Daniel. "Take the ends of the strap above your head and pull those against the pain. I'll warn you, it's going to hurt like the fiery blazes."

"I lived with your sister for three years, so I'm comfortable with torture."

"You're injured so I'm going to let that go." Elizabeth grinds her fist into the palm of her other hand, but winks down at Daniel. "For now."

"Alright, hold still and try not to scream while I get this disinfected."

"Do I look like some kind of—sweet mother of the Cardinal, kill me now."

Eric moves with speed to dab at the wound with whatever was in the bottle. "Open up and bite on this." Daniel accepts the short leather piece and clenches down with his jaw.

"Thomas, sit on his ankles here to keep his legs still." Eric wipes down a needle with the same liquid he used to clean Daniel's leg. "Girls, hold his shoulders back as much as you can, but watch out for elbows. Once I start, he's going to jerk and we don't want any broken noses."

We all move into position, but our eyes stay glued to the needle. With a practiced hand, he pulls Daniel's skin together and places the first stitch. Daniel convulses against our hold and the tree branch creeks where the leather strap hangs over it. I look away so I don't have to see Daniel grimace from the pain. Three more times, Daniel spasms against my hands. Even with the leather gripped between his teeth, his screams tear at my heart.

"Okay, that's enough." Eric sets the needle down and presses a clean square of gauze over the wound. He wraps some stretchy cloth around that before sitting back and wiping his wrist across his forehead.

Daniel's arms drop from the leather strap and he spits the piece out of his mouth. "Thank you." His voice comes out breathy.

He's covered in a layer of sweat. I wipe his face with the bottom of my shirt and wish there was more I could do.

"That will keep it clean until we can get back and have Doc look at it." Eric closes the kit and stands up. "You need to stay off it so you don't cause any more damage."

Elizabeth and I ease his pants back up while the pain is still on edge. Better to get it all over with now than drag out the agony.

"Stay here." I lean in and kiss him on the forehead. "You promised me I never have to be alone again so don't you dare die on me now. Understand?"

Daniel nods, though his lips are pressed into a thin line. His eyes close, and it only takes a few seconds before he's out.

A few yards away Liam is standing in front of the captured guards, his bow swapped out for one of their guns.

Eric grabs my arm before I make it over to Liam. "We have to speed this up."

"But you stopped the bleeding, right?"

"I fixed what I could see." Eric puffs out a slow breath. "I have no idea what kind of damage that bullet might have done inside."

I nod and run over to Liam. The faster we get this done, the faster Daniel gets what he needs.

"Rebecca," Liam says, without taking his eyes off the guards, "is Daniel okay?"

"Eric has him patched up as best he can out here, but he needs us to hurry up. What's the story with these two?"

Liam nods at the tied up guards. "They refuse to tell us if there are any more guards inside. I would think they would have come running with that gunshot if there was anyone in there."

"But we can't assume there isn't. We need to get in there."

"Any suggestions?"

I survey the camp. Our arsenal is up now from a few bows to include two guns. We still have the manpower. We can do this, but it needs to be now before someone comes looking for our guards. And we need to do it without drawing the attention of the guards at the schoolhouse.

"You and Ethan take the guns and go in through the front." I point to the edge of the forest at the unseen destination. "I need the two best shooters to go in the back with loaded bows. If you go at the same time, it should disorient any guards still inside long enough to take the advantage. The rest of us will be right outside with bows, ready to charge in at the first sign of trouble."

"Simple, but effective. I like it. We should be good to go in five minutes." Liam runs off to find Ethan and the others.

"Hey, how are you holding up, princess?"

"Me?" I turn to Elizabeth even though I can barely see her. "Swell, really. Great even. You know, just leading a military coup while my freshly minted husband watches on with a gunshot wound. I'd say pretty typical day, all and all."

"Good." She punches me lightly on the arm. "I was a little worried you might crack under the pressure."

"Crack? No, that would be for people who have no idea what they're doing."

"Rebecca." Ethan comes running up putting an end to our conversation. "Liam wants to see you."

Thirty-Three

"Are you guys ready to go?"

Liam stands in a small grouping with several others.

"Ethan and I are taking the front with the guns. Jeremy and Mary are going in the back with bows."

"Mary? Are you sure about that? She hasn't slept in at least a day and the emotional toll—"

"I'm sure I'm the best shot in this village or any other."

I hold up my hands in surrender. "Alright then. We'll all be right outside the back door waiting."

What else is there to say? 'Good luck' feels weak, like something you say to someone hoping to snag the last of Carol's rolls at dinner. They all look to me, but I've got nothing. I nod at Liam, and that's all it takes.

The armed foursome splits into two groups, and they head for opposite ends of the dining hall. The rest of those brave enough to come with me on this ridiculous mission crowd behind me at the edge of the forest. The night is silent, but deadly loud at the same time. All around me dead leaves crunch as small animals scurry along the forest floor in search of their next meal. Crickets and frogs sound against each other like competing sections of an orchestra. And not far from here, the river rushes over rocks and sand.

From the front of the building, a flash of light pierces the darkness. The signal from Ethan that they're ready to go in. I hold my breath and wait for subtle noises to fill the night.

Boots on wooden planks, a door creeping open, shouts from inside the building.

A bang, just like before, breaks through every other sound. Another gunshot.

"Archers with me." Everyone with a bow jogs behind me as I make a path straight for the back door. I'm a few steps away and the door opens. I freeze and from the corner of my eye, the archers lift their bows to aim.

"Weapons down." I run up the stairs to the back door. "Mary, who's shot?"

"No, it wasn't us. We thought you guys were found."

"We're all fine."

"The schoolhouse."

She doesn't have to explain. If the gunshots didn't come from them or us, there's only one other place in town, and that sound can't possibly be good news.

"We're going to get them. Are you clear in here?"

Mary snaps her head back from staring off into space. "Yeah, there was only one more guard, and he gave up the second we came in."

I run back out to the tree line and hustle the rest of our group inside. Eric and Thomas carry Daniel between them. His face has lost its vibrancy, turning his dark skin almost gray. He needs Doc, but that has to wait for now. I follow them inside and pull the door tight behind me.

The room is packed with people. Some of them huddle on the floor in small groups while others move about, asking anyone and everyone what's going on. It's chaotic and way too loud.

I jump up on the bench behind me and cup my hands around my mouth. "Attention."

At my shout, the din quiets down and everyone turns to me.

"I know you are all scared and worried right now, and you probably have a million questions. But we need to keep the noise down so we don't draw the attention of the other guards." Several faces in the crowd pale at the mention of more guards coming back. "We're going to do everything we can to keep each of you safe, but we need to move quickly and don't have time for questions. For now, I need everyone to go have a seat, and please keep your voices down." They all stare at me expectantly, but I don't have anything else to say. "Okay, then. Uh, thank you."

I jump off the bench and quickly shake hands with a few people standing nearby. I nod at a few others and then move away from the group. We don't have time for niceties.

"Liam." I push my way to the front of the room where he's standing with Ethan and a few others. "What's the plan?"

"The schoolhouse only has one entrance, and there are a ton of windows by the door that would leave us completely exposed. This plan won't work over there."

"Think, think." I step away for a second, pounding my fists against my head. There has to be a way to get in there. "Okay, talk to me about the building."

"It's old," Mary chimes in. "We let it sit for a long time, but the older kids needed their own room for school. They've only been in there a few months."

"Okay, that's a start. What else?" I pace a bit to keep my brain moving. What I really need is a nap, but there's no time for that. "Was it remodeled inside or left alone?"

"They didn't do too much to it. Fixed a hole in the ceiling and sealed up the windows. They just got the new parts for the furnace installed last week so we'll be ready for winter."

"Wait. The furnace. You're sure it's working now?"

"I don't think they fired it up. The ducts need cleaning first, but the guys working the crew seemed pretty confident."

"Ah ha, that's it." I stop pacing and spin around the room. "Where's Thomas?"

I don't wait for a response and take off down the hall. He's parked on a bench munching on a piece of bread and watching over Daniel's sleeping form.

"Thomas." I sit down next to him and pinch off a piece of his bread. It's stale, but better than nothing. "Is there a way to activate a furnace without using the switch on the home control panel?"

"What are you talking about?"

"The furnace in the schoolhouse. They just got it working but haven't cleaned the ducts yet. You told Daniel about clearing the systems of debris. I want to flush out the guards, but I need to turn the system on from the outside."

Understanding flashes in his eyes. "Someone would have to shimmy under the building if they can. It'll be a tight fit. Most of these buildings have a manual override panel hidden under the house just in case all the programming goes wonky."

"And I could use the override to start the furnace."

"No, but someone else could. Daniel would kill me if I let you get into trouble."

"Someone else small enough to wedge themselves under a building and activate an ancient heater?" I stare at him until he's forced to meet my eyes. "It has to be me and we both know it. Daniel can't protect me from everything. Now tell me what to look for."

"It will be an open metal box, maybe with a door, maybe not. Inside, you'll find switches that are hopefully labeled. If not, then get out of there because your only option is to try every switch until you get the right one and that will give you away instantly."

"So which ones do I turn on?"

"Look for something labeled either CUH or EUH. You'll need to flip one of those on, plus check to make sure the fan is on. Otherwise the debris will leak out and barely cause a stir, let alone send them running in panic."

"Anything else?"

"Don't go." A now awake Daniel lifts up on his elbow and grabs my arm with his free hand. "I'm a selfish, overprotective husband."

"Rebecca." Liam comes up from behind me. "We need to get moving. The sky is already starting to turn a little pink."

I kiss Daniel on the forehead and lean in until our noses meet. "I have to do this, and the sooner, the better."

I pull away and walk with Ethan to where the others are waiting. "Okay, we have a plan. It's not exactly air tight, but it will have to do." I look around the room bustling with quiet activity. "Where's Jeremy?"

"Right here," he calls out from behind Mary.

"Perfect, listen up, everyone. The ventilation system of the schoolhouse hasn't been cleaned out yet. Thomas walked me through how to activate the furnace from under the building. Hopefully, I can get it going full blast and the whole place will fill with dust, sending them running for the front door."

"So we're going to flush them out?" Liam asks.

"Exactly. There's only one way in or out so we know exactly where they'll come running."

"And we'll be ready." Mary hoists up her gun like she's ready to storm a castle.

"To disarm." I push the tip of her gun back toward the ground and pause while I catch the eye of each of the shooters. "We need information about what the Cardinal is planning, and we can't question dead men."

"What happens if the furnace doesn't kick them out?" Ethan shifts next to me.

"Once the furnace fires up, they'll know something is going on. They're coming out no matter what. The question is if they'll come out ready for us or not. We won't know until the door opens."

"No way." Liam grabs the gun from Jeremy and reaches for Mary's. "I'm not putting the rest of you at risk. I'll stand out front and take care of whatever comes out."

"Over my pile of smoking ashes." Mary pulls her gun out of reach. "We have no idea how many guards are in there. If they come out with a heads up, you're a dead man walking."

"Better to have one dead man than four." Liam matches her glare, and the family resemblance between them has never been more obvious. Same green eyes, same wrinkled nose, same stubbornness.

"Okay, how about a compromise?" I push them apart to force an end to their staring match. "What if Liam stays in front of the building. Slightly out of sight, but with a clear view of the door. The rest of you can wait on the sides of the building and get a lock on the guards from behind after they come out."

"That still puts Liam in the most danger. Alone." Mary stares at me like there must be more to the plan, but that's all I've got.

"Someone has to be out front to keep them from running back here." Liam reaches around me to grab Mary's arm. "We have to put the village first."

Mary nods and Liam nods back at her.

"Let's go then."

Thirty-Four

The walk to the schoolhouse takes forever. Even though the building isn't that far away from the dining hall, we have to go around the village so we can approach from behind. By now, the pink rays of the sun are growing, though it's still dark thanks to all the trees. We have to hurry or we'll lose the benefit of surprise. The guards could go back to the dining hall for another torture victim at any time.

As soon as we get to the back of the schoolhouse, I don't waste a second. It takes a minute, but I find a board along the base of the building loose enough to pry off.

Ethan helps me with another one to make a bigger hole. I grab his light and I'm diving under.

"Rebecca."

"What is it, Liam? I need to go."

"I know." He scratches the back of his neck. "I just want you to know, no matter what happens, in case I don't make it, I'm really proud of you. Ana would be, too."

I can't have this conversation with him, not right now. I have to focus. "Listen for the system to kick on."

I dive back under the building before he can call me back.

There isn't enough room in the crawl space to stay on my hands and knees. I drop down onto my stomach and slither deeper in. I have no idea how far in the electric box will be, so I have to keep stopping and rolling over onto my back to check the ceiling.

The sounds of Ethan, Liam, and the others can't reach me down here, but everything going on above me is amplified.

No one says a word, but there is a lot of movement. Someone with a heavy shoe, like a boot is right above me now. They are walking in a little three foot circle, changing direction every couple of laps.

Whoever it is, is highly agitated, and that can't be good.

Two more sets of feet come close. One is a clipped pace, but the other might as well be dragging their feet. I have to keep moving.

"Where is she?"

"I don't know who you're talking about."

"Yes, you do." A chair scrapes across the wooden floor and sends a shower of dust down onto my face. "Rebecca Collins. She was here, and we know it."

It hits me, lying on my back in the dirt, under a schoolhouse. That person they are looking for, Rebecca Collins, doesn't exist anymore.

Rebecca Collins was a naive little girl who spent her whole life cowering behind an overbearing mother. Rebecca Collins wanted nothing more than to follow the rules and go along with the plan, even if she knew it was flawed. Rebecca Collins was ready to accept that she was some kind of deranged monster, just because someone else told her it was true.

Rebecca Whedon isn't any of those things. And not just because I married Daniel, though picking a husband without her mother's approval is definitely outside of Rebecca Collins' approved activities. I'm not that girl anymore because I choose to be better than that. I can be whoever I want to be, and right now I choose not to be a coward.

I roll over onto my belly and use my arms to pull myself across the ground. I have to be getting close to the center of the building. My neck aches from holding it at such a weird angle. I need to finish this fast.

Another few feet and I roll over, holding the light stick at an angle above me so none of the light seeps through the floor above. Nothing.

I roll back over and out of the corner of my eye, something dangles down in the darkness. Please let that be it.

I slither over several feet to my right and something hits me in the face. I flash on my light and let out a soft exhale. I found the box, but my heart is stuck in my throat.

Wires are everywhere, some of them connected, others dangling into the dirt, useless.

About like I'm feeling right now. If Daniel were here he could sort this all out in less than a minute. I am not Daniel, but my choices are pretty limited to fixing the panel or running away like a scared dog. Since option B includes watching a lot of innocent people beaten and killed, I have to figure this out.

I slide over until I'm right under the panel and peel back some of the wires. I need to find the right switches before I can even think about fixing anything.

The fan switch is on the side of the unit and there aren't any exposed wires near it. I have to assume it works okay, but only because I don't have any options if it doesn't. The CUH toggle is harder to find, but it's there, just like Thomas said it would be. There is one wire near it that is loosely wrapped around an exposed metal prong.

The connection looks shoddy at best. I twist the metal around with dirty fingers and mold it until it's butted up against the prong. I shine the light on all the other disconnected wires. What do I do? If I try to put them back, but put them in the wrong place, I could blow the whole system up.

I don't have many options other than firing it up and seeing what happens. I flip the switch and nothing happens. I toggle the CUH switch and hold my breath.

Nothing but more shouting from above. There must be another more central line that isn't where it should be. After everything we've done to get this far, we're stuck. Because I can't get the furnace to kick on.

I feel like I'm back in the PIT listening to Daniel explain all the inner workings of the Cardinal's system and how he was hacking into the system. I get that there are wires that should be connected, but that's where my understanding runs out.

I could attach wires to the various tabs until the sun is at high noon and still not be any closer to getting this system running. Plus, I risk setting everything on fire. I can't waste any more time. I'll have to crawl back out and come up with a new plan. We could storm through the front door and hope for the best, but that almost guarantees someone else ends up with a bullet hole. We could wait until they come out of the building to get another torture victim, but who knows how many lives would be lost before then.

I spin around until my head is facing the back of the building and roll back over. I stop myself before I'm fully on my stomach and let my back sink into the dirt. What are the chances?

Right above me, several wires twist together and connect with a metal capsule at the end. Each of the wires is a different color, different from all the black of the other box. This has to be important.

I run my fingers along the edge of the box until I hit an indent that feels like it could hold the metal connector. Please let this work. I wedge the light between my chin and shoulder and guide the connection of wires over to where my index finger holds the spot. When something isn't working, Daniel blows on it. Might as well stick with what works. I blow all the air in my lungs on the wires and stick the metal connector into the slot.

Lights on the panel go crazy flashing green and red over and over again. Somewhere in the building, the furnace kicks to life with a soft moan followed by the steady thrum of an engine.

The voices above me change from shouts and orders to confusion. More people moving, walking from room to room. I lay my head back in the dirt and close my eyes. My heart beats out a frantic pace and pounds against my ribcage. Please work. Please work. Please work.

Coughing joins the noise upstairs, and it's the sweetest sound I've heard in a long time. I squeeze my eyes tighter and picture the room above me filling with dust and debris. The shouting picks up again and pounding feet all rush toward the door. Please let Liam and the others be ready to move.

The door squeaks open and shouts tumble into the early morning.

"Freeze. Hands in the air." Liam's voice is unmistakable.

More shouting and the sounds of heavy objects hitting the ground. I have to hope those are the guards' weapons and not ours. The voices are indistinguishable now, between those shouting orders and those yelling profanities.

The shouts deaden. Gags. Whoever lost their weapons just lost their voice as well.

"Split up. Ethan, head inside and get everyone out. Jeremy, run back and let the others know we're okay." Liam. Liam is calling out orders.

Warmth fills my chest and spreads down my arms and up into my face. We did it. It's over and no one dies. I press a steady hand to my heart and open my eyes, staring at the now empty floor above me.

I roll back over onto my belly and work my way to the opening. My legs are useless noodles behind me, and wiggling out of the crawlspace is harder than it was wiggling in. Without all that adrenaline pumping through my veins, pulling myself across the damp soil with only my arms is harder than it was a few minutes ago.

I push my way out of the opening and stop, leaning on my knees to suck in deep breaths of fresh air.

"Rebecca!"

My head jerks up. Patrice runs straight at me with Eric right behind her. "What are you doing here? You're supposed to be back at Allmore with the others."

"She stole a horse and followed us here." Eric stands with his arms crossed, glaring at Patrice.

Patrice wraps her arms around him and Eric relents into the hug. "What was I supposed to do, just sit there and wait for all of you to come back? Or not come back?"

She turns around to face me and the look of love on her face makes her look even more like Daniel. I'm not sure if I should slap her or hug her. Daniel would probably do both.

"Once upon a time you told me that there would come a day when you all would become my family and I'd be glad to be stuck out here with all of you." Patrice lets go of Eric and grabs my hand. "You were right. This is my family, and families stick together."

I pull her into a hug and Eric wraps his arms around both of us. All that's missing is Daniel. I sink into the relief of everyone being safe for another minute and then let go and switch into command mode.

"Alright Eric, I want you to find Marcus and get that bullet out of Daniel's leg now. Patrice, stick with me so I can make sure you stay out of trouble. I need to find Liam so we can get out of here and back to the rest of our family."

* * *

I push open the door to Alan's house without knocking. When you save someone's life, I guess there's less of a need to follow formalities.

"Rebecca." Liam gestures from his seat in a formal cushioned chair. "Come on in. Have a seat. Alan was just about to fill me in on what happened."

Alan glances up from his chair and I cover a gasp with my hand. He's aged ten years since I last saw him. Margaret sits next to him, her arm looped through his as if she's ready to fight wild lions to keep him safe.

I ignore them for now and turn to Liam. "How is everyone?"

Liam leans back in his chair and pinches the bridge of his nose. "Scared, shocked, mourning. I'm not sure they know how to feel."

I take a seat on the couch opposite Alan. He's exhausted, like the rest of us, but we need to know what happened before we can plan our next move. "Tell us what happened."

Alan stares at me with bloodshot eyes, his face unreadable. "It was a normal night. We were all done with dinner and everyone was getting ready to call it a night. I was still in the dining hall talking with Dan about a project he's working on." Alan shakes from a chill. "It all happened so fast. One minute we were sitting around just like this, and the next minute Mary comes racing in screaming about guards finding her."

"Why would the Cardinal send so few men out to attack?" Liam sounds more frustrated than curious.

"I'm guessing they were a scouting mission, but running into Mary forced them to act or risk us not being here when they got back with reinforcements."

Liam nods. "Then what?"

"We were powerless to fight against them. They had guns and our bows were all put away. It's not like we expect violence on a daily basis." He pats Margaret's arm and keeps going. "Once they had everyone inside, they grabbed me and several other men, and hauled us over to the schoolhouse. They tried to torture information out of us."

"Information about me?"

Alan's eyes meet mine and he doesn't have to say it. "When the torture didn't work, they started shooting."

"How many?" I don't want to know, but I need to. I need to know how many more deaths the Cardinal is responsible for.

"Five. Five brave men who will be remembered for their sacrifice. Everyone will want to have a release for them before we leave."

"We don't have time, but we'll make time for this. Did you learn anything from them? Do they know the location of the other villages? Are more guards coming?"

"No, they didn't say anything to us. Liam, I'm so sorry." Alan leans forward and reaches for his son's hand. Liam pulls back, and Alan has to settle for patting his knee. "I was wrong. About Ana and all the other Rejects. I let the Cardinal poison my thoughts all the way out here, and if I could go back and change it I would."

"Did you tell the other villages to stop trading with us?" It's so inconsequential right now, but I have to know the truth about this man who we all just risked our lives to save.

"Yes, but only because I wanted you to come home." Alan stares at Liam, tears making his red eyes even worse. "I thought if enough villages refused to trade with you, you'd be forced to give up on Allmore and come home. Even Ana."

"Well, that's not going to happen, because Ana is dead." Liam jumps up and wrenches open the front door. "I have my team loading up supplies from your storehouses. Mary and I are working on the exit strategy to get everyone out of here. I'll see you in Allmore."

The four us of sit in silence as Liam stomps down the front porch and off into the village.

"I never meant for any of this…" Alan stares at the door, his shoulders hunched and his face blank.

There's nothing else to do here. I grab Patrice's arm and stand up. Margaret catches my eye and nods at the same time she tightens her grip on Alan's arm. They need so much healing, but at least they have each other.

I nod my thanks and we head back out into the village. There are people moving about everywhere, but the cheerful banter and ease of everyday life is gone. For the moment, Arbor Glen is stripped of its happiness.

I shake my head at the stark difference. "I can't imagine what he's going through."

"Are we talking about Alan or Liam?"

"Both." I thread my arm through Patrice's. "Alan was so desperate to win his son back, but he couldn't just admit that he was wrong. Now Liam pretty much hates him. Then poor Liam. All those years without speaking to his father, wanting to prove himself so bad. But no one wants to be right like this."

"I miss my dad. I wish I could have told him how much he means to me one last time."

I've been so wrapped up in my own world, I never stopped to ask Patrice how she was handling the news of her father's disappearance. "Don't give up hope yet. I haven't."

She nods. "Okay."

I nod back, but I don't have any confidence in my own words. Now I know just how far the Cardinal is willing to go to maintain his delicate hold on control and power. I've been officially missing for months now. Maybe he can feel the rule of his little domain of force-fed perfection slipping from his fingers. A man like that doesn't let a member of his inner circle break out alive.

But the Cardinal is getting reckless.

Thirty-Five

"How is he doing?"

The lobby of Marcus's office is packed with people waiting to be treated for their injuries. Eric stands from where he was wrapping a woman's ankle in stretchy gauze.

"Better now." He grabs Patrice and wraps her in a firm hug. "Marcus got the bullet out and repaired the torn muscle. He's going to have a long recovery, but he'll be okay."

"Can we see him?" It's not that I don't believe Eric, but I need to see Daniel with my own eyes.

"He's probably still out from the anesthesia, but you can wait with him if you want."

Patrice looks up into Eric's eyes. "Can you come with us?"

"Let me finish here, and I'll come back in a minute, okay?"

Patrice nods, and he kisses her gently. My chest warms a bit at seeing the two of them together. They deserve to find some happiness.

Eric turns back to his patient. Patrice loops her arm through mine and we push through the door to the back rooms of the infirmary.

Daniel is asleep on a bed in the back. An old-fashioned machine beeps out a steady rhythm, like a heartbeat, and harsh lights cast his skin in yellow hues.

Marcus walks over after checking on another patient. The room is packed with beds. "He'll be waking up soon and probably in a lot of pain. I don't have IV meds for him so I can't give him anything until he can swallow a pill."

I nod and grab Daniel's hand. His palm is warm against mine. I thought it would be cold, so the warmth is reassuring. "Eric says you got the bullet out."

Marcus lifts Daniel's other hand and pushes two fingers against his wrist to check his pulse. "It wasn't too deep, but it did some serious damage on the way in. It'll be a while before he can walk, and he might always have a bit of a limp."

"So long as he keeps breathing, the rest we can live with."

Marcus nods and sets Daniel's hand back on the bed. He punches something into his Noteboard and adjusts his shirt, avoiding meeting my gaze.

"I...I want to say thank you." Marcus's eyes flicker to mine before looking away again. "Rumor has it you were the one who argued for coming back to help us. After the welcome you got here…well, you certainly didn't owe us anything."

Daniel stirs on the bed and lets out a low moan.

"Daniel?" I grip his hand a little tighter.

"Take it easy." Marcus pulls a bottle of pills out of his pocket and grabs a glass of water from a nearby table.

Daniel's eyes flutter open, and his hand grips mine tight enough to hurt. "Cardinal on a cracker." He hisses the words out between clenched teeth.

"Here we go," Marcus says, holding a small pill to Daniel's mouth. "Swallow this before we do anything else. It should kick in pretty fast."

Daniel opens his mouth and takes the pill without any water. He grits his teeth and closes his eyes against the harsh lights.

"I need to check on a few other patients, but I'll be back in a bit." Marcus picks up his Noteboard and heads over to another row of beds.

Patrice stares at Daniel's tense body, her arms shaking from holding back tears. I give her arm a quick squeeze with my free hand. She grips my wrist like I'm her last lifeline. We stand there, all of us joined together, and wait in silence for the pain meds to give Daniel some relief.

Less than ten minutes later, Daniel's jaw unclenches and his breathing evens out. His eyes blink open again, and this time he's able to look around and focus on Patrice and I still holding each other tightly.

"How are my two favorite girls?"

My held breath releases in a chuckle. Patrice's tension escapes as a single sob. Daniel tries to smile at both of us, but it comes across as more of a grimace.

"Daniel." Tears streak down Patrice's face as she lets go of me and throws herself across Daniel's chest. "I'm so sorry."

"Whoa, what's this all about?" Daniel lets go of my hand so he can wrap up Patrice and pat her back while she cries all over him.

"I was awful to you and Rebecca and everyone and all I did was complain about everything and try to make everyone else as miserable as I was after all you did was find me a safe place to live and try to make me happy." She sucks in a deep breath and lets it go in another sob.

"All I ever wanted was for you to be happy."

Patrice stands back up and wipes her nose. "I am."

Eric pushes through the door and walks over to our gathering. "Look who's awake." He nods at Daniel, but marches straight to Patrice and wipes her tears away with the edge of his sleeve.

Patrice looks back at Daniel and smiles with watery eyes.

"I should apologize, too." Daniel reaches out and grabs my hand again. "When I left for the PIT, you were still a little girl who needed her big brother to take care of her. But you grew up while I was gone, and it took me a while to realize it."

"I will always need you."

"Good, because I don't intend to stop being your big brother. I'll always be there." Daniel lifts his eyebrow at

Eric's arm draped over her shoulder. "And that includes screening boyfriends."

"Daniel…" I shoot him a look that I hope comes across as 'tread carefully.'

"Fine," he huffs out. "Eric passes."

Patrice laughs, and Eric tightens his hold on her. I close my eyes and laugh along with her. This right here is worth fighting for.

Daniel yawns and fails at covering it with a hand.

"You need sleep." I lean down and kiss him as gently as I can. "Try to rest while you can. Hopefully, we'll have everyone ready to head home soon."

"Okay, but you have to promise me something first."

"Anything."

"Can you go scope out the tech room and see what we can take with us?"

"Barely out of surgery and already itching to get your hands on some gears and wires." I give him another quick peck on the cheek, then shoo Patrice and Eric out of the room. "Now I know you'll be just fine."

* * *

Patrice and I push our way into the supply room, right where Margaret said we'd find it. My heart aches at the sight. Daniel would love this. The room isn't big, but every inch of it is filled with more electronics than I've ever seen. It reminds me a bit of Daniel's room back in the PIT. It has the same smell, like an Airtrain engine. The difference comes in the details. Where everything in the PIT was thrown around and mostly in a state of disrepair, this place is as organized as my mother's closet. All the equipment is labeled and sorted, with the tools perfectly clean and hung up for easy reach.

"I'm not really sure what to take." I look around and grab a mostly empty box from a bottom shelf. "Put anything important-looking in here. Just remember we have to be able to carry this all home. Any idea what Daniel wants?"

"Do you know what you want?"

I drop the box on a bench. "What are you talking about?"

"About this." She waves her hands around the room, but she's not talking about a storage room. "Have you even taken a second to think about what you did here?"

"No, and I don't plan to." I turn away and fiddle with a stack of wires on a shelf. This is not a conversation I want to have. "We came in and did what needed to be done. And now we are going to go home to live our lives. That's what Daniel and Elizabeth and everyone else keep telling me. My defiance is living a life the Cardinal never wanted me to have."

"And what if they were all wrong?"

Nope, not doing this. "Is this copper?" I spin with a bundle of wiring in my hand. "I think I heard Thomas mention we could use some more of this."

I put the wire in the box and move a few more items around, though I'm not really seeing anything. All I can focus on are Patrice's words.

"Rebecca." Her hand reaches out to stop my fidgeting arms. "Daniel might think you need his constant protection, but I know better. I've watched you these past few months and you're stronger than you give yourself credit for."

"I can't do this. I can't be two different people." I push away to the other side of the room. "I used to want to fight back, but I can't do that. I can't hang on to that anger and hatred in one hand and keep loving everyone else with the other."

"So, that's it." She lounges on a bench with her arms casually draped behind her like nothing is wrong. "You and Daniel can just head back to Allmore, set up shop in your new house, and pretend like nothing happened?"

"Yes, and that sounds perfect to me."

"And what will we do when the Cardinal comes looking for you in Allmore? What will it do to Daniel when the Cardinal finds you?"

I shake my head back and forth. I don't want to think about any of this. I deserve a break. I deserve to have some happiness and a chance to live my life without looking over my shoulder waiting for the Cardinal to come after me.

The more I think about it, the angrier I get. I played his game and did everything I was supposed to. I followed all the rules and then he sent me to the PIT. Because I'm dangerous. Because I have the audacity to question. But I'm not trying to question him anymore. I just want to be forgotten.

I sweep my hand across a shelf and knock everything to the floor. It feels good. I reach up and knock another shelf clear. And another. I turn around and grab a heavy box off a bench, hurling it at the wall. I use all the strength in my arms to crash something bulky against the door. It smashes to pieces and showers the room in bits of plastic and metal.

Patrice doesn't move from her perch. "Oh, are you angry now? Ready to stop pretending like this little altercation here was the end of it?"

"It's not fair. I just want a chance like everyone else." I pull my hands back and run them through my hair. "The Cardinal turned me into some poster child for the PIT to save his expansion deals, but now the council won't let it go. As long as he's in power, I'll never be safe. You'll never be safe. We can never have our happily ever after."

"So what does that mean?" She leans forward, resting her elbows on her knees. "What do you want to do?"

The Cardinal is never going to stop. He can't. If he doesn't bring me to justice in front of the Territories, the council is going to force him out of power. Oh, they'll let him retire to save face, but he'll go down in the history books as the first Cardinal to allow a Reject to escape from the PIT. Everything he's done will be just a footnote to this huge mistake. Any man who would send a council member's daughter to the PIT out of spite will never accept that kind of future.

As long as the Cardinal is in power, I can't be safe and neither can Daniel or anyone else within three feet of me. I have two choices. And what I want doesn't have anything to do with them. I can keep running, hide from village to village. Or I can fight back.

"The Cardinal and his Machine Rejected me because I'm a threat. If he wants a threat, he's got one."

I pick up the empty box again and hand it to Patrice. "Can you pick out supplies for Daniel? I need to talk to Liam."

"Sure, but—"

A sharp bang rings out. I flinch at the sound. By now, I know exactly what that was, and it can't possibly be good.

Thirty-Six

I'm out the door before Patrice can move off the bench. Outside, everyone is packed together toward the end of the road, the horses loaded up and ready to go. Thomas and Eric have Daniel strapped into a cart tied behind a horse. They are all frozen mid-motion, staring at the schoolhouse. I freeze, too. That's where the guards are being held. Shouting pours through the walls of the building, and I know the voice instantly. She's yelled at me enough times that it couldn't be anyone else.

Liam and I both make a run for the door at the same time. Two men from Arbor Glen run out of the schoolhouse, the door flapping open behind them.

I sprint up the stairs and rush back to the room where the guards are supposed to be. Elizabeth stands like a soldier in front of them, each one gagged and tied to a chair. A gun raised above her head points straight at the ceiling, now complete with a bullet hole.

"Elizabeth, what are you doing?"

"Taking care of this." She turns to me, and there's something new in her eyes. A hardness I've never seen. Not even after Molly was killed.

I wave a hand back at Liam to keep him from coming in the room. Elizabeth isn't going to hurt me. "Okay, let's talk about that."

"There's nothing to talk about." Her voice is flat. No anger, no sadness. Just fact. "They killed Molly, and now they need to pay."

The guards shift in their seats, but there's no way they can escape.

"These men didn't kill Molly. You know that. Those guards are back in the PIT."

"But they did kill people here. One guard is the same as another." She lowers the gun and points it straight at the head of the first guard.

I'm losing ground. She's right. These guards are responsible for the deaths of five men.

"What about Eric? He was a guard. Does he deserve to die?" Her shoulders twitch, and her gun drops a bit. "He was wrong, but he can be forgiven. So can they."

She shakes her head and steadies the gun. "No, Eric was confused. The Cardinal lied to him. He knows what he did was wrong." She waves the gun back and forth from one end of the line of guards to the other. "They aren't confused. They think we're monsters. They deserve to die."

"Elizabeth, they are only doing what the Cardinal told them to do. What everyone out there does." I take a step closer. "The Cardinal lied to them, too. He lies about everything and just like everyone else, they accept the lies."

"Not you. Even when you thought the worst of yourself, you never saw the rest of us as criminals." Elizabeth jerks her shoulder up to wipe her eye. "You saw goodness in me even when I was trying my best to drive you off. You were the first to forgive Eric, and when this village said we couldn't stay, you just kept going."

She takes a shuddering breath and steadies her hands. "You see everyone for the goodness they could have, but they don't. They will always look for the bad, and nothing is going to change that. They are responsible for Molly, Ana, and the men who died here, and every pile of stones back in the PIT. And someone has to pay."

The guards twist against their ropes and shout from behind the gags. She pulls the gun up and lines her eye up for the shot like she's been handling weapons all her life.

"No!"

Six shots ring out in sequence. The guards fall over, perfect red circles in each of their chests. I turn away from the carnage as nausea sweeps through my stomach.

Elizabeth turns away from them and hands me the gun, heat pouring off the end. "It's done. I want to go home now." She walks out of the room without even glancing back.

I can't look at the men she shot, so I stare at the gun instead. She's right. Eric was scared and selfish and made a horrible mistake. These guys might have been assigned the role of guard, but no one forced them to hate. Am I supposed to be glad that there are six less guards out there to do the Cardinal's bidding? If I fight back against the Cardinal, will I have to give up my humanity? Can I see these men in the red jackets as people? Can I kill them if I do?

Liam marches into the room and hisses out a breath at the scene of death. The sharp tang of iron fills the room, and I have to get out of there before I lose it.

Liam takes the still-warm gun from my hand. "It's done and there's nothing we can do about it." He shakes his head, the strain of the past twenty-four hours etched into his face. "Let's get out of here. I'll have some others take care of their bodies."

Outside, the whole village watches Elizabeth walk down the street toward the waiting horses. Their eyes follow her movement, and I can almost read their thoughts. Is this our new future? Elizabeth may have drawn first blood, but it won't be the last. The Cardinal isn't going to stop until we stop him.

Liam walks out and talks to a few men standing nearby. They nod and head into the schoolhouse. "Alright everyone, we need to head out. Load up and start moving."

Two men walk out of the schoolhouse holding one of the guards between them. I walk away to find the others for the long haul back to Allmore. I need a distraction. Anything to keep my mind from imagining how many more scenes like this one I might see in the future.

The front of the long line of Freemen takes its first few steps into the forest. Daniel's cart is in the back, so that's where I head.

His face is still paler than I'd like, but the pain med Marcus gave him seems to be working. I reach over the side of the cart and run my thumb over his hand. Daniel's eyes flicker open.

"Hey there, handsome."

"Hey, you." His lips lift up in a tiny smile. "Where's Patrice?"

"Right here." Patrice slides in next to me and wraps her arm around my waist. She smiles at me, and my heart grows a little bit so I can add her in with the rest of my family.

"Don't worry, she's fine." I wrap my arm around her shoulder. "Better than fine, actually. Did you know your sister is kind of a bad ass?"

Daniel rests back against a pile of blankets. "I think these pain meds might be working a little too well. I just hallucinated that my sister is smiling like she might actually like it here, and then my wife used the word 'ass.'"

Patrice and I laugh, and it feels good. Our world is most likely falling apart, but these moments of normalcy remind me exactly what we have to fight for.

Someone shouts behind us, but before I can turn there's a loud bang. Another gunshot.

"Oh." Patrice crumbles under my arm.

I reach out to catch her before she falls, but her weight pulls both of us to the ground. A dark, red stain spreads across the front of her shirt. I pull us underneath the cart, but there's no way to know what I'm hiding from.

"Patrice!" I kneel down next to her, my hands pressed against her heart, but the blood is coming too fast.

Her fingers inch over and brush my knee as her eyes close.

"Don't you dare," I order her as I pick her head up and rest it in my lap. "Don't you dare die on me."

Daniel is going wild in the cart above us, screaming Patrice's name, but unable to get to us or see what's going on. I scan the streets, but I can't see anything between the hundreds of legs running in every direction.

"Help, please! Someone help us." My shouts are lost in the chaos of people.

Another gunshot rings out and the voices around us get louder.

Patrice coughs and a trickle of blood runs down the corner of her mouth and stains her already paling skin.

"No, please." I choke out the words between sobs. "Not now. I need you to stay here and be happy and help me keep Daniel in line." I wipe away the blood from her lips, but another thick line replaces it. "Please."

Her eyes are almost closed, but they find mine and I stare back at her, willing her to live even as I watch her slip away.

"Love him." Her words are less than a whisper, falling from her mouth seconds before she goes completely still.

A wordless scream rages out of my throat. Eric comes running and skids to a stop next to me, already on his knees. His face collapses in agony, but I can't hear what he's saying. The whole world has gone silent as chaos reigns around me. Eric pulls Patrice off my lap and clutches her lifeless body to his chest. His body shakes so hard her limbs flail around like a ragdoll, smacking against the broken road.

I grab her hand, still warm in mine, and hold it up out of the dirt. She wasn't even supposed to be here. She should still be back home in Cardinal City. Tears fall on our joined hands and mingle with the blood stains. It's too much. It's all too much.

I stand up, every movement as if in slow motion. The screaming has stopped. Daniel still thrashes in the cart next to me. Thomas and Ethan hold him down while Marcus jabs his thigh with an injection. Daniel jerks once more, then his muscles relax and his eyes close, tears leaking out from under his thick lashes.

Elizabeth moves into my line of sight. Her lips are moving, but I still can't hear anything. She shakes my shoulders, until I focus on her eyes. "There was another guard hiding in the woods. They got him."

I nod, as if her words mean anything. They don't. Patrice is dead. She says something else, but it's lost to me. Letting go of my arms, she takes my hand and gently wipes away Patrice's blood.

Thirty-Seven

Three days later, a sad line of exhausted horses and people march into Allmore and head straight for the dining hall. Three days of Eric walking in silence and crying himself to sleep. Three days of sedatives so Daniel would lie still and not open his surgery scar. Three days of too much time to think about everything that led up to Patrice dying in my arms.

The room is packed with all the villagers from Arbor Glen. We'll have to figure out how to accommodate all these new additions, but that can wait. First we need food, rest, and healing.

The doors to the basement store rooms open up, and the people who stayed behind slowly filter into the dining hall and get their first look at the survivors. Liam grabs a few riders who stayed back to protect everyone hiding in the store rooms. "We left a huge trail from Arbor

Glen straight here. I don't know how much can be done, but go see what you can do to cover up our path."

Carol walks through the door with Nellie. She squirms out of Carol's arms and sprints over to Liam, leaping up into his arms and burying her face in his neck. My heart hurts for the missing member of their trio. Liam turns around and walks over to the table where his parents are sitting. He pauses, but then sits down and introduces Nellie to her grandparents for the first time. And because she's every bit her mother's daughter, she climbs into Alan's lap and shows off the fluffy white dandelion clutched in her tiny fingers.

Constance finds us in the crowd and runs over, launching into Thomas's arms. There will be time for tender kisses later, but right now their faces only hold relief. I'm too tired to think about how short-lived that emotion will be. I sink down onto a bench, and Elizabeth settles across from me. She hasn't said a word since we left Arbor Glen.

Liam, Eric, and Ethan come over with a basket of bread and some water. They join our exhausted group, and we all sit in silence, passing around the food and trying not to think about what we've just done.

Daniel went straight the infirmary, still knocked out from the sedatives, but he'll be waking up soon. I'll need to be there, but I'm not ready to think about that yet. I turn my focus to what I can control. We have so much to do and who knows how much time to get it done.

I take a big gulp of water and wash down a bite of bread. "We need to send some riders out with a warning to the other villages that the Cardinal is looking for me. They need to be prepared."

Liam nods. "Fine, but then I want everyone back here, pronto. No more trading. We'll just have to make do with what we have."

"And then what? Sit and wait for the guards to show up here?"

"We have the cellar store rooms, and we'll keep scouts watching from every side of the village. At the first sign of red we all head to the cellars and wait until the guards move on."

"Are you serious?" I set down my bread to stare at him. "Let's just pretend that plan has a chance at working. What happens then? They don't find us and move on to hunt down another village?"

Several others at our table turn at my raised voice.

"What other choice do we have? You saw what happened." He swallows hard, the past several days of strain pulling at his face. "I won't let any more of my people die like that."

I stand up, unable to contain my anger. "If not us, then it will be another village, and then another." More people around the room turn to stare at me, but I don't care. "The Cardinal is not going to just stop. He won't lose interest and leave us all alone. He has too much on the line to walk away."

"Rebecca, please." Liam reaches out to pull me back down. "We need to sit down and talk about this."

I pull out of his reach. "The time for talking is over."

Someone from Arbor Glen stands up and shouts from the middle of the room. "So what do you want us to do?"

I stare over at him and then pause to take in the room. Hundreds of exhausted and terrified faces stare back at me. Eric looks up at me. His eyes are rimmed in red, and dark circles prove he hasn't slept. And yet, behind the exhaustion, there's a determination.

"Fight back."

Nervous laughter and huffs of disbelief fill the room. They've bought into the lie that the Cardinal is unbeatable. I used to think that, too. I stand up on the bench and raise my voice above the chatter.

"I've seen first-hand what the Cardinal is willing to do to have his way. He won't stop until he controls it all. One loose thread threatens everything he's worked to build.

"He seems unbeatable, but he's not. I'm just a scrawny girl who, eighteen months ago, only worried about finding the perfect Acceptance dress. But I stood up to him, and now he's scrambling. Imagine what we could do if we all stood up."

I have their attention now.

"Everything the Cardinal has is built on a lie. This is bigger than just us. Guards just following orders lost their lives because of the lie. Innocent people lose their freedom and everyone lives with blinders on, all to maintain the lies of one man who considers them nothing more than pawns in a sick game."

Several people nod. Most of these people were born in these villages. They've never lived under the Cardinal's thumb. But the rest of us know. I find Elizabeth. She isn't nodding, but I can see the truth in her eyes. She's lived with the painful consequences of those lies. Eric is crying again, but his face is tensed with anger. Thomas holds Constance tight in his lap, but they both nod at me. They know. We tried to meet his ridiculous demands and lost. We've seen how far he's willing to go to create a distorted version of perfection.

"We can't sit this one out and pretend it's someone else's problem. I don't know about you, but I'm done living in fear. I'm tired of wondering when the Cardinal is going to rain blood and fire down on the people I love. If we ever want to be free, we have to stand and fight."

A handful of people around the room stand, and more follow suit.

"We have to stop hiding and pretending that it's okay that we live without. That we don't need the medicine and technology that could save the lives of so many."

I look down at Liam, and he's staring at the table, ever so slightly nodding his head.

"There's never a good time to fight." I'm shouting now, reaching to be heard over the calls for action. "It's easy to say we'll leave it to tomorrow. But the Cardinal just showed us that we aren't promised a tomorrow."

All around the room, people bang their cups on the tables and shout encouragement to each other. The laughter is gone and everywhere I look, determined stares meet my gaze. This is it. This is the beginning of everything.

I hold my arms out wide to include the whole room. Two villages combined as one because the Cardinal thinks we're disposable. We call ourselves the Freemen, but we aren't. Not as long as we let ourselves live in fear of discovery. But we could be.

"Brothers and Sisters. We've proved that if we stand together, the Cardinal is no match against us." I stare into the eyes of so many people I love, and my heart aches for all the loved ones I'll never see again. "Before you stands the future."

The End

Dear Reader,

Well, here we are again at the end of another book. A book, I might add, that I never thought I would write. But I did. Because so many of you asked me to. Because you needed to know what happened. And because there was more of Rebecca's story to be told.

I have loved hearing from so many of you. Your words of appreciation kept me motivated and sharing in your joy has made every late night editing session more than worth it. So keep it coming. You can find me at SarahNegovetich.com or just email me at SarahNegovetich@gmail.com. Reader mail is my favorite kind of email.

Your reviews helped new readers find Rite of Rejection, so if you are inclined, I would be eternally grateful for any reviews of Rite of Revelation. If that's not your thing, telling a friend is a great way to spread the word.

Thank you for being a part of this story and for continuing to keep these characters alive. Stay tuned for more because Rebecca's story isn't over yet.

Before you stands the future!

Sarah

Acknowledgements

First, thank you to all the readers who demanded for Rebecca's story to be told. This book would absolutely not exist if you hadn't asked for it.

Thank you to all my beta readers Ashley, Katie, Andrea, Nikola, and Ethan. You guys were amazing. Special thanks to Ashley for being my writing task master and to Ethan for being the late night catch all for my diva drama.

Thanks to my amazing editing team Zoe and Kate. You guys whipped this hunk of a manuscript into shape. And to ER who stepped in and saved the day to make sure readers never know how poorly I grasp the English language.

Last, but never least, thank you to my amazing family: Nick, Sophia, and Isabella. There's nothing quite like hearing your daughter say "Look, mommy, there's your book". Thank you for always being my joy. Love you, mean it.

About the Author

Sarah Negovetich knows you don't know how to pronounce her name and she's okay with that.

Her first love is Young Adult novels, because at seventeen the world is your oyster. Only oysters are slimy and more than a little salty; it's accurate if not exactly motivational. We should come up with a better cliché.

Sarah divides her time between writing YA books that her husband won't read and working with amazing authors as an agent at Corvisiero Literary Agency. Her life's goal is to be only a mildly embarrassing mom when her kids hit their teens.

You can learn more about Sarah and her books at www.SarahNegovetich.com or follow her antics on Twitter @SarahNego.

Want more?

There are only twenty-four hours between Rite of Rejection and Rite of Revelation. But a lot can happen in a short amount of time.

Sign up for my author newsletter and get a free mini ebook containing scenes from the point of view of each of the main characters, including the Cardinal! Find out exactly what happened when the cameras turned off.

Plus, get two bonus scenes from our leading men, Eric and Daniel.

Get your free ebook today by signing up at www.SarahNegovetich.com!

54147969R00202

Made in the USA
Columbia, SC
26 March 2019